W9-BON-699

Notes on Extinction

Notes on Extinction

JANICE DEANER

DUTTON

DUTTON
Published by the Penguin Group
Penguin Putnam Inc., 375 Hudson Street, New York, New York 10014, U.S.A.
Penguin Books Ltd, 27 Wrights Lane, London W8 5TZ, England
Penguin Books Australia Ltd, Ringwood, Victoria, Australia
Penguin Books Canada Ltd, 10 Alcorn Avenue, Toronto, Ontario, Canada M4V 3B2
Penguin Books (N.Z.) Ltd, 182–190 Wairau Road, Auckland 10, New Zealand

Penguin Books Ltd, Registered Offices: Harmondsworth, Middlesex, England

Published by Dutton, a member of Penguin Putnam Inc.

First Printing, October, 2001
1 3 5 7 9 10 8 6 4 2

REGISTERED TRADEMARK—MARCA REGISTRADA

LIBRARY OF CONGRESS CATALOGING-IN-PUBLICATION DATA

Deaner, Janice.
Notes on Extinction / Janice Deaner.
p. cm.
ISBN 0-525-94415-X (acid-free paper)
1. Women screenwriters—Fiction. 2. Americans—India—Fiction. 3. Female
friendship—Fiction. 4. Separated people—Fiction. 5. Plantation life—Fiction.
6. Terminally ill—Fiction. 7. Assam (India)—Fiction. I. Title.

PS3554.E1743 A94 2001
813'.54—dc21   00-060395

Printed in the United States of America
Set in Adobe Garamond

PUBLISHER'S NOTE

For Nik Malvania

ACKNOWLEDGMENTS

I would like to express my gratitude to the Jalan family of India for opening their homes to me in Calcutta, New Delhi, and for graciously allowing me to stay on their tea gardens in Assam. In particular, special thanks to Madhu Jalan, without whose help and guidance my trip to India would never have been possible. And gratitude to Manoj and Vineeta Jalan for so generously extending themselves during my stay on their tea gardens. And I thank my husband, Nik Malvania, who introduced me to India and who has never failed to believe in me as a writer.

I would also like to express my gratitude to Deborah Anderson who has helped me immeasurably with all of my books, and who so kindly accompanied me to India and helped me with my research, and then contributed enormously to the preparation of this manuscript. I'd like to thank her husband, Gene, and their children, for their generous support in allowing me to take her away for hours and days at a time.

My love and gratitude to Shelly Mars who contributed enormously both in spirit and in mind to this book, in more ways than I can articulate.

I also want to thank my agent, Suzanne Gluck, for her patience and support. I thank my editor, Rosemary Ahern, for her allegiance to me, for her wise and kindly editorial guidance, for which I am most grateful.

Thanks also to Yaddo for my summer stay in 1999, during which time the novel took its greatest shape.

And special thanks to Jonathan Santlofer for his wonderful editorial input and for the moral support he provided steadily over the course of my writing this book.

To Paul Calabro, a particularly heartfelt thanks, for his unflagging belief in me.

And to Jack Burlison, so many thanks, for so many things.

"The great object in life is sensation—to feel that we exist—even though in pain."

—Lord Byron

Notes on Extinction

The dodo never lived anywhere on the earth except on the island of Mauritius where it had once flourished. The island had very few natural predators, in particular no mammals, and though there were reptiles, the dodo bird had a beak that was like a claw hammer. As its body gradually evolved to great size, its wings did not, and at some point, it ceased to fly.

Being land bound, it ate mostly fallen fruit, and it developed such a large throat, it could swallow fruits whole. Since it had become quite large, it couldn't get around very quickly, but without any real predators, this didn't matter. In consequence, its largeness actually helped it survive—bulked up, it could live through long periods of scarcity.

But then around 1598 the Dutch came, and they ate a lot of dodo birds. Dodos were easy to catch, because they were big and lumbering, but they were also ecologically naïve and unafraid of human beings. Eventually, they might have been eaten into extinction, but when the Portuguese came they brought pigs, and the pigs feasted on dodo eggs, if not on the dodos themselves. Within a short period of time the pigs went feral and proliferated, and in 1709 they were so numerous, it was reported, that a posse of eighty men killed more than a thousand of them in a day. And then, though no one knew how, monkeys were introduced to the island—crab-eating macaques—and, like the pigs, they feasted on dodo eggs. The same man who in 1709 had reported the pig massacre, mentioned in passing, how he had seen, as well, a group of four thousand monkeys in a nearby garden.

No one knows the actual moment of the Dodo's extinction. Most likely it was a quiet, unprecedented moment. Certainly one that went unheralded. Perhaps there was a witness, however unknowing. The moment conjured: one mating pair has managed to survive on the island. With both of them alive, there remains the possibility of the survival of their species. But while the female searches for fallen fruit, a Dutch sailor spies her. He saunters over, and without a thought, he draws back his club. He does not know, nor does anyone, the ramifications of his ordinary act. He is simply attending to his supper. But with the light swing of his bat, he has driven the dodo into extinction. He has left the male without a mate. It is an irrevocable act, a deeper death—the death of a species.

From Notes on Extinction, *by Will Mendelsohn*

Chapter 1

First he loses his book, a voluminous work on world extinction, then he loses his wife.

It was not uncommon for her to burn candles in the evening. She put them around their apartment. Sometimes on a shelf above his desk, but usually in the living room on the coffee table. The night she left one burning on his desk, she went out for a pack of cigarettes. She ran into a woman she knew, and when she rounded the corner some two hours later, she saw the fire trucks parked outside their apartment building on Sixth Avenue.

When he comes home, she is sitting on the steps just outside the apartment, red-eyed and silent, having already wept for an hour. The only thing she says is, "Your work is gone." She looks old to him, forty-six instead of thirty-six, the lines at her mouth slack, the underneath of her chin a puddle of flesh, her lean frame, sparer.

From the doorway of his apartment, he stares into his living room. He's never seen a room consumed by fire. He is struck first by how blackened everything is, then by the overpowering smell of smoke. The white sofa is blackened, ravaged, the drapes, gauzy Italian silk, sizzled except for a few threads which dangle from the uppermost edges where the hooks hang from the rods. His library of books, which must have given the fire its great impetus, are mounds of ashes, the shelves themselves, a stark network of burned crosses. When he sees his desk, the finality of it comes to him in an instant. It is now a burned hull, the computer a melted, blackened blob. Nothing remains of his ten-year effort but bits of black, scalloped paper which float in ashen water.

He and Geena sit in the Mexican restaurant across the street while they wait for the firemen to leave. It is crowded and difficult to concentrate, the look of sombreros dangling from the rafters ludicrous.

From his gloom, he listens as she details every moment of her evening. She lit the candle at seven. When the phone rang, she took the call from his desk. She set the candle on top of his stack of Oxford dictionaries while she talked. It was eight o'clock by the time she got off the phone, and she'd run out of cigarettes. She thought about moving the candle before she ran out, but decided to do it when she got home.

"Then, Rose," she says. "She stopped me on the street, and you know what happens when Rose stops you on the street. I couldn't get away from her, and I was standing there nodding and nodding, trying to find a way out, but she just loops from one thing to the next. Then I saw the fire trucks, Will, and I knew it was the candle. And when I saw inside. Oh, God, Will, I'm so sorry. It's so small a thing to say, but I am sorry, so sorry. Sorrier than I've ever been about anything. You don't know how sorry I am."

Her black curly hair is in wild disarray. Her lips are cracked where she's bitten them. The backs of her beautiful hands are red and welted where she's pulled at them. Twice he says to her, "It wasn't your fault. It was an accident," and it seems true, at the very least the thing to say, but by the third time he says it, he no longer believes it.

He feels his heart pounding, but his thoughts are sluggish, the usual quick pace with which he reasons, frozen. His shoes are soaked from having stepped into his flooded living room, his pants too, the water bleeding up the cloth to his knee.

He looks over her shoulder every so often to the fire trucks outside, to the crowd which is still gathered on the street. It doesn't seem quite real to him. He sees his reflection in the glass window. He looks like a haggard man, the line between his eyes, deeply furrowed, a trough, he thinks. He is forty years old.

After an hour her solicitude begins to grate on him.

"Stop apologizing, Geena," he finally snaps.

She goes silent, her mouth pinching shut, and she looks down at her hands.

Nothing about her is either excellent or repugnant, except her hands, he thinks. They seem possessed of an exquisite dexterity that has nothing whatsoever to do with the rest of her, as if they'd been appended as an afterthought.

Although she has fine, delicate features, they somehow have not accumulated into beauty, he thinks again—a straight, thin nose, large brown eyes, a full mouth, her teeth small and white. But when put upon her face they amount not to stunning beauty, but rather to plainness, to disappointment. It seems it is the same with her body. He is handsome, a fact that makes her plainness prick him more sharply, for he knows he could have married a more beautiful woman. Why he considers this now, he doesn't know.

He always imagines himself shallow when he looks at her and suffers this small disappointment. He has always tried to content himself with the impermanence of beauty, of how unimportant it is in the scheme of things, but it was not always possible. It seems it would have been nice to have admired her from across the table for the twenty years or so granted one before old age stole one's looks.

Now, with the loss of his work, this fact oppresses him even more.

Still, he cannot deny he has had no greater admirer than her: Geena, who has sacrificed going out at night so that he could work; who has given up any thoughts of a long vacation, who has even learned to cook so that he wouldn't have to waste time going out to restaurants, who has read his latest pages aloud, pronounced each and every passage "good."

He wonders what their friends will say when they learn that she had left a candle burning on his desk. They often remark how kind and generous she is, how lucky he is to have her. He wasn't always so kind to her. It is true, perhaps, he has taken her for granted. Twice he'd been unfaithful.

When they arrive at his mother's apartment on the Upper West Side, his doom feels complete. The place has not changed since he left home over twenty years ago. The walls are scuffed with black markings, the wooden floors bare of varnish, except for small strips along the halls where no one has ever walked. The furniture, though vaguely passable—a green-blue divan and matching swivel chairs—is outdated. Everything about it oppresses him.

After Geena goes to bed, he sits in his mother's decrepit kitchen, in her ironlike presence. She is trim and vital still, her hair barely grayed; she still dresses elegantly in dark skirts and white cotton blouses.

Over a cup of tea, Will tells her, "Geena must hate me." It is an idea that has bloomed in his thoughts in the restaurant and has reached a greater blossoming in his mind now.

In her thick Polish accent his mother says, "Nonsense. It was the burning limbs of your relatives that toppled the candle, to remind you of your past, a past you have never believed in." She sits back in her chair and folds her arms, regarding him with her narrowed black eyes.

It has always been a contention between them, the relatives lost in the Holocaust. Every day of his childhood she'd sounded their names—a roll call of the dead. He had spent his earliest years straining to feel them all, stretching what little sentience he had across an ocean, but he couldn't.

Despite her obvious distaste for an American son, he was hopelessly this; his own ancestry went back no further than his mother and father, both Polish Jews, who had survived. To avert it, she dressed him as a little Polish boy from the thirties, speaking to him in only Yiddish or Polish. His only defense was to answer her in English.

If he'd been embarrassed of their accents, of how dark his mother kept the house, of the fact that she saved every plastic bag, milk carton, paper bag, and rubber band that ever entered their apartment, his shame was complete when she sat at the kitchen table and told his friends how he had no cousins, no aunts, no uncles, no grandparents. His friends could not have been sorrier; but still, to have come from a slaughtered people.

If his father had taken the flowering of the Holocaust and turned it inward, its great roots choking him without witness, his mother had turned it out. She was its trellis; its stalks and leaves and flowers grew upon her for all to see. She knew whose shame it was.

He resents that she brings it up now. "I just lost ten years' worth of work, do you think I want to hear about that right now?" His voice has risen, and his hands now drop down to the table. It is a moment in which he clamors for her sympathy, for her compassion, but she won't grant it.

Like some old parchment come to life, she says, "Now you see what it is to lose things you cannot get back."

In the morning, he and Geena go looking for apartments. While she turns in the empty spaces asking, "Do you like it? What do you think, Will?" he cannot help but see her acquiescent behavior in a new light. Before, it had seemed to him innocent enough, a wife trying to please a husband, but now after the burning (which he has taken to calling it) he cannot help but regard it as a sham, a delicate cover for something ugly.

As she peers into the closets and cabinets, he thinks, Such a perfect act. She was not in the room when the candle burned. It had not been felled by her hand. She had the perfect alibi: "I always burn candles and I often go out and nothing has ever happened before."

Their lunch is markedly silent. Often their dinner conversations are quiet, if he hasn't felt like talking. She will speak then of things that don't interest him.

He suspected quite early in the marriage that they had already assumed the roles of the middle-aged couples he'd seen so often in his early youth, dining in silence, intent on their food, either mildly disinterested in one another or quietly hateful.

They take the third apartment they look at, though neither of them particularly likes it. It is smaller than they are used to, and dark, but it is preferable to living with his mother. In the late afternoon, they go furniture shopping. He can't raise his interest, and tells her to go ahead and pick out some things. As he tags after her through sections of dining tables and sofas, he discovers that had his own tastes not prevailed in the past, they would have been reclining on large floral-patterned sofas, gazing into mirrors edged in small, pink roses.

She watches the disappointment in his eyes, and in an uncharacteristic moment she says, "Fine. You don't like what I pick, you go and pick it out yourself."

He finds her three blocks later, walking quickly against the wind. As he trails her down the street, he has a small hope that she will finally fight, that they might say to one another all that has gone unsaid. But when he reaches her, he grabs hold of her shoulder, and she turns to him, her lower lip already trembling. "I'm sorry," she says.

"Don't apologize," he says. "Don't, Geena."

Her fingers grasp his coatsleeve. "But I am sorry. I shouldn't have yelled in the store."

He takes her under his arm, and they walk back to the store and settle for buying a mattress and some bedding. As he pads behind her through the aisles of sheets and pillowcases, he has never been more certain that he is living the wrong life, with the wrong woman. It is all wrong, every bit of it. He can feel somewhere inside of him what the right life is, but it seems he has trudged so far along this wrong life, that now everything, even down to the shoes he wears is wrong.

That night they sit on the mattress in the emptiness of their new apartment. There are no distractions—no television, no radio, the phone has not even been connected. In the quiet, he suggests that perhaps she has harbored an unconscious anger toward him, or at the very least toward his work, and that something, quite unconscious— he emphasizes it delicately—had caused her to place the candle on his desk, and then furthermore had caused her to stay away talking with Rose on the street while his desk burned.

But she looks at him as if he has made up the whole idea of the unconscious mind and simply reiterates the facts. "I've told you everything," she says with measured patience. "I often burn candles, and I've run out before to get something from the store, and nothing has ever happened. It was purely a coincidence that the phone rang, and I put the candle on your desk. There is nothing unconscious going on. You always think there are reasons for everything, and sometimes there just aren't. I would never do anything to hurt you, Will. Nothing, ever."

Her words fall on him flatly. He gives her a bland look and closes his eyes.

"What?" she says.

"I just want you to talk to me, Geena. I just want you to say something, anything," he yells. "I want us to talk about it. Can't we talk about it? Be true, Geena. For once be true."

But she disappears. He sees the vacant look in her eyes that comes whenever he presses her. The fight leaves her; she retreats deep inside of herself, and in her absence he feels strangely too much.

"I said I was sorry, Will. What else can I do?" Her lips compress, and he sees the beginning trace of smoker's lines radiating from her upper lip. When his silence unnerves her, she falls to her knees in the all but empty room, and presses her forehead against his kneecaps. "I'm sorry, Will. You can't imagine how sorry I am."

But it is the apology a supplicant gives a master, words that are expected, rather than true, and he wants now to kick her away. His marriage has always been like this, he thinks. Its mechanism is simply exaggerated, the fire having burned away the facade, exposing its working parts. In the face of her obeisance, he becomes the tyrant, the one lucky to have her. For years he has walked around with this guilt, possessing it the way one possesses their fingers—without question of them.

Oddly, he now takes grim satisfaction in the fact that she has burned his work.

She looks up into his eyes, her own brimming with tears. He puts his arms around her and pulls her to his chest, and when he smells the scent of her shampoo, a smell he has come to hate, he knows that it is over.

He lays next to her on their new mattress, and though he feels guilty at having already left her, he experiences the strange, heady emotion that attends such endings, the exquisite mixture of relief and sadness, the tally of the inevitable losses—she listened to his every word, she kneaded his shoulders well, she read every word he ever wrote—added with the losses he feels now glad to incur—he would never have to look at her and feel the disappointment of a face that failed to please, he would no longer have to settle for sex that never quite inspired him.

For days he considers all these things, secure in the secret of them, their inviolability within his mind. When she asks, "Is something wrong?" all he has to do is to invoke the loss of his work, and she says no more.

Then comes the task of telling her. Yet, he need not have worried himself, because while they eat dinner in a Chinese restaurant, she tells him that she has found herself another apartment and is moving out. The tiny cob of corn he's taken into his mouth feels foreign, the crush of his teeth against it, irony.

"Where?" he asks, instead of why.

"On Jane Street, off Hudson."

He listens to her reasons for wanting to leave: she can't do anything right; she is certain he will never be able to forgive her for having left that candle burning on his desk; that he will forever hound her about her unconscious reasons; and she is certain, absolutely certain that it isn't true; that she has always loved him and has always wanted the best for him. There is a tug of thought, to change her mind, but all her talk about loving him and always wanting the best for him has such a ring of falseness, even the caress of her hand on his arm seems so inauthentic that it drains away his interest.

When a few days later he watches her walk from the apartment, he does not feel compelled to open the window, to call after her, although he watches her small, compact body walk down the street. He has only one fear—that she will weaken and turn back.

Extinct:

Akioloa, Alauwahio, Amazon, Arabian Ostrich, Bonin night heron, Caracara, Chatham Island bellbird, Chatham Island fernbird, Conure, Courser, Delalande's coucal, Dodo, Duck, Dusky Seaside Sparrow, Elephant bird, Emu, Eskimo curlew, Finch, Gadwall, Great Amakihi, Great auk, Grosbeak, Guadalupe Caraca, Guadalupe flicker, Gaudalupe rufous-sided towhee, Guam flycatcher, Heath hen, Huia, Ivory-billed woodpecker, Jamaican pauraqué, Kioea, Laysan apapane, Laysan millerbird, Lord Howe Island blackbird, Lord Howe Island fantail, Macaw, Mamo, Merganser, Moas, New Caledonian lorikeet, Norfolk Island kaka, Nukupuu, O-O, Oahu akepa, Omao, Owl, Painted vulture, Passenger pigeon, Petrel, Quelili, Réunion fody, Ryukyu kingfisher, Saint Kitts Puerto Rican bullfinch, São Tomé grosbeak, Serpent eagle, Shelduck, Solitaire, Spectacled cormorant, Tanna dove, Towhee, Ula-ai-hawane, White eye, White gallinule, Cisco, Killifish, Lake Titicaca orestias, New Zealand grayling, Pupfish, Speckled dace, Spinedace, Sucker, Thicktail chub, Utah Lake sculpin, Agouti, Arizona jaguar, Aurochs, Badlands bighorn sheep, Bali tiger, Bandicoot, Blue buck, Burchell's zebra, Caribbean monk seal, Caucasian wisent, Christmas Island musk shrew, Dawson's caribou, Greenland tundra reindeer, Hartebeest, Hispaniolan hexolobodon, Hutia, Ibex, Isolobodon, Nesophont, Potoroo, Puerto Rican caviomorph, Quagga, Quemi, Rufous gazelle, Schomburgk's deer, Sea mink, Shamanu, Steller's sea cow, Syrian onager, Tarpan, Wallaby, Warrah, Antarctic wolf, Carolina parakeet, Rufous fantail, White-throated ground-dove, Micronesian honeyeater, Mariana fruit-dove, Guam flycatcher, Drepanis pacifica, Hawaii mamo, Drepanis funera, Black mamo, Ciridops annu, Layson honeycreeper, Koa-finch, Kona grosbeak, Hawaiian rail, Oahu nukapuu, Amaui, Kiola, Marsupial wolf . . .

From Notes on Extinction, *by Will Mendelsohn*

Chapter 2

*E*very morning he is grateful to wake alone.

He tries to rewrite the work, but the vastness of what he has lost overwhelms him—nearly three thousand pages of scholarly research on island biogeography, two hundred detailed drawings of animals, seventy pages of footnotes, bibliographies, and indexes, not to mention the manuscript itself, which was well over a thousand pages. He has written about islands, how they represent simplified, exaggerated versions of the evolutionary processes that occur on the mainland. With artful precision he has illuminated the crucial link between evolution and extinction, discussing how evolution is best understood with reference to extinction and extinction with reference to evolution. In studying the evolution of unusual species on islands, it casts light indirectly on the greater problem: the extinction of species in a world being hacked to pieces.

Although his first book had made him rich—a short work on the life of Alfred Wallace, a man who had arrived at the theory of evolution concurrently with Charles Darwin—it was this book, *The Extinction of Species,* that was to bring him acclaim.

He attempts the research again, but his heart is not in it. His mind wanders, and he drifts, working less and less.

He doesn't know what to do with his time and goes out more often with his friends, but something about losing his work and his wife has removed him. The sort of talk that has always gone between them, of everyday problems, no longer interests him. It all feels like a waste of time.

Often he meets his friend Bradley at a coffee shop, and they talk about the opera Bradley is still trying to write. He's been working on it for fifteen years, but there is always a job Bradley has to endure to tide him over financially, and invariably the job never ends. The idea that he and Bradley might sit there in this coffee shop, growing older and older, talking about the same thing begins to terrify him. He wants to say, "Let's face it, Brad, you're never going to write the opera." But he can't. His friendships have hardened into sympathies and acceptances and tolerances that seem to do nothing but hold one another in place. When he begins to hear himself complain about one friend to another, suddenly the whole purpose of friendship seems defeated.

Nights he lies on his mattress, blinking up at the white ceiling. He entertains thoughts of suicide, but even they are not compelling, and in the silence that follows their dismissal, he thinks: He does not quite possess himself. Perhaps he never has. He's employed his poor wife to inhabit his tiny world, to patrol it and keep its boundaries. But why? he wonders, and at night he listens for the quiet ripple of his own thought. Slowly it comes to him, over the course of a few weeks, the idea that the hands that have shaped him have been terrified and a little inept. It isn't his fault, he concedes. It is never any man's fault for the hands that have shaped him. It has simply become his responsibility. That's the bargain everyone makes when they consent to their own creation: to assume responsibility for these hands that have shaped them, no fault of their own.

After this thought, he can't sleep, and late, after 3:00 A.M., he gets up and burns the few pages he's managed to write. As the ashes fly in the breeze outside his bedroom window, he decides what he will do.

He will write another book on world extinction. But this time, he will write it from the world; he will witness its hacking. He will issue the warning.

In the morning he buys himself maps of the world, spreads them across the wooden ribs of his barren living room floor, and in the early light he charts his course with the red fingernail polish Geena has left behind.

Species on islands tend to differ from those on the mainland. Communities on islands differ from mainland communities as well. Islands even differ from one another in their species and communities.

Yet islands differ in ways that are similar.

Islands harbor rarer species than mainlands. Species become rare for two reasons: geographical isolation and evolution.

Creatures tend to evolve more quickly on islands, and their evolution conforms to a strange pattern: On islands, large animals like elephants, hippopotamuses, rabbits, deer, pigs, and foxes tend toward dwarfism. While smaller animals like birds, tortoises, geckos, skinks, night lizards, and iguanas tend toward giantism.

Such a strange, flightless bird, as the dodo, in all of its improbability, could never have evolved anywhere but on an island.

Extinctions happen more quickly on islands, and rare creatures meet extinction with even more regularity.

Yet, islands represent uncomplicated, hyperbolized models of the evolution and extinction that occurs on the mainland. That is why they are so illustrative in a world being carved into islands.

From Notes on Extinction, *by Will Mendelsohn*

Chapter 3

*H*is travel is circuitous and subject to change, and the schedule he follows is often very different from what he's planned. Sometimes the projects lose their funding or they simply have no room for him or they have room for him now but not later. He goes first to the Galápagos Islands, next to the Midriff Islands, then on to Madagascar.

He has romanticized the travel. His idea of it had been a blithe journey, or, if there was inconvenience or even suffering, it was all without any affect—a picture of the suffering, without the attending feelings. He imagined himself in his hiking clothes, standing on bluffs, on cliffs, cutting a rugged figure against a backdrop of blue sky. He had not known that when he finally stood at these places, he would be worrying about whether he was being swindled by his guide, or obsessing about the awkward conversation at breakfast he had hours ago with one of the scientists, a pompous man who had suggested that his understanding of modern genetics was less than adequate.

It disturbs him that the beauty of the places before him is not always foremost in his mind. There is such majesty in the valley of treetops below him, through which he might glimpse verdant fields of sugarcane or glaucous tarps of oceans. He stands instead flawed. There are no pure moments, he supposes.

He next goes to the rain forest in Brazil, where a group of scientists study the effects of a rain forest hacked to pieces for the sake of cattle ranches. Isolated from one another in a collection of islands, great populations of deer and New World monkeys were diminishing by the year. When Will sees them, mangy and terrified, blinking at the edges of their increasingly circumscribed habitats, he knows that no book he can write will save them.

Sitting outside a cave of Vanikoro swiftlets on the island of Guam, he watches the birds dumbly building their nests on the ceilings. Where once they had inhabited hundreds of the caves, they now have drawn instinctively together into one. He knows they are doomed, their extinction inevitable.

The entire avifauna population of Guam—the Vanikoro swiftlets, the rufous fantails, the bridled white-eyes, the Micronesian honeyeater, and the Guam flycatchers—are disappearing almost overnight, and no one knows why. When he sees them dropping dead, holds them in his hands, he has a deeper, more disturbing revelation: the world will eventually unravel. He is now simply a witness to it. There will be no salvation. It has been an amazing event, man's presence on the earth, a grand experiment, but it has failed. He feels this deeply, as if he has been let into a secret, a member of an exclusive club of those who know. Everywhere he sees shadows.

Perhaps this is why a young assistant named Rita, a twenty-one-year-old graduate student from the University of Chicago, so captivates him. She is filled with a girl's passion, with an Idealism he now feels himself being slowly drained of. He finds her silly, in the ways the old always find the young ridiculous, but while he tracks across limestone plateaus with her and a group of six scientists in search of the endangered birds, he never loses sight of her. When they pair up to sit watch in various designated stations of the forest, he makes certain he is assigned with her. They all keep vigil in the forest, watching birds through field glasses, like mothers.

It is adolescent, he knows, when he and Rita make a game of it, and he would not have wanted any of the scientists hearing him say, "Rita, there's Don Juan doing it with Marilyn Monroe," when he spots a mating pair, but he cannot help himself.

He finds it impossible not to sit next to her inside the makeshift office while she records data in a ledger with her lucky pen, a peppermint stick ballpoint with a smiley face eraser, and talks enthusiastically about saving Guam's birds from extinction.

"I know it's not very scientific or anything," she says, "but I've been sending small prayers out to the birds at night. I mean, I think about them and try to concentrate, like meditation. I'm trying to get to the source of it, you know, like pick up on the vibe of it. I'm not the religious type either. I mean, I never go to church or anything, but since I've been here I've gotten really spiritual."

She is sitting cross-legged on a bench, her blonde hair in a ponytail, her green eyes filled with wonder.

She is one of those Save the Whales people, a type he has always done his best to distance himself from. He must admit that he listens to her so that he might watch the way her tongue moves delicately across her full lower lip, so that he might gaze at her skin, so smooth and poreless, so that he might bathe in her enthusiasm.

He never pretends to feel the same way as she does, but he does not mention either that he has never been interested in the salvation of one species over another. His interest has always been in preserving the ecological system, for the purpose of salvaging man. Rufous fantails and Guam flycatchers are but one thing.

She smiles now, folds into herself. "Have you gotten more spiritual since you've come?" she asks.

Her youth suddenly embarrasses him, and he cautions himself not to say anything that will insult her. "I don't think so," he says carefully. "I've never really been a very religious man."

"Me either, but I can *feel* those birds, and last night I actually sent prayers out to them. If we could figure out what is killing them. I mean, if we could *really* figure it out, you know. Doesn't it give you the chills to think of it?" She tosses her blonde ponytail over her shoulder, her eyes shining.

"I'd like for it to, but I must admit that it hasn't happened to me yet. I'm waiting, though."

She laughs when he says things like this. "You're so funny, Will. You remind me of my uncle Julius."

"I hope he's not the one in the nursing home," he says.

Another peal of laughter; he will take what he can get.

"If it was in my power," she says, "I would collect them all and put them in a house and take care of them *all* day."

"Maybe you should get work in an orphanage."

She laughs and bites the smiley face eraser. "If only there was a true culprit, you know. Like if it was man, and we knew, we could protest and take legal action. But it's a silent killer. It comes out at night, like, and it's creepy, like it's the dark hand of evil or something. You know?"

She inserts these "you knows" often. The shakiness of youth, the unsure attempt to formulate larger ideas, but he is no teacher, and simply nods.

He finds her silly when she cries over one of the Guam flycatchers they find dead on the forest floor, but he shags after her down to the beach and holds the flashlight while she buries it in the sand. He even repeats the prayer she asks him to recite with her. He forgives her this. He has once had ideals too.

At night alone in his tent, he struggles to understand what claim Rita has on him. He thinks of her when she is not there. He finds himself looking for her. He has never been attracted to women younger than him by twenty years. It is not so much her body he is attracted to, he reasons, though of course he is, but rather the steady flicker of life on tap inside of her, as if his has diminished so drastically in supply he needs to siphon off someone else's.

When he finally kisses Rita's neck, she is crouched down next to him, tears streaming down her face as she wraps yet another casualty of the night—a Guam flycatcher—in the Kleenex he takes from his pocket. He opens the specimen box so that she can put it inside. When their hands accidentally touch, he leans in and kisses that perfect, tender white skin at her throat.

She moves away from him, and he sees in the brief moment of her alarm, that she has never looked upon him romantically. To her, he is an old man. She does not say it, but she says something that brings it to his mind. She says, "I love talking to you. You know? I mean, I just love to talk to you."

That night, in his tent, he looks at himself closely in the small mirror he uses to shave. There is gray at his temples that he has never quite noticed. It is as if it has come to him overnight. He looks too at the underside of his chin and discovers that the flesh there has slackened. He has been unaware of this onslaught. The line between his eyes is like a slough, he thinks. He has worried too much and too often. Even without frowning, he can feel the groove with his fingertip.

The sudden thought of a middle-aged couple performing passionate love on a bed in the afternoon sunlight repulses him. Their graying hairs, their sagging stomachs, the crepey skin slack along their thighs. No one wants to see withering flanks in the throes of passion. Yet his feeling for it has not diminished.

In Mauritius Will tramps through the forest with another team of scientists, climbing the nearly vertical purple basalt cliffs along with them, making the hand-over-hand ascent up thick vines that grow flush against the rock, as they make their way up to where the kestrel, the world's smallest falcon, lays its eggs in the scrapes. They replace the real eggs with glass ones and incubate them in a makeshift laboratory, later returning the fledglings to their nests to be reared by their mothers. The kestrel figures prominently in his book—it is rare now, and the measures that a wily Scotsman named Mr. Jones and his team take to rescue it from the edge of extinction verge on the saintly.

Where once he felt their efforts noble, they now strike him as futile. At night he sits alone in his tent, and types up notes on an old typewriter, tracing the Mauritius kestrel's decline to the French, who had come in the late eighteenth century. By carving up great tracks of the forest to plant fields of sugarcane, they isolated the kestrel's breeding grounds into three mountain chains—the Moku, the Bambous, and the Black River Gorge. By 1973, there were only eight of them left in the entire world. Now, in 1983, there are three times as many. Even so, it is nothing, he thinks. A drop in the bucket.

When one night a few of the scientists pass around photographs of their wives and their children, he feels stricken. He is a man who has so often written about the fate of a lone male, wandering a forest, a desert, and now he feels himself to be such a solitary figure. It surprises him the power of this image, the sway it suddenly holds over him; his work, his marriage, both have been fruitless. It raises panic in his heart, to glimpse so surely the ships that have passed.

When Diane arrives at Mauritius, he feels vindicated. She chooses him above the rest. Granted, it is not the best selection, but he accepts the honor graciously. She's come from Chicago, on assignment with a scientific journal to write an article about the preservation of Mauritius' kestrel. She is moved to see him sitting in his tent with his knuckles swollen under white topical cream and an ice bag strapped to his knee. Women were often touched by his awkwardness, by his self-deprecating manner, traits that made him appear endearingly harmless.

She offers friendly advise on the quickest way to heal rock scrapes, and manages to extend her stay by asking questions about his book, until he finds himself the recipient of her notes on the kestrels, though they are far more than he will ever need.

She is pretty, pleasing to look at—short brown hair, blue eyes, even white teeth. She's an able-looking woman, strong legs, nice lean arms. She's forty-four, an age he now finds comfort in.

When she comes to his tent a few nights later, it is to say, "The men are prowling around my tent. Can I come in for a while?" They are, of course, the same men who have passed around photographs of their wives and children.

"Come in," he says.

"God, that guy, Wally Shire. What's his story?" She sits on the floor, with her legs drawn to her chest, while he sits on the edge of the cot. A kerosene lamp burns on the floor, the soft light taking ten years off of her.

"He's the resident bore," Will answers. "There's always one in every camp."

"It's true, isn't it?" she says. "And they always find me. They glom onto me because I'm nice, and I don't have the nerve to blow them off. But this guy. He's got to be the most tedious man I've ever met."

"It's true," Will says. "He's one of those stentorian bores, a man who hides himself behind a wall of facts, offering dry oats of knowledge. I hurl myself into ditches to avoid him."

"Why didn't you warn me?" she says. "He pinned me in the lab for nearly an hour, telling me about the annual rainfall on Mauritius for the last ten years. And then I was treated to a complete listing of the plant species it decimated. Come on."

"I heard about tenrecs," Will says. "He knows everything about tenrecs—little blind mice, if you don't know. And don't make the mistake, like I did, of asking him why he did research on tenrecs."

They laugh, and he knows that it's been accomplished. They've conspired against Wally Shire, and have created a bond whose central code is to keep people like Wally Shire out.

"I bet he didn't try to kiss you, though," she says.

"He tried to kiss you?"

She shudders visibly, nods.

"It was thrusting, like if you mated a jellyfish with a walrus and it projected itself at you."

They have another laugh over this, and he knows the other men can hear their suppressed giggles. Their tents are in an encampment, pitched in a row. Someone sneezes and everyone hears. Their huddled shadows inside his tent will not escape notice either. It is a small victory that she has ended up in his tent, while the other men inhabit theirs alone, but a victory nonetheless.

"Oh, this is awful," she says. "The way we all talk about each other. I wonder what they say about me?"

"Since they all want to sleep with you, it's probably all very flattering. It may change over the course of the next few weeks, but right now I think you're probably in good standing."

"What do they say about you?"

"In my deepest insecurity, I fear that when I leave the lab, they make fun of my first book, on Alfred Wallace, the man who came up with the theory of evolution at the same time as Darwin. I imagine them whispering that it is a pseudoscientific hack job, a cheap exposé with very little scientific merit." He leaves out the fact that it made him rich, and that apart from that, it is an embarrassment to him now.

"I think they say my ass is too fat," she says.

Over the next week, he follows her through the forests, climbing the purple basalt cliffs, sitting with her while she makes certain that the mothers have not rejected the glass eggs. Through the canopy of trees below them, they catch glimpses of green fields of sugarcane, which give way to a far-flung tarp of blue ocean. Up there, they speak easily, offhandedly.

"I always feel myself apart from everybody," she says. "I mean, I find myself sitting with everyone and talking and all the rest, but what really interests me isn't what's being said. You know?"

"They say life is lived internally."

"Is that true? Is it?"

"There are so many things in the way of our ever communicating anything real to one another."

"I know, but I hate it."

"I do too. There are so few people I ever feel any affinity to." Yet he longs for it, and he holds out the hope that it may be with Diane.

She begins to sleep with him at night, and he is honestly glad for her company. She is cheerful, a fact that helps counteract his moments of gloom. They fit together nicely somehow, the feel of their limbs entwining a deep comfort to him. They often lay together in one another's arms and make good, pleasant conversation. He finds honest moments of happiness and pleasure in her body, and makes love to her often, though it is never with much passion.

He is not quite moved by her, a fact that he is sorry for, and when after two weeks, it doesn't grow beyond a pleasure, remaining instead comfortably small, he contents himself with the idea that it will be confined to this time, to this island.

But she has fallen more deeply, and when one night she brings up the future, he dreads the conversation.

"There is no future," he admits softly. Abruptly she sits up and pulls on her shirt. The expanse of her back is broad and white, pleasing in the flickering yellow light of the kerosene lamp.

"Of course not," she says.

"Why of course not?"

She glances over her shoulder at him. "You are one of those men who does not love women."

She pulls on her shirt and stalks off. He knows she will be back— she has all but moved in with him.

It is an idea that does not astonish him. He considers it while they walk through the jungle, while they climb the basalt cliffs. He thinks it must be true. Because women have often loved him, it seems that he must have loved them too, but it is obvious to him now that he has misunderstood something vital.

He is not certain why, but a few days later he tells Diane a story from his life, telling it to her in greater detail than he might have ordinarily. The forest, and the fact of their eventual parting give him license.

He is sixteen and is holding Heather Holden's hand in Central

Park, he says. She is a blonde-haired, blue-eyed girl with German ancestry. She comes from people named Beckman and Schroeder. The
Goy of Goyim, he says.

When his mother saw him in Central Park sitting there with
Heather Holden on a bench, holding her hand, he knew immediately
that she was seeing something that was not there, a treacherous nightmare of betrayal, but before he could say anything, his mother turned
and fled the park.

When he got home she was in bed panting for air. Her room was
dark. It was always dark and shrouded, even in midday. He came to
the foot of the bed and touched the thick, dark scrolling of the footboard.

"My own enemies," she said, "and you consort."

She closed her eyes against the horror, and he gripped the scrolled
footboard.

"She is only an American girl," he said. "She doesn't even really
know about the Nazis."

His mother propped herself up on her elbow, and in the cloistered
semidarkness, she shook her finger, a finger now crooked from arthritis.

"You trace her history, there's a Nazi there who killed your people,
Will. Your own blood. Now, I am going to tell you a story, Will, and
I want you to listen."

He knew already the story she would tell. She had told this story
so many times that had she fainted dead away, he could have taken
her place and recited it. This story, out of all of her stories, seemed to
be his provenance.

"One night, one of the Nazis came into the bunks and asked
which girls could dance," she said. "Of course no one speaks. There
is no one who wants to die, so not a word out of anyone. His name
is Schmidt, this man, I remember this, and he speaks again, and he
says now that whoever can show him they can dance, they can go free.
Imagine this. The word free, in this awful place. All the young girls
raise their hands, of course. Who would not? Not knowing what this

really means, I raise my hand. I am foolish and young. Not yet do I know how evil are these Germans. I am chosen, along with three others, and we are made to dance like spinning tops on the cold floor with shoes with no laces, they are so clumsy, and we are cold and hungry, but we dance to get free. So this Schmidt, he takes us to a house. Ah, it is warm in this house, and the table just after dinner. I can smell the food, and I see scraps of meat and potato dumplings left on the plates. I want so much to steal them and put them in my pocket. The men, they are Nazis, and there are six of them. They are smoking and drinking, and I think, oh, I will dance my best. Maybe I will be free. Free, you can't imagine.

"So they take us to another room, a room with books, with leather sofas and chairs, and they turn on the phonograph and play French songs, cabaret songs, songs I once loved, but now I cannot bear. Then they ask for us to dance, and so we go into the center of the room, and we dance for them. They make us dance for hours. Even when they are not watching, we are still to dance. They are talking to each other, but they still make us dance. I keep dancing; I think maybe I will get free. I don't know how long it is before one girl drops and then another. The men laugh, and I am happy these girls fall, because now maybe I will win. The girls that fall, they send away. Now there are only two of us, and I think if only I can keep going, I must dance longer than she can. And then the sun rises up, and I see the blue sky, and then my prayer is answered, the other girl falls down. She struggles to get up, and she tries to say she just tripped, but they tell her no, she must go. And I think, I win, I think, I win, I finally win, I will go free. And I am proud, so proud, and I think how proud my papa would be. He didn't want me to have dance lessons, but now these dance lessons, they have saved my life. And I am happy, happy as only a girl who wins can be. But they don't let me go. They toss me back, like a fish, and my hope is ruined. I learn to hide my assets, not to be so ready to show them. I learn to never dare hope again. Never to hope again. This you can never forget. You cannot forget your own blood, that these people, they kill your own blood. Your own blood. Do you hear me, your own blood."

His mother fell silent, and her eyes slipped away, robbed again by the past. He did not say anything. Never once in all the years she had told him this story did he ever speak a word.

But late at night, he dreamed of blood transfusions, of genetic mutations; he imagined other possible origins. To be the rare one, the only offspring left from his family's tribe was a burden. To escape the entombment of his room, he went up to the rooftop of his apartment building, and lay shivering on the black-topped floor. He stared up at the sky, comforting himself with the knowledge that the world was large, that it went far beyond the two-bedroom apartment he lived in with his mother and father, a household stopped in time. The universe was timeless, a haven unconcerned with whether one was Jew or Gentile, a place where one was simply alive.

When a few nights later at dinner she repeated the story to him and his father, Will threw his fork down on his plate, where it bounced and fell, oddly, acrobatically, tines down, into a dish of butter.

"Do you know how many times you have told us that story?" he yelled. "Hundreds of thousands of times. I can't stand to hear it anymore."

And then he mimicked her, her Polish accent, which to her horror, he did to perfection. "Oh, Will, they make us dance. I think, oh, to dance as best I can. Maybe I will be free. Free, Will, you can't imagine. But they throw me back like a fish, and my hope is ruined, Will, and I never dare hope again."

He savored the grotesque mask that stole across his mother's face.

Then she said, "You are lucky, Will. You are the lucky one, not me, not your father. You, Will. You can afford to say such a thing. But you know nothing. You who were born in this country, the lucky one."

"I don't want to be the lucky one," he yelled. "I don't want to be the lucky one anymore."

But his mother was already groping down the darkened hallway on her way to her bed, the womb she climbed into at the worst moments.

"I will make it not true," he yelled. "I will not be the lucky one." But his mother's door slammed shut, and he had nowhere to retreat but to his own room.

Later his father came in and closed the door behind him. He sat down at Will's desk, while Will lay on his back on his bed, his hands beneath his head. He never looked at his father. His gaze was fixed on the ceiling above him, on the cracks that had festered beneath a coat of off-white paint.

"Will," he said, "that night they make your mother dance, she is only sixteen years old, like you are now. She thinks she wins, because she keeps dancing, but the men take her afterward, because she is the strongest Jew. They tell her, they don't want to copulate with a weak Jew, only a strong Jew, so they do this to her. All of them, one after the other, on the leather sofa, Will, and then they make her walk back to the bunks naked, through the mud, and the other girls—everyone knows what has happened. There is blood on her legs. They don't let her wash. If it had only been one night, Will . . . You don't know what kind of shame is this for a woman."

Will never turned his head, never looked at his father. He fixed his gaze on the ceiling, though he no longer saw it. It was as if the ceiling had opened and had become the sky, for what happened when he lay on his back beneath the stars, happened now—he felt the loss of his own boundaries, his perspective. The sky was not a good mother. Then his father's hand touched his shoulder, and he listened for the sound of the door closing.

When he looked at his mother across the breakfast table the next morning, he saw her beneath piles of Nazis, a sliver of a girl, the light dying in her eyes. When he looked at his father, he appeared to Will as someone vast on the inside, yet wholly diminished on the outside, like a small shack, beneath which lay whole catacombs.

"I took different paths home from school," he quietly says to

Diane, "and viewed things I was accustomed to seeing from different angles: my apartment building nested on the block when I came from the east instead of the west. The pattern of building against sky when I lay at the foot of my bed rather than at its head. I saw now the underhang of the Brooklyn Bridge, no longer the suspension cables. The peaks of the buildings, rather than the stoops. The small ledge of the subway, rather than the broad platform, where I found a book on the extinction of passenger pigeons of America. It was like a great murder mystery I couldn't put down.

"I read every book I could find about extinction, and in the course of my reading I came upon Charles Darwin. The theory of evolution and extinction was a gospel without irreconcilable complications, without contradictions. It was provable, quantifiable. Life was a matter of chance, of randomness, and within the hands of chance, there was a kind of order.

"I began to haunt the Natural History Museum, where I pursued two things—the study of extinction, and the meeting of shiksas. I kept a notebook, where in the front section I listed the animals in terms of their kingdom, phylum, class, genus, species, and began to draw them. Then, in the back, in a special section all of its own, under the title SS, for Secret Shiksas, I am embarrassed to say, I recorded every one of my conquests—their names, their parents' names, the names of their grandparents' parents. I listed their physical characteristics—their hair color, the color of their eyes, their breast size, their scent. I wrote down the hour, the minute when I'd had them, where precisely I had had them, how often I had had them, and exactly where we were and what time it was when I shattered their dreams."

When he finishes his story, he finds himself crying briefly, inexplicably. After a moment's hesitation, Diane enfolds him in her arms. He doesn't let himself go, like he might have. Grief glimpsed, must by needs be short.

He wonders if she imagines he has revealed some vital secret to himself. Women often believe such things, he's found. He wonders why he has told it, and considers that he's told her so that she will know, as his wife did, that he is not a good nor a kind man, so that she will know she has not lost much.

When he leaves for India a few days later, he tries to imagine that he will never forget her, but he knows it isn't true.

Chapter 4

He has a heavy schedule in India—five wildlife preserves beginning in the state of Gujarat and ending in the state of Assam. It is there he will visit his mother's friend, Mim Ritchards—a woman his mother knew from the camps—and since Mim has recently lost her husband, his mother has asked him, as a favor, to visit her. He will stay with her in Dibrugarh for a week, and then go on to Guwahati, to the Kazaringa Wildlife Preserve, where the endangered one-horned rhinos are found.

He is unprepared for India. He's read about India's teeming masses, its stultifying poverty. He's seen photographs of her streets, filled with her people, where barefoot boys hustle wooden crosses ladened with cheap plastic trinkets, and marketplaces are startled with the reds, oranges, blues, purples, of women's saris and stacks of fruit, of pyramids of spices.

He has never seen so many eras represented at once, entire centuries, in fact, moving side by side like unlikely dance partners. Advertisements for air conditioners loom over hot, wide thoroughfares, where small, reedy, dark-skinned men pull rickshaws barefoot through the streets, and cows sleep imperiously in the mediums.

The mark of the British is indelible, their grand architectural wonders, a stark contrast to the drab, concrete structures that are India's own, at the base of which creeps this black mildew, spidery and ruinous, a rot from air corroded with fumes mixed with the wet of monsoons. And the smell, always slightly musty, as if all of India is a vast closed-up closet.

His first day in India, he gets lost in one of Bombay's most crowded slums. He has come from the train station, has taken the wrong direction and wandered into intolerably narrow lanes between the hovels, the hovels themselves, structures with no space between them, made of anything that is available—blankets, sheets of tin, of metal, cardboard. Here, India runs to brown; the skin of the people, their rags, the earth from which they seem distinguishable only in form.

It is their eyes that crush him; they stare out from the darkness of the hovels, filled with the stupor misery leaves behind, a residue of exhaustion and a hopelessness that differs in quality from eyes that have once known hope and then lost it. The smell of piss and shit bakes in the oppressive heat. The sound of swarming flies, of the din that comes when people are crowded together fills his ears. Up one claustrophobically narrow lane, then another, he panics when he cannot find his way, and is finally rescued by an old man in a dhoti, who quietly leads him out.

That night he takes an auto rickshaw to Juhu Beach, a swath of sand along the Arabian Sea. It is a waveless sea, copper-colored, capped by a cerulean-blue sky, the sand like brown sugar. He buys a *samosa* from a stall just off the road, and wanders down the empty beach. He is momentarily enchanted by the silhouetted image of a turbaned man giving camel rides to children on the shoreline. Out of nowhere a boy of eight years old maneuvers over to him on crutches and holds up his amputated leg, cut off from the knee. The boy makes a gesture with his cupped hand, moving it vigorously from his mouth to his stomach to indicate his hunger, and without thought, Will hands him the *samosa*.

He walks down to the shore, to escape the boy, and within minutes he is being followed by a ragged mother with a naked child on her hip, by a small girl who wears a sodden red dress, by an old blind man and his wife. The blind man has some English, and grips Will's arm. "Sir, I am blind. I am blind." Will looks briefly into his cloudy white eyes. He has no idea where they have come from. He hasn't seen them. They follow behind him, and the man who gives the camel rides pauses as Will passes with this parade of beggars.

He finally stops, and they crowd around him, the woman and the girl in the sodden red dress making the cupped hand gesture from mouth to stomach, moving their heads from side to side, a seesawing, importuning motion that he is not able to decipher; the boy holds up his amputated leg, the blind man and the woman tug at his shirt. He looks into their faces, into their pleading eyes, all of them greedy for life, and he takes money from his pocket and hands them each a few rupees. They wait for more, but when he shrugs, shows them his empty hands, they turn and move away wearily. The kestrels on Mauritius are treated with greater care than these people, he thinks, and later in the back of an auto rickshaw he finds himself crying into his sleeve.

He has no idea how delicate and finicky he is until he travels on India's trains. No matter how thirsty he is, he will go without water rather than to drink it from the greasy glasses old men dip up from plastic buckets on the train platforms. He will go without food rather than to take a paper plate of a yellow, mushy substance he can't recognize. He stands in despair in the doorway of a public bathroom in the Jaipur train station: to get to the doorless stalls, where there is a row of holes for toilets, he would have to pick his way gingerly, on tiptoe, through hundreds of piles of shit.

As he travels from preserve to preserve, the airs of India are potent and profuse and fall over him. He moves steeped in her mystifying vapors. She has strong, inescapable flavors; images and smells and sounds that impose themselves, that insist. Yet he feels eased here. In India, there is no hurry. Each day seems long and satisfying in its apportionment of time.

At the fourth preserve, the Kanha National Park, where he is to study the endangered tiger, his accommodations fall through, and he must stay with one of the rangers, a man named Mr. Belani and his dutiful wife, Raisha.

They live in a simple apartment on the eighth floor, and since there are no elevators, the open-air flights must be climbed. By American standards the two-bedroom apartment, with its linoleum floors and boxy drabness, would be considered a project. But in India such an apartment is the mark of solid middle class, and he must rave about it as Raisha proudly shows it off.

"It has two bedrooms," she says, "not just one." Will follows her from the living room into the first bedroom, then into the second; they are unremarkable rooms without much furnishings.

He finds himself saying, "It's beautiful."

"And Americans think all Indians live in hovels," she says.

Mr. Belani hangs back, as if slightly embarrassed, while Raisha takes Will into the kitchen, a room he finds starkly esthetic in its absence of all modern conveniences; there are no coffeemakers, no electric can openers or microwaves, no blenders. There is only a small altar on the wall, with a photograph of Ganesh and a small lit oil lamp, the fresh heads of orange marigolds adorning it. She has brought him in to show him the refrigerator, a small rounded Frigidaire-like box that Americans had in the thirties. She opens the door, proud to show him how cool it is inside.

"It's a real beauty," he says.

"And we have a washer too," she announces. She speaks quickly to the young girl servant in one of the Indian languages, and the girl moves out of the kitchen. She has been chopping vegetables with her head down the whole time they are admiring the refrigerator, and now they follow her to the bathroom, where she struggles to pull out a wringer washer Will remembers from his childhood.

"And you think we're not modern here," Raisha says.

"It's amazing," he says, patting its metal side.

Mr. Belani speaks sharply to her in their language, and Raisha quickly motions for the servant to put the washer away. Will is not certain what he's said, but he imagines Mr. Belani has let her know that they have washing machines that are far better in America, and now Raisha is embarrassed.

They insist he take their room, which is the large bedroom and the only room with air-conditioning.

"No, no, please," he says. "I couldn't possibly. I insist on the guest room. I will be much more comfortable there." His voice is importuning.

"No, no, we insist," Mr. Belani says. "We won't hear of it."

"You will stay here, in this room," Raisha says. "No, now, you must go inside and relax after your trip. You must be feeling very tired. Will you take tea?" In one of the Indian languages he understands not a word of, she instructs the servants to put his suitcases in this room, and after a few minutes, he finds himself sitting on the edge of their bed, blinking. He doesn't know if it is the thought of sleeping in their matrimony that so repels him, or if instead it feels as if it is an unearned right, one that he will have to pay for in ways he does not want to pay, in politeness.

He feels awkward. He senses their blind duty, which they are bound to dispense to all guests, independent of their true feelings, which he is certain are masked and will never be revealed. The idea that they must now play at this game of guest and host unsettles him.

After tea he washes up and goes out. The dust on the unpaved roads chokes him; the squalor is too close; hairless brown pigs root through thick, foul-smelling sewage that flows openly on either sides of the narrow roads. Scrawny children in rags stand barefoot in it and watch him pass. The air smells of backed-up water, stagnant and festering.

He sees a Hindu temple set back from the road, slips off his sandals, and walks across the cool marble to the temple inside. Somehow the strange doll-like gods of Vishnu and Lord Shiva give him comfort. They stand on a stage, offerings of coconut and marigolds at their feet. He sits down on a bench and gropes inside for some semblance of himself. He dreads going back to the apartment. He doesn't particularly like the couple, nor perhaps do they like him, and now they are going to have to go through a charade of politeness.

An hour later he climbs back up the eight flights to their apartment just in time for dinner, which is prepared in the small, dark kitchen by the servant girl, who stands in the doorway and stares open-eyed at him. When he looks back, she quickly averts her eyes and disappears into the kitchen. She is no more than twenty years old, and briefly, without much appeal, he considers having an affair with her as a form of comfort against Mr. and Mrs. Belani.

It would not have been so bad had there been some affinity, but there is absolutely none, which makes their dinner a strain. When their two daughters and their husbands come after dinner to meet him, he is forced to sit in the living room in the extreme heat, offering polite conversation, asking them all manner of questions, occasionally eating the desserts of *gulab jamun* and *rasmali* they pass him regularly, though he finds them cloyingly sweet.

One of the daughters, a heavy though pretty woman of twenty-four says, "You must be feeling very overwhelmed right now. You have never been in India, and to arrive here not knowing anything and anyone." She gives him a look as if to say, "To end up here is a sorrow."

He barely sleeps—he is not a man who feels at ease with strangers. He endures the nearly silent breakfast in the morning, then the car ride with Mr. Belani to the preserve, in which Mr. Belani, separated from his wife, talks incessantly about a variety of subjects; his son-in-law's small law practice, his neighbor's restaurant venture, his own hobby of collecting coins.

Two weeks stretches out before him like a year.

He dreads now having promised his mother that he would visit her friend Mim, in Dibrugarh. When he calls her to make the arrangements, he makes it clear that she needn't go to any trouble on his account, that he prefers fending for himself in terms of meals, that she must not feel obliged to spend time with him or coordinate any social functions for him.

The future is no longer a great tract of undiscovered land. It now has perimeters, its size no longer infinite, but finite. He must be careful with whom he spends his time.

There is trouble in Assam, and for twenty-four hours movement in and out is restricted, and he must stay an extra day with the Belanis. He knows nothing about Assam, but discovers that there is talk of ending the provisional government, of holding state elections. In 1979 the All Assam Students Movement began an anti-immigrant movement, and in 1980 they so effectively blocked a state census that the state government was paralyzed, the legislature dissolved in 1981. Since then Assam had been ruled by central government. The students were now stepping up their demands for the deportation of the "foreign" Bangladeshi, who they claimed were robbing them of their identity. They had been coming to Assam in great numbers since 1911, but Indira Gandhi's government said to deport them would be inhuman. There is now talk of disenfranchising those Bangladeshi who settled illegally in Assam between 1961 and 1971, but the students want them deported.

Nonetheless, he flies to the northeast jungle of India, to Assam; it is India's most remote appendage, cupped between the foreign palms of Bangladesh and Bhutan to Dibrugarh. The airport is no more than a large barn in the midst of rice paddies. There are pails on the floor, here and there, to collect leaks, and wild green parrots swoop in the rafters above. The only modern convenience is a conveyor belt which creakily ferries in suitcases.

Mim is waiting for him there. She is a tiny Polish woman, a far-flung piece of the Diaspora, he thinks, wearing the Penjabi, a traditional Indian dress of tunic and loose-fitting pants. Had he not known she was Polish, he might have taken her for an Indian woman.

She married an Englishman named Harold Ritchards a few months after her liberation from Auschwitz, and went with him to his tea gardens in Assam.

When he tries to retrieve his bags from the conveyor belt, she won't allow it. The driver, who has stood quietly off to her side, on her word, moves forward and hauls Will's suitcases outside.

Mim leads him out into the heat, which is so extreme he totters for a moment as they stand waiting for the driver to pick them up.

In the backseat of her blue Ambassador, Mim sits with one leg crossed delicately over the other. Her short dark hair is casually elegant, the red lipstick on her mouth, a becoming trace.

The road is so pocked and rutted from the rains, the driver must drive very slowly. It is quite drastic, as if they are on rocky terrain, and as the two of them bump and jar in the back, Mim seems unfazed.

"They don't repair the roads?" he asks.

"This is Assam with a provisional government," Mim says. "Hopefully, after the elections the roads will be repaired. But the elections, they are another nightmare. They are still six months away, but already there is trouble. The All Assam Students Movement will protest and there will be strikes. And now there is a more militant group emerging, the People's Liberation Army of Assam, led by a terrorist named Aban Bezbaruah. This is what has got the tea-garden owners nervous." She touches her forehead with the back of a delicately bent hand.

Outside, India moves in its medieval skirts along the edges of the road. Dark-skinned men the color of water buffaloes trod alongside bullock carts heaped with long green lengths of sugarcane, women walk in single file, baskets balanced on their heads, barefoot boys herd cows with sticks.

"I'm so glad for your company," Mim says, patting his hand. A mote of grief passes briefly through her eyes, and she dabs at the corners of her mouth with a Kleenex. "Harold's passing has come as a great shock to me. Not sick a day in his life, and then one night he has a coronary. For him, it was over quickly. But for me," she says, "it will take a long time." She smiles bravely, her fingers moving back and forth across the hill of her knee.

It is never easy to offer condolences, especially when you know neither the deceased nor the widow, but he tries. "I am very sorry, Mim," he says.

"Thank you." She touches the Kleenex to the corners of her eyes, then shifts herself toward him.

"I feel as if I already know you, Will. Your mother has told me so much about you. I have pictures of you from the time you were a small boy."

There has been mention of her all through his life too. He knows her to be the girl his mother knew in the camps, the girl whose ovaries were plucked from her, in a Nazi experiment, when she was eleven years old.

"Your mother was a very spirited girl," Mim says. "We girls all looked up to her. She was our inspiration. She refused to let her spirits sag. There was no girl more spirited than she."

She never mentions that it was in Auschwitz, that it was in the confines of a concentration camp that his mother had displayed such spirit, speaking as if it might have been an especially bad Kraków winter they had all endured.

"Your mother tells me you lost your manuscript in a fire," Mim says. He is surprised by how swiftly yet delicately she maneuvers herself to this fact.

"Yes," he says. "All the research, the drawings, everything."

"You poor man," she says.

When the driver turns onto a quiet lane, the chaos of the road is quickly replaced by the fertile green of the far-flung tea gardens of her tea estate. On either side of them stretch enormous fields of green waist-high tea bushes, dotted regularly with slender shade trees. Far in the distance, Will can make out the colorful shapes of dozens of women pluckers whose sweat and toil and misery is so removed both by distance and immediate experience, that they simply look beautiful within the gardens.

The gates to her compound open to a British-styled bungalow—a plantation house, with wide top and bottom verandahs. It is painted ochre, shuttered in green, and set back on a lawn of English design—a network of hedges and rose gardens, complete with arbors and marble benches. Three servants are at work pruning the hedges, mowing and sweeping the lawn.

The car pulls to the front door, and immediately two servants, dressed in ochre-colored safari shirts and trousers open the car doors. With one word from Mim, they quickly take Will's luggage and disappear inside.

It is a spacious, airy house, built to offset the oppressive heat; the ceilings are high, the windows tall and abundant, ceiling fans hoop in every room.

Her rooms are filled with Indo-English furniture, a marriage of teak and cane, each room well appointed with chandeliers, Persian rugs, gold-edged mirrors. The floors are tiled in white and blue, some marbled. Amid the British silver tea sets, banker's lamps, and delicate porcelain vases, are statues of the Indian gods, Durga and Ganesh among them—a comely marriage of two disparate cultures.

In every room, it seems, there are barefoot servants, men, women, of various ages, dusting, sweeping, polishing. When he and Mim enter, Mim speaks to them, and they nod, casting a quick, furtive look at Will, the younger women suppressing smiles. He counts at least twelve. It seems they each have a small role. This one dusts. This one sweeps. This one peels. This one cooks. This one drives.

When she shows him to his rooms—a suite in her bungalow—she says, "You do just as you like. I don't have delicate feelings. You stay as long as you like. Please yourself. It is the only thing I ask."

She leaves him alone, and he settles into a large cane chair with gargantuan arms, admiring the Persian rugs, the mahogany tables, the blue-tiled floors. After the tents and huts he's lived in over the past year, the opulence is overwhelming. Within minutes the servant he learns will be his, a quiet teenage boy named Aruun, enters tentatively with a tray, offering Limcas, tea, and small sweet biscuits.

So this is what it feels like to be the lordly white man in another man's country, he thinks. It is a complex feeling, an unfair pleasure, amusement even, coupled with an abhorrence.

After he's washed up and put away his things, Mim takes him on a tour of her estate. They drive slowly down the dirt lanes that traverse the tea gardens, and he now sees the women pluckers at close range. They wear ragged saris in bright colors, reds and oranges, purples and greens. A coiled cloth is set on their heads to cushion the weight of the gray cotton bags which hang from their heads and fall down their backs. They pluck the leaves quickly with both hands—two leaves and a bud, Mim tells him, and when their hands are full, they reach back and drop them into the bag. They are delicate, slender rhythms in the gardens, its dark moths.

"Where are the men?" he asks.

"The men don't pluck," she says. "The women make better pluckers. Their hands are more delicate, their temperaments more patient. The men do the pruning and keep the drainage system clear."

He sees a few of them, knee-deep in what looks to be a moat that surrounds the garden.

But it is mostly the women they see walking single file down the long lanes, reedlike in their sheaths of saris, treading slowly, only their thin hips moving, their upper bodies perfectly still, as they balance large baskets on their heads. Their faces lack all expression, as if the heat and the plucking have taken something from them which they can never get back.

They are tribal people recruited over a hundred years ago by the British from the state of Orissa, and they no longer know anything of their origins. Whole generations have grown up and died on her tea estate, she says, without many of them having ventured off more than a few miles in either direction.

They are the tea gardens' disconsolate children.

They drive slowly through one of the small lanes on the edge of the gardens where they live, a place called the Line. Will stares out the window at the rows of serried hovels, made of bamboo and mud, at pale, bony goats and chickens scratching in the dirt of the front yards, at the children who play in rags, the old people who sit slumped in doorways in the stupor of misery.

He says nothing, though he is shocked by the squalor, by the obvious difference in lifestyles. It is nearly slavery, he thinks, but he says nothing.

"It's an old system," Mim says. "It's much better than it used to be. They've now got running water and electricity. Harold put it in a few years ago. A lot of the tea-garden owners have not done this."

They drive by the small hospital on the premises, a large camplike infirmary, run by a kindly middle-aged doctor named Dr. Chaund, and though Will is apprehensive about meeting the paralyzed boy Mim has described to him, he follows her into the room where he lives. He is one of the tribal boys, she tells him, who fell from a tree at the age of four, and would be so honored to meet an American scientist. The boy is fifteen now. Paralyzed from the neck down, he is confined to bed, to this small hospital room, but as soon as Mim walks in, he breaks out in a grin. When she speaks to him, his eyes shyly shift to Will.

"I've told him you are a scientist, who studies extinction," Mim says. "He's very interested in science."

"What kind of science?" Will says. As Mim asks and the boy replies, Will's eyes gingerly take in the boy's lifeless arms, the tiny brown hands that have curled over.

"He is studying biology right now."

Will nods, smiles, and the boy smiles, makes that seesawing motion with his head. Something breaks open inside of Will, a pity, coupled with a strange gratitude for the boy's cheerfulness.

"What will happen to him?" he asks when they leave.

"He will be taken care of until the day he dies," she says.

He has dinner with Mim out in her garden, an English-inspired garden, lush with mums and roses. When her girl servant, Latisha, brings out coffees and bread, Will reflexively thanks her.

After she leaves, Mim smiles and says, "You don't need to thank them. I know the temptation is very strong, but you will wear yourself out. You will find that they do everything, and if it makes you feel better, I tell you I pay them well, better than the Indian tea-garden owners."

She smiles again. "I think of them as my children." And when a few moments later she adds, "I was not able to have children of my own," he remembers why and the look in her eyes, an acceptance of life at its cruelest, crumples him.

Two hours slip by in good conversation, and in the morning, she has the beautiful oil maps of the world he has bought in Cairo hung on the walls of his living room and then has a long desk set beneath them. He finds himself writing there in the afternoon, the first words he's typed since he conferred his last pages to ashes and let them fly in a breeze outside his bedroom window: *When the Siberian white crane is lost, it will be like losing fingers. Losing the Asiatic elephant, like losing a limb, the tigers gone, an eye . . .*

They fall easily into the routine of having breakfast over the papers in her lavish dining room, where they eat toast and marmalade and discuss the political situation in Assam. Without her husband, she feels defenseless.

"I am just a Polish Jew tea-garden owner now," she tells him. "No one would say so to my face, but this is what I am. I am a foreigner here, Will, and right now the Assamese call the Bangladeshi foreigners, but I fear one day they will turn and call the tea-garden owners foreigners. And I will be the first to go. I am not Indian born, and even those Indian born, if they are not Assamese, they are considered aliens. A bride comes from another state, from the state of Gujarat, say, and for years she will struggle to gain acceptance here. In India the alliances are very narrow."

"They are not interested in the tea-garden owners," Will says. "It is the Bangladeshi they want out."

"It is only a leap of thought away," she says.

Though he tries, there is nothing he can say that will soothe her.

After breakfast he works well in his rooms, and in the afternoons he often takes her Ambassador car and driver into Dibrugarh and wanders around. It throngs with a thick tide of bicycle rickshaws, oxen-drawn bullock carts, cars and diesel buses, the traffic chaotic, every man for himself. The dust is always ankle-deep, rising and falling with every step, every turn of wheel.

The shops are concrete cells, open in front, with no windows to look into, no doors to walk through, stuffed with saris and plastic buckets and small electric appliances, things he could not conceive of ever wanting. Some are just wooden stalls where bearded dark-skinned men sit cross-legged or squat on their haunches next to jars of spices, or neatly arranged fruits. The men are often so still, flies cluster at the watery edges of their eyes.

He goes every day to Sari's News, a newspaper store where Mr. Hazaraki, the proprietor, mails Xeroxed copies of his latest pages to a safety-deposit box in New York.

This is where he meets Stella Fars. When he comes in, she is leaning heavily against the counter, asking for Hot Stuff, a salty mixture of fried lentils and chickpeas. When Mr. Hazaraki doesn't understand her, she says it loudly, precisely. "Hot Stuff. Hot . . . Stuff." Then, spotting it hanging on a rack behind him, she points. "Right there," she says impatiently. "There, behind you. No, to your right. No, up. No, I said up. I said *up*." The poor man is in a panic, reaching for one thing after another. Finally he touches the right bag, and Stella says, "Finally."

He watches as she tears open the bag of Hot Stuff and pours some into her small hand. She throws it back into her mouth and stands for a moment chewing it. He can tell she relishes it. She leans a hip against the counter, and tosses back another handful. Only then does she acknowledge his presence, surveying him, without the slightest self-consciousness.

"Where you from?" she says.

"New York," he answers.

"Oh," she says. "I was afraid you were one of those British left over from the Raj." She is a small woman, petite and blonde, and wears a pair of bright blue corduroy shorts that fall just above her knees and a pair of lime-green sneakers. She reminds him of a teenage boy, though he guesses she is about thirty-five.

"Where in New York?" she says.

"I live on Charles Street."

She brightens. "I live on Perry, at Bleecker Street. Do you ever go to the restaurant on Charles and Bleecker, the Trattoria?"

"All the time," he says.

"Do you go downstairs with the fountains?"

"Sometimes," he says. "But I never liked it much down there."

"Me either. I think it's tacky. They have good lasagna, though."

"I like their calamari."

"What is your name?"

"Will," he says.

"I'm Stella."

She invites him to go across the street to sit in a small restaurant, and they order tea and talk about the things New Yorkers always talk about—rent and apartments and restaurants—and they discover, in the midst of it, that they are both Jews. Had they met in New York it would have meant nothing, but now, meeting one another in Dibrugarh, it takes on a startling, almost fateful quality.

"What's your last name?" she asks.

"Mendelsohn," he says. "My name is actually Elisor Mendelsohn, but my mother let me change it when I was ten. I named myself after Will Rogers."

"Well, mine is Stella Greenblatt, but I go by my stage name, Stella Fars." She tosses her blonde crop of hair back and assumes a feminine air.

He finds her unusual. She seems to possess equal amounts of masculine and feminine, slipping between the genders smoothly, almost imperceptibly.

"If you promise not to tell Grace Tagore, I'll tell you what just happened to me," she says. She shrugs forward, shakes her hair so that it falls over her eyes, and he sees again a teenage boy.

"I don't even know Grace Tagore," he says. "Who is Grace Tagore?"

"She's a filmmaker. She's from New York too. We're writing a screenplay together. That's why I'm here. You'll meet her," she says.

In exchange for meeting Grace Tagore, it seems, he must now hear the story of her meeting with two young men from the All Assam Students Movement. She's just paid ten dollars to see their machete. She followed them down a side street and through a shop that made clay statues of the goddesses Durga and Kali, and out the back, where she waited on the banks of the Brahmaputra River for them to bring out one of their machetes. When they put it into her hands, she first touched its rounded steel hump, then did a capoeira dance (a Brazilian martial arts), *jingaing* back and forth, squatting into stealthy poses.

"Did you ever kill anyone with this?" she asked them.

They looked at one another and laughed.

"Did you whack any Moslem heads off? Come on, tell me. Did you?" she said. She moved back and began to slice slowly through the air with the machete. When she asked them if they had any machine guns, they laughed nervously.

"Come on, you've got them, don't you?"

Anup, the thin, quiet one stepped back.

"Maybe we know where there is one," Bhupen said, stepping forward. "But we would have to take you into the jungle. It would cost ten times the amount."

"I told them I might come back in a few days," Stella says. She gulps the sugary remains of her tea.

He has never met anyone like Stella Fars.

"So you like machine guns and machetes?" he says.

"Yeah," she says. "Don't you? They're hot and sexy. They're beautiful, well-made machines. Don't you think?"

She suddenly reminds him of a kid brother, and though he doesn't often think of machine guns or machetes, he doesn't want to hurt her feelings. Her enthusiasm is so genuine, and he answers, "They are beautiful, aren't they?"

It is the right answer, he discovers, and imagining they have bonded on this matter of machetes and machine guns, she invites him to meet Grace Tagore. "You'll like her. She's smart and funny, but you can't tell her about my meeting the students. She would flip. Okay? She goes nuts about things like that."

Will is not quite sure why he agrees to this arrangement, but he does, and finds himself jockeying down the street with her, plunging through the thronging traffic by her side, in fact, helping to put her bicycle in the trunk of Mim's Ambassador.

When they are in the backseat, bumping through Dibrugarh, he wonders why he has come. Does he really want to meet Grace Tagore?

"I should tell you that Grace is married to Vikram Tagore. But not exactly. They haven't had sex in eight years." She takes a cigarette from the pocket of her shorts, lights it delicately, and sits back against the wide seat, crossing her legs gracefully. She turns and smiles at him, a woman.

She is a small beauty, he notices. Her mouth is full, and for those few minutes the wind blows her hair back and the smoke swirls around her, she seems so radiant a being that his life with Mim is suddenly thrown into stark contrast. It feels heavy and plodding, his existence with her the life of a married couple advancing in years.

When Mim's driver turns off the main road onto a quiet lane of the Tagore Tea Estates, he is struck again by the beauty of the gardens, the women, a hundred in a field, spread out in various rows, the stillness, the utter quiet beneath the sound of the crows.

The sun above is set in the sky like a lidless eye that bears down so fiercely and with such intense heat that it stills everything. The unrelieved blue that surrounds it, a perfect flawless veil, hides the bones, the veins, the flesh that belong to this radiant eye that never blinks and that gives release only at night, when it retreats beneath a dark blanket of sky.

The car stops at the gates that surround the Tagore bungalow, and Stella pokes her head out of the window and waves.

The gates open to a bungalow set back on lawns that are violently green, edged perfectly in orange masandra and pink bougainvillea. It is a British-style bungalow, similar to Mim's—a large house with spacious top and bottom verandahs. Attached to the bungalow by a long, slender sidewalk arbored in yellow hibiscus, is a small house, a simple Swiss chalet-looking structure with a wide porch.

Will follows Stella across the drive and nods to the servants, who stare openly from underneath the shade of a mango tree. Stella points to the little chalet. "That's the Small House," she says. "Vikram lives up there." When Will glances up, his eye, as if by some force, is carried to the second-story window, where he sees the face of an Indian man, a man who appears to be no older than himself. He is lying in a bed. Will can only make out the left side of his face, the delicate curve of his shoulder.

"He's dying, you know," Stella says.

He suddenly feels as if he is trespassing, entering a private scene into which he perhaps should not. He has misgivings about coming now, a strange lark that had begun innocently enough, but the moment he had felt such satisfaction in the back of the car disappears. When they finish the sidewalk and slip onto the tiled verandah, a dozen blue-black crows take sudden flight from the eaves. It is odd, the suddenness of it, their near proximity, the multiple sound of their wings.

Stella leads him through a tidy drawing room of straight-backed white sofas and dark-wooded tables, over which ceiling fans hoop, and soundlessly, two young servants, both dressed in white safari shirts and dark trousers, emerge from the kitchen. One, Ajit, a teenage boy, is shy and withdraws immediately, while Vedeshpra, older by at least ten years, stands waiting.

"Where is Grace?" Stella asks.

"Memsahib is upstairs," he says.

Will follows Stella up a dark wooden staircase and down a long marble hallway, the walls painted a pale apple green. When she leads him into a large bedroom with blue-tiled floors and a white English canopy bed, he feels again as if he is trespassing, but nonetheless he follows Stella out the French doors onto the verandah, where Grace sits in a cane chaise, writing in a notebook. She looks up at the last moment, and suddenly he finds himself staring into the pale blue eyes of a blonde, leggy woman.

"Grace, this is Will," Stella says. "Will, this is Grace. He's writing about world extinction, and is going to the Kazaringa. He's another Jew from New York. I'll be right back," she says, and she goes off to change her clothes.

"Hi," Grace says. "Have a seat." She gestures with her hand for him to sit down in the chaise next to her. Her hand has a delicacy to it, quite unlike Stella's. In fact, she is altogether unlike Stella. He doesn't know who he has expected, but it is not this blonde, leggy woman.

"But I am interrupting you," he says. His awkwardness is suddenly apparent. He can't keep his hands from touching his throat, from pushing up his shirtsleeves. He even knocks his knee against one of the small tables.

"Of course you know now that I am a Jew from New York," he says. "We're noted for our athletic prowess." Her laugh, so immediate and deep, surprises him.

"No, no," she says. "Please, sit down."

Her words put him at ease, and he sits down in the cane chaise next to her. The view is extraordinary—a tea garden stretching down a quarter of a mile to the banks of the Brahmaputra River, a gray-blue water that lies before the Himalaya like a vast moat; the mountains look vaguely ethereal, shrouded in blue. He feels for the moment as if he has happened upon Daisy Buchanan and Jordan Baker on a tea garden in India.

"Where did you meet Stella?" she asks. She's put her notebook aside, given him her full attention.

"Buying Hot Stuff at Sari's Newspapers."

She nods knowingly.

"She meets everyone. As soon as she got to Dibrugarh, she was having tea with the woman who runs the bordello, and bargaining behind the market with the men who deal in illegal contraband. She's got all sorts of things up in her room. Tiger's teeth and Tibetan monks' robes and Buddha heads," Grace says. She says it like a mother who tolerates, even feels a certain guarded affection for her child's strange passions.

Her blue eyes, blonde hair, and skin are a shade lighter than pale, he notices, a shade for which he can find no word. As if they've gone through a delicate bleaching, a subtle lightening, yet there is no trace of sickliness. He guesses her to be his age, maybe a few years younger.

Her servant, Vedeshpra, comes out to the verandah with two cups of tea on a tray, and she motions for him to put them down on the little table that stands between them. She is particularly solicitous with his tea, stirring it for him, which he takes as boldness, particularly when she glances up at him, as if to acknowledge the boundary she has crossed, small as it is.

She is lonely, he thinks. The idea of having an affair crosses his mind, and he suddenly wonders how close her husband is to death.

"How do you and Stella know each other?" he asks.

"I used her in a film I made. She played a part based on my aunt Jacqueline. I'm writing an action adventure for her now," she says. "I was dying of boredom here and had to bribe her with something. She wants to be like Linda Hamilton in *The Terminator*. There are motorcycle scenes, leaping-from-train scenes, car-chase scenes, a harrowing swim through an alligator pit." There is a sudden brightness in her eyes, an alluring mirth. "It bores me to tears, but don't tell her."

"I won't," he says.

"Now she wants to know the rebels. She wants to see someone's head get lopped off, you know. I've told her she can't get involved with them, but she doesn't listen. I suspect she's talking to them."

She takes a sip of her tea, looking over the rim of the cup, as if to suggest the question: "Did she say anything to you?"

He considers warning her that Stella has gotten involved, but it seems the act of a tattletale, and he says nothing.

"So you're a writer, traveling the world, writing about world extinction," she says.

"Yes."

"How interesting," she says. "You'll tell me about it, but first, how do you know Mim Ritchards?"

"How do you know I know Mim Ritchards?"

"Because I know her Ambassador. It's the only blue one in town."

"She's my mother's friend."

"She's very plucky, and everyone loves her."

"So you know her?"

There's now a steady line of contact between their eyes.

"Everybody knows her. Mim is the Grand Madam of the Tea Gardens. I am but Hester Prynne. I love Mim, but Mim doesn't like me."

"Why not?"

"You'll hear it from Mim because her driver will be incapable of not mentioning that he's driven you here with Stella Fars, so I'll tell you the rumor. That my husband is dying, and I have a lesbian lover living with me."

"It's not true?" he asks.

"Well, my husband is dying, and I have a lesbian living with me." She smiles and wipes a drop of tea from her lip, and he stares, transfixed. Her lips have a faint trace of red lipstick, her teeth even and white. Her cheekbones are high, rounded, her blonde hair cut in a classic page-boy style, which she has the habit of pushing behind her ears. His eyes stray discreetly down the length of her—the dress she wears is thin and he easily discerns the fullness of her breasts, the shapeliness of her legs, the alluring curve of her hipbones.

By the time Stella appears in the doorway, in a pair of green corduroy shorts and a black jog bra, it has already happened. His alliance
has shifted.

"You guys were talking about me," she says. Her eyes move between them.

"I was telling him you are crazy," Grace says. "That you are interested in machetes and machine guns."

Stella glances quickly at him to see whether he has told on her. His eyes
are innocent, and for the moment he counts himself in her good graces.

"Ajit," Stella calls out. The shy young servant boy appears, head
bent, in the doorway. "Go get mango at the market. Man-go."

"Usko suno mut," Grace says delicately, and the boy looks suddenly
grateful and disappears.

"But I want a mango now, not papaya, and he didn't get any man-
gos. Just let him go out. He doesn't care."

"No, Stella. He's not going out again for your mango. You asked
for papaya this morning. If you want mango now, you go out and get
it. He's not a slave." She turns to Will. "Stella loves the idea of having
slaves. Nothing would please her more."

"He's a servant," she says. "That's what he's here for, to serve."

"He's my servant, then, and I don't want him serving you."

"You don't know how to treat servants."

"And, of course, Miss Fars is an authority on servants," Grace says.
"We won't mention the poor retarded housekeeper in Indiana, who
practically drooled on herself, while Stella and her brother taught her
that one clap was for pretzels, two for Cokes."

Will and Stella both laugh, and just after Stella drops into the chair
next to Will, she says, "Grace didn't speak until she was eleven years
old, you know."

"Stop it, Stella, and behave," Grace says.

She gives Stella a sharp look, then turns to him. "You'll have to
forgive us, Will," she says. "We're like Gertrude Stein and Alice B.
Toklas, except that I'm not a lesbian, and Stella doesn't make tea."

When Will laughs, Stella goes silent. She crosses her arms against her chest, regards them both from under the cliff of her brow. She is in love with Grace, he thinks, and she regrets having invited him. She has miscalculated Grace's response.

"Grace is German, you know," Stella says.

"I'm American," Grace says.

"She's three quarters German, and one quarter French," Stella says. "She speaks German and French fluently. Say a sentence in German and another one in French," she says.

"Don't be ridiculous," Grace says.

"Come on, Grace," Stella says. "Just say one sentence in French and one in German. Tell her to say it, Will."

"I would like to hear," Will says carefully.

So Grace accommodates them. *"Je suis fatiguée, tu sais: J'en ai assez de toujours courir, de travailler tout le temps. Ich weiss, dass kommt ungelegen. Das tut mir auch leid."*

"The German rolls off her tongue, don't you think? And she looks so German, that pale Aryan skin—"

"Stella," Grace says. "Please."

"Her first words were German," Stella goes on. *"Ein, zwei, drei, vier, fuenf."* Stella pronounces each number with commanding force.

Will is surprised at how sternly Grace says, "Stop it, Stella."

Stella plays off this reprimand; it gives impetus to her sudden rise from the chaise. She clicks her heels together briskly and salutes Grace in the way of Nazi officers.

"Heil Hitler," she pronounces.

It doesn't seem quite possible, but Stella begins goose-stepping past the end of Grace's chaise, crying, *"Ein, zwei, drei, vier, fuenf."* Spittle flies from her mouth.

It is the tirade of a jealous lover, he thinks. She means to dislodge his alliance with Grace, pitting two Jews against the German. What doesn't quite figure is the look of sudden, unveiled sorrow that floods into Grace's eyes, in stark contrast to the alluring mirth he has seen just minutes before.

The moment passes and they go on to other things, but part of Will's mind is held captive by those moments when Stella has goose-stepped past Grace's chair. He finds he cannot keep his eyes from Grace, and sometimes the look she returns is bold, at others it is faltering and ineffably sweet.

When he uses the bathroom just off Grace's bedroom, he is surprised to find himself interested in her possessions. He quietly slides a drawer of a small bureau open and discovers that she uses French soaps and lotions. He touches the pink slip and a silk navy blue robe hanging on the back of her door between his thumb and forefinger.

When he returns to the verandah he hears a brief, unexpected snippet of their conversation.

"I should never have told you anything about me," Grace whispers. "And you goose-stepping past me. I can't believe you did that, Stella."

"You shouldn't have embarrassed me in front of the servant, then."

"I am sorry about that, but—"

"You can't get involved with him, you know," Stella says.

"Don't say it, Stella," Grace says, and Stella holds her tongue, when they see him in the doorway. It is an omission that never quite leaves his mind.

He leaves late in the afternoon after the fierce Indian sun has swooned in the sky.

Grace walks him to the car, and when he glances up at the Small House he again sees Vikram in the window. It feels strange now, not as it had earlier, but worse, as if he has not only trespassed, but has cuckolded the dying man in his own house. Especially when their hands accidentally brush, and neither moves to alter it.

He wants to say something, to invite Grace somewhere, but he can think of nowhere but the Umananda Temple that Mim has suggested he see. He mentions how nice it was to meet her. She smiles and looks down at her hands, which she clasps for a moment.

"Come back," she says.

He nods and climbs into the car.

On his way back to Mim's, the traffic is thick on the rutted road, a vein coursing a strange, uneven blood of bullock carts and auto rickshaws, buses, a blood that clogs and flows, pumped from an unseen heart. He watches from the backseat. Certain looks she's given him, he can't get from his mind; when she glanced up from stirring his tea, when after she said, "Come back." There was longing there, coupled with something else, something which he can't quite name.

He senses a powerful recognition between them, something that has happened maybe once or twice in his life, and he finds himself imagining a life with her. There is no basis for the feeling, nothing remotely concrete that would lead him to such thoughts; it is only an intuitive feeling, for which he has a certain healthy skepticism.

When he and Mim eat dinner, it is as Grace has said. As she sips her tea, she says, "So you've met Grace Tagore and Stella Fars today."

"Yes," he says. "I met Stella at the newspaper store, and she took me to the Tagore Estate."

Mim rolls her eyes and sighs. "Her husband is dying, and she's got a lesbian lover living with her."

"I don't think they are lovers," he says. "I think they write screenplays together."

"Her husband is dying, and he rents out a hall to show her film, *And Some Chose to Forget*. I am told by those who saw it, that they wished they could forget."

She lays her napkin down on the table and looks across at him.

So there will be a wrinkle in their otherwise smooth relationship.

In the 1890s, field naturalists noticed strange afflictions on many of the Hawaiian bird population—lesions and tumors around the face, on the legs and the feet. They were perplexed: The birds' food sources and habitats were intact. Inexplicably, from a total of eleven species of endemic perching birds inhabiting Oahu, six species were extinct by 1900. Little by little, the forests of Hawaii were being silenced.

No one knows for certain what happened, but there have been speculations, one quite plausible.

Until 1827, there were no mosquitoes in Hawaii. Not having a name for them, they first called them "a singing in the ear." It has been postulated that they came in with the British ship Wellington. The ship stopped at Lahaina on the west coast of Maui, having come from Mexico the year before, and a group of men disembarked to freshen their drinking water. Before refilling their casks, they emptied the dregs into an adjacent stream. An uncalculated, seemingly innocuous act, which had serious ramifications for the birds of Hawaii: The water was swarming with the larvae of Culex pipiens fatigans, a night-flying mosquito found along Mexico's west coast. Within ten years the mosquitoes were well established in Oahu and Kauai and Maui. As it turns out, Culex pipiens fatigans is the principle carrier of avian malaria.

The tally of ensuing extinctions grew long:

Drepanis pacifica	Kona gros-beak
the Hawaii mamo	Hawaiian rail
Drepanis funera	greater amakihi
Black mamo	Oahu nukapuu
Ciridops annu	amaui
Layson honeycreeper	kiola
the less Koa-finch	akialoa

From Notes on Extinction, by Will Mendelsohn

Chapter 5

Two days pass. He sits at his desk beneath the oil maps of the world and stares out the window at the heavy rains. He watches the women servants crouched under a covered walkway as they roll out with wooden pins small clay-colored sausages of crushed lentil. They work slowly, flattening them into thin round discs, every so often wearily shouldering the drapes of their saris.

When the rain stops, Will climbs into the back of Mim's Ambassador and asks to be taken to the Tagore Estate. As the car pulls away, he sees Mim draw the curtain back from the window. The driver will tell her where he has gone. When they pass rice paddies so green it is startling, he consoles himself with the idea that he has always followed his reason and it has not gotten him anywhere. He has lived too carefully, and every hour that is wasted is wasted now and will never be returned.

The gatekeeper lets Mim's car into the Tagore Estate without a word. He imagines that Grace has told them to let him in, and it breaks open unbidden hope. When he climbs out of the car, he looks up at Vikram's window. Mercifully, he is not there. The Tagores' driver, a sulky older man who sits beneath a mango tree, nods for him to go unescorted to the bungalow. Will feels his gaze follow his movement down the arbored sidewalk.

Vedeshpra answers the door, and after Will asks for Grace, the servant nods and disappears up the front stairs, his feet so light they are barely discernible. As Will stands in the foyer waiting, he is surprised by the sudden violence of his heartbeat.

In a few minutes Stella sulks down the wooden staircase, barefooted, with a blue-and-white silk robe tied loosely around her waist.

"You're back so soon," she says. She arches her eyebrows suggestively. "Vedeshpra," she calls, and within moments the servant appears in the doorway. "Two teas with milk," she says. She leads him into the drawing room that is much like Mim's, with its high ceilings and ceiling fans, with its Persian rugs, yet there is a trace of youth to it—white sofas and chairs, modern Indian paintings, sparely arranged.

Stella stretches out on one of the straight-backed white sofas, crossing her legs over its delicate arm. The robe falls open a bit, revealing a triangle of thigh. It is the silk bathrobe that has given her the cue to be a woman, he thinks. Without the prop, it would disappear. Had he not met her before, he might have been fooled. He pictures her taunting men with her femininity, attracting them with her wiles, only to laugh at them when they come to her aroused.

He sits down across from her.

"You got a cigarette?" she says, and when he hands her one, she leans over the coffee table for a light, and as the end burns to life, she looks up into his eyes.

"She got under your skin," Stella says. "Poor dear, you're pining."

She knows the look; it is in her own eyes, he thinks. She sits back on the sofa, holding him fixed in her gaze. He is trespassing.

"Is Grace here?" he asks.

"I wondered when you were going to ask," she says. "You may as well forget her right now. She's *very* married." The way in which she narrows her eyes lets him know they have entered a contest, one in which he is certain he will win. But it is Stella's mistake, he thinks. She makes judgments based on her own: she is not attracted to him, thus she imagines Grace would not be either.

"Is she here?" he asks.

"It depends," Stella says.

"Depends on what?"

"It depends on how badly you want to know." She slips forward on the sofa, crosses her legs, playing at being a woman.

"What would you be willing to do for the information?"

"What do you mean?"

"I know where she is, and it would be a perfect place for you to find her. Beyond perfect."

When he asks what it is she wants, she answers, "A hundred dollars."

It is so indelicate a moment, so unlovely, and yet it has a gamelike quality to it, as if they are betting now, pitting their luck. He does not know why he takes it from his wallet and lays it on the coffee table, but he does, and Stella's fingers close around it. As she folds it into the pocket of her silk robe, she smiles at him, the way one smiles at fools.

As he walks through three dark tea gardens to a banyan grove that grows, shrouded, along the banks of the Brahmaputra River, he is not certain what exactly has been transacted. Is it a bet on who can win Grace? he wonders. He and Stella cast as rival suitors?

He encounters a few tribal men climbing the shade trees, breaking off branches for firewood. When they see him, they shimmy down and duck into the tea bushes. The men on the tea gardens are useless. It is the women who do all the work.

He finds Grace alone in the midst of the strange, dwarfed banyan trees. She wears a thin white dress and black riding boots. There is now such a direct link between her womanhood and his desire, it surprises him. With Diane the link had been comprised only of a few threads.

He stands quietly, the river slipping by soundlessly, dotted by a few lights trailing from the junks which pass further out. The black Arabian horse she has ridden shakes its long neck at the edge of the river, its metal chains jangling.

It is awkward, his coming here. What is he to say now? He thinks of turning around and retracing his steps through the garden, but the idea of nothing happening, of stasis, is suddenly an agony.

"Grace," he says quietly.

She is startled by his presence, and lets out a small gasp.

"Stella told me you were down here," he says.

Her hand goes to her throat. "I thought you were one of the tribal men," she says. It is her relief that allows him to enter the banyan grove.

But he senses her guard. She has not thought of him as he has thought of her. She has a full and complex life, he thinks—a husband who is dying, but nonetheless one who needs her, another woman who loves her, with whom she works, not to mention the tea gardens. While he is alone, living with an old woman, tied to no one, to nothing, with a vague need to visit the Kazaringa in the near future. A man lost. He feels the hole of his own need. Yet, oddly, on the edge of oblivion, it comes back to him, the first look she gave him when she stirred his tea. Hadn't it beckoned him closer?

While the horse wades near the edge of the river, they sit on the banks of the Brahmaputra. They talk awkwardly of the heat, of Stella and Mim. It is the sort of conversation he dislikes, but he does his part. Perhaps it has been a fluke, their ease with one another the day they met.

But when it comes, it comes quite suddenly, on the most banal of subjects—baths. They mention how hot it has been, and discuss the various methods they employ when the air-conditioning fails.

"I try to take cool baths sometimes," she says. "But I can't ever get myself to sit in the bath, no matter what. After a minute or two, I don't know what to do with myself, and I get up."

"I don't like them either," he said. "I do exactly the same thing. It's too leisurely somehow."

"Yes, exactly. I guess you have to be the sort of person who knows how to relax."

He is not certain why it is suddenly so exciting, this similarity.

They discover how many strange little things like this they have in common. Neither of them likes jazz music or dusty antique shops. They hate parties and small talk—they suffer the same discomfort.

"What do you think of India?" she says.

"I feel seduced," he says.

"Yes, it's true. You fall under her spell. Don't you?"

"Yes."

They go on trying things out on each other. A few times he fudges so as not to break the rhythm. He exaggerates his dislike of a few books she has hated. He lies about liking opera. She loves it, she says. In fact, her mother had been an opera singer, but it is going so well, he doesn't have the heart to admit that he despises opera.

He watches the slow way she pushes her hair back behind her ears when she admits softly to preferring Wagner because her mother had sung it best; the long incline of her neck when she bends forward, the delicate slope of her breasts, the way she rolls a fallen banyan leaf between her fingers. There is still something of the girl about her.

He finds himself telling her about his stay with the Belani's: his immediate discomfort when he was forced to take the couple's room, the meals he felt compelled to keep afloat with questions, none of which he cared to hear answered, the days he was forced to spend with Mr. Belani, who put him in a stupor with his dull conversation, and how in his room one night, he actually stood on the balcony and looked down with the thought of jumping.

She tells a similar story and the internal experience is so exact, the understanding so precise, they laugh. It is a spontaneous, deep laughter born of complicity, and for those moments, he feels the exquisite absence of loneliness.

He leans over suddenly and kisses her mouth. He is astonished by the eagerness of her response. It is immediately potent. He can't remember ever having felt the same mixture of passion and heat, coupled with this—he knows no other word to call it—affinity they've discovered together. They part for a moment and stare into one another's eyes, sharing an open, startled look. She slips away then. It isn't abrupt, but rather silken.

"I've got to give Vikram his medicine," she says.

When she slaps her thigh, the horse clamors up the banks of the river. His mood is quickly altered. Has she inserted her husband at this moment to come between them? Or is it something else? She grabs the reins, and in an instant she swings onto the horse's back and holds out her hand to him. She slips her foot from the stirrup so that he can mount.

"Hold on now," she says. He puts his arms around her waist, and midway through the tea garden, he touches his lips to her neck, and she moves her head to make it easier. Without expecting it, he is flooded with relief.

Inside the stable they dismount, and he watches as she takes the horse by the reins to groom. It suddenly feels absurd, the way he watches her, the way his heart races ahead. An aging Romeo, watching his middle-aged Juliet. But what else is there to do?

They walk across the fragrant lawns, their hands clasped behind their backs, as if they are just friends strolling, admiring the infinitude of the Indian sky. He glances up at the Small House and sees Vikram in the window.

"What is Vikram's illness?" he asks carefully.

"No one knows. He just seems to weaken every day. When I first came, he used to be able to walk through the gardens, but not anymore."

The line between her eyes deepens, and her hand pulls absently at the seam of her dress. "He's been sick for two years," she says. She has only been with him the last year. The first year, she had been living in Paris with Stella. Before that they had not lived together for a few years.

"Why don't you come up and meet him," she says.

"Should I?"

"Yes, you should," she says. They exchange a glance, which he cannot decipher.

He follows her up the stairs of the Small House to the second floor. Vikram has his own staff of servants who stir at the top.

He has taken refuge in the front bedroom. He lays beneath white sheets, in the wooden slat bed he'd slept in as a boy, his brown skin perfectly poreless, like the skin of a baby. He is tall for an Indian, his hands especially delicate. His lips are dark red, his nose fine. He is thin now from dying.

"Vikram, I've brought someone to meet you," Grace says. From habit, she moves to the side of his bed. Vikram struggles to sit up, but she tells him not to.

"I saw you two come in on Gypsy," he says pleasantly, but his eyes move restlessly between them. They have that clarity that death's approach only sharpens.

He is not at all what Will has imagined. He has expected someone with that endearing wobble of head, the singsong accent, the deep smile. But Vikram's Indianness has been subverted, lost. He is American.

"Yes, Stella told him where I was, and he found me in the banyan grove with Gypsy," Grace says. She touches his hand to dispel his fear, and he relaxes. "Vikram, this is Will. Will, this is Vikram. He's staying with Mim Ritchards, and is going on to Kazaringa soon."

Vikram smiles and reaches out his thin brown hand. It is the frailest of hands.

Will sits down in the chair Grace offers him and follows her movements as she walks around the room, straightening it up, moving the vase of flowers from one place to another.

"When I met Vikram, he was a man without a country," Grace says. "There were no photographs of his family in his house, no clothing from India, no bedding, no books, none of India's music. The only thing he had were Indian spices in his kitchen cabinet, and when he counted, he counted with his digits and not his fingers, like all Indians do."

Vikram enjoys her talk of him, as if he is some curiosity she needs to explain, and he obliges her now by a show of counting his digits. "*Ek, do, tin, char, panch,*" he says. "*Chhe, saat, aath, nau, dus.*"

She sits down in the chair next to the bed and begins to peel an apple for him. Will cannot yet decipher her intent. Is she displaying her marriage for him, or is she putting on a show for Vikram's sake?

"Vikram moved to the United States when he was seventeen," she says. "He went to Harvard. Everyone tells me he is very brilliant."

"They have to tell her because she cannot tell on her own," Vikram says. Will glances at Grace and sees a flash of impatience cross her eyes.

Have they entered into a conspiracy together to have an affair under Vikram's nose? he wonders. Were they going to play at being friends? Steal down to the banyan grove? Meet in dingy motels?

On his way out of the Small House, he glances through the railings briefly and sees her bent over him, unbuttoning his white pajama top.

"I walked to the bathroom myself," he hears Vikram say.

"That's good, Babu." She kisses his smooth forehead, still so untrammeled, even in his dying. Her voice is tender in a way he has heard only rarely. In some way, she loves him.

In the lush dark in the back of Mim's car, he wonders how he can consider taking a dying man's wife. He feels no guilt, only pity. A dying man is no competition. He is only sick at the thought that he might not be able to accomplish it. His sudden greed astonishes him, his mind now lingering on thoughts of her naked body coupled with his own. He pries into every place of her, without fear, with devout interest and curiosity. He pulls off her riding boots, kneeling between her legs, sliding his hands beneath her dress, taking her breasts into his hands. It startles him the sudden power of the fantasy, the many erotic shifts it takes in only a moment's time. He had imagined this sort of power of feeling was lost to him.

Mim is still up when he gets home. She comes into his rooms and sits in one of the cane chairs. He assumes she knows that he's gone to the Tagores'. The driver has been in and out of the kitchen already, but she says nothing about it.

"I find out today that Latisha is in love with Aruun," she says. "I found them holding hands and giggling out in the back garden." She sits with one leg crossed delicately over the other, a white silk scarf tied loosely around her neck, a trace of red lipstick on her mouth.

"Could they marry?" he asks.

"Yes, I don't see why not. They are both from the tribal people who work on the gardens. They marry and unmarry each other all the time. They often make such messes of things. Harold used to have to go down to the Line and settle their love disputes. This one is married to this one but is in love with this other one. There would be drunken brawls when one man laid his hands on another's wife. All sorts of intrigues."

He wonders why she is telling him this, if there is an underlying reason, but she doesn't pursue the subject, and he thinks perhaps he is being too sensitive.

Later, when he loses to her in canasta, he lays his cards down. "Have I overstayed my welcome?"

"You've done nothing of the sort," she says. He looks at her and sees a fear in her eyes. "I don't want you to go."

So he will be staying, then.

Chapter 6

He wakes in the middle of the night into a rare state of mind, a vision-state, one marked by sudden clarity: He married his wife to guard himself against the very feeling that Grace has now aroused in him. He married her to keep himself, in fact, from all feeling, to freeze him into a middle position where he was kept from either extreme: passion or utter loneliness. His marriage was wholly dishonest, his wife never his partner, but rather his shield.

Now, his mind has seized upon Grace. He is suddenly frightened. He does not love often nor easily, but when he loves he loves intensely, often to his disadvantage. He has tried to change this in himself, without any success. He has never been a man given to wide variety. He has always envied those men who spread themselves wholeheartedly across wide gulfs, whether it be social circles, books, travel. He has always secretly believed that they possess much more than he does. He is a man who stumbles accidentally upon one thing only, giving himself to it with an exclusivity that borders on the perverse. He has been known to read one book six times rather than to read six different books, to take from it nearly the very glue and spine of it, until he exhausts it. And yet when his interest departs, it leaves finally, never to be revived or solicited again.

He has the rhythms of a desert dweller: a man who comes upon an oasis every now and then, but who mostly walks ploddingly forward; a man who has walked too often guided by the illusions of the land, and has found out quite late, that it is the stars from which he should seek direction, for unlike the land, which shifts according to the winds, the stars are fixed in an inalterable pattern.

When he gets up, the revelation has lost some of its clarity. All morning he works, but she is never far from his mind. Not since he sat outside the caves of the Vanikoro swiftlets has he had much taste for writing this book, he must admit. He no longer believes in spreading the gospel of saving the world. He can only document the destruction, which somehow feels small, diagnostic. His work has betrayed him. Each morning, like a jilted lover, he returns to it apprehensively. He cannot rely upon it with the same trust. He continues to light the oil lamp each morning beneath the photograph of a Ganesh that Mim has put into his bedroom, with some vague, dry hope that it will not only protect his work, but will inspire him as well. He doesn't understand himself. He has never had even a fleeting belief in such things.

He writes about the day he held the last rufous fantail on the earth in the palms of his hands, how he took it to the sea with Rita while she cried in the roar. It seems sentimental now, and he gets up from his table and goes outside to sit in Mim's gardens and watches the servants bent over sweeping the dead leaves and petals from the earth. He envies them the ease and clarity of their work.

In the afternoon he looks up from his work and finds Stella in the doorway. Aruun has shown her in. She is overheated from her bike ride and slumps down into the chair across from him. There is no trace of the woman who wore the navy blue silk robe. The teenage boy has returned in green corduroy shorts, a white T-shirt, and a pair of black high-top sneakers. From the headphones of a Walkman hanging around her neck, he hears the faint sounds of Bruce Springsteen. The whole time she is with him, she leaves it playing. It is a small tinny sound he is never quite unaware of.

"I went into the jungle last night with Bhupen and Anup," she says. This is why she has come, to tell him the story. He understands now how their relationship is going to work: when she is with him alone, he is her friend. When Grace is present, he is her rival.

"I paid them a hundred dollars, and they let me shoot off their machine gun. We had to walk an hour through rice paddies to get there." There is a flickering of uncertainty in her eyes, as if she is unsure of her experience.

Nonetheless, he is disconcerted to realize that the hundred dollars he'd given her to discover Grace's whereabouts has been used to pay the students to shoot their machine gun. He and Stella have now inadvertently entered into a pact of secrecy against Grace, one for which he has not bargained.

"What happened?" he asks.

"It was great—the shooting the machine gun part."

"What happened?" He feels his heart begin to beat faster.

She tells him she followed Bhupen and Anup through miles of rice paddies. All she could hear was their breath and hers, the sound of waded-through waters, the metallic screak of the kerosene lamps as they swung from their handles.

They took her to a clearing where a stuffed white dummy hung from the branch of a tree. It was there that she met their leader, Chetia, who she describes as being the only Indian man she has ever found remotely attractive. He was tall and slender, no more than thirty years old. His body was an inviolate line, his bones strung in flawless alignment, the muscles laying upon them defectlessly. When he walked toward her, he did so with the air of a dictator.

He made a quick motion with his hand, and Anup and Bhupen disappeared. She had no idea where they had gone, but quickly Chetia spread an Indian cotton blanket out on the tangled weave of vines.

"Please," he said. "Sit here with me." He gestured with his hand, and Stella sat down on the blanket under the great canopy of the jungle. After she gave him the hundred dollars, Chetia whistled long and high, and within moments Anup and Bhupen appeared out of the darkness of the jungle in the clearing. Anup brought Chetia the AK-47, and he quickly snapped the magazine into place, the sound of the click so clean and abrupt that it severed them completely from their last moments.

Chetia placed the machine gun in Stella's hands. She felt its heft and fitted it into position under her right arm, her left hand cradling the barrel. Squeezing her left eye shut, she peered through the sight with her right eye. She walked around the circle until she found the optimum place from which to shoot. When she took aim and fired, she was a terrorist, an insurrectionist, a member of a family of murderers. The sound of the machine gun in her ears was deafening. It filled the whole of her consciousness, no words now, just this sound, the voice of power, amplified now within the coil of the jungle, rapid fire bursting nonstop, metallic ejaculations decimating in seconds. The sight of the dummy jumping as if on the strings of a demented puppeteer inspired her. Then she heard the plash and saw the dummy severed in half on the ground.

When Chetia took the gun from her hands and dismantled it, they heard the sound of a man cry out in pain no more than a hundred yards away in the pitch-black.

"Who was that?" Stella asked. Chetia said it was their prisoner.

"Let me see him," she said.

Chetia paused and considered it, finally shaking his head. "It is not a good idea," he said.

"Oh, come on. Just let me see him. I won't do anything."

He took her then, Bhupen leading the way with the kerosene lamp, Chetia right behind her telling her what the prisoner had done. His voice was soft, restrained, as he detailed the atrocities.

The man was Bangladeshi. He had gone to the houses of many Assamese farmers while they were in the fields and had raped their wives at knifepoint. He had left a few dead, lying in pools of blood in their kitchens. He had thrown one in a scalding bath. He had raped girls, some as young as four, and had dismembered one and thrown her limbs into the fields. One woman's heart he had cut out and nailed to the wall above her bed.

No one said anything when they came upon the prisoner. The man was on his knees, his hands bound behind his back. A black cloth was tied around his eyes. His mouth was twisted in grief, his body strung taut in fear. He looked no different than Anup or Bhupen or Chetia. He had the same black hair, the same brown skin, the same reedlike slenderness.

Chetia reached down and yanked the blindfold from the prisoner's eyes. The man blinked in the light, trying to take it all in quickly.

Chetia prodded him with the toe of his boot and spoke harshly in a language Stella did not understand. The man shouted something back and spit at the ground near Stella's feet.

"What did he say?" Stella asked.

"I asked him if he was ready to talk, and he said that he would not speak in front of a—" He stopped speaking.

"Of a what?" Stella said.

"A whore," Chetia said quietly.

"Fuck him," Stella said.

Chetia kicked the prisoner in the stomach, as if to defend Stella's honor, and Bhupen hit him over the shoulder with a wooden bat. The man howled in pain, and Bhupen struck again with the bat, this time across his chest, Anup kicking the tender places on the man's back that marked his kidneys. Chetia slammed his knee into the man's jaw, and the prisoner responded in a sickening, pleading voice that needed no translation. A thin stream of blood leaked from the back of his head.

When the prisoner fell over on his side, the four of them gathered around his disconsolate form. Bhupen raised the kerosene lamp up from the ground, and the soft light fell over his stilled body. The evil of it ravished Stella.

"Are you going to kill him?" she breathed.

"Perhaps," Chetia said softly.

"When?"

"It depends."

"Could I watch when you do?" Stella asked.

Chetia looked down at the prisoner, then up at Stella.

"It will cost you," he said.

"How much?"

"One thousand American dollars."

"That is a lot," Stella said.

"Your friend must have it."

"I'm sure she does, but she won't give it to me."

"No, I suppose not," he said, and they all laughed.

It is quiet in Will's room after Stella finishes the story. He is sorry to know the details. That his money has paid for such a thing sickens him. He pushes a plate of scones toward Stella, and she takes a bite of one without relish.

The eagerness that had animated her story drains from her face. "I feel kind of bad about the prisoner. I've thought of going back into the jungle to see if he is okay."

She says it in all seriousness, and he sees beneath the bravado, a softhearted girl.

"You have to forget it," he says. "You have to let it go. Forget the prisoner. He is probably already dead."

"I know," she says.

She sits blinking. She is in need of advice, and he must give it to her. These are desperate men, he tells her, men for whom a hundred dollars is like a thousand, a thousand like ten thousand. Men with machine guns often use them, and however brave and adventurous she is, she is no match for them.

She nods obediently, wipes her tears with a napkin.

He's not sure what it is about the situation that prompts her to tell him the facts of her life, but now he must hear how she was raised in a small Indiana town, that her family, the only Jews, owned an appliance store. He learns that as soon as she finished high school, she moved to New York to become an actress. He must also act as confessor to her admission of having worked in the sex business, doing erotic massages. It is unwanted, the image of Stella's short boyish hand stroking a multitude of penises, but there it is. He imagines Grace has tried to rescue Stella from this life.

When there is nothing more on Stella's mind, he asks how Grace is.

"She's fine," she says. "She's with Vikram right now. She's always with Vikram." She looks up from her teacup knowingly.

He wonders if Grace has told her anything.

"You know, she really didn't speak until she was eleven years old," she says.

"You already told me. Maybe you shouldn't have," he says. "It didn't seem like she wanted me to know."

"Oh, she's so secretive. It was nothing really. Her father used to take her with him so he could carry on his affair with this woman named Mrs. Henry. He'd put her in the backseat when they were in the front, and under his desk when he and Mrs. Henry were on top of it. He told her if she ever spoke a word, he would kill her."

He is shocked. "You think that's nothing?" he says.

"No, I guess not." She laughs, and falls silent for a moment.

"Her first words really were German. She said them when she counted the blue sailboats on her pajamas."

"Why German?"

"Her mother spoke only German and French to her when she was small."

She points her finger at him, shakes it. "Now you're asking me questions. You better not tell her that I told you any of this."

"Don't tell me anymore," he says. "I've got too many secrets already."

Before Stella leaves, he feels he should warn her again that she shouldn't have anything more to do with the students. "They are involved in things we can't comprehend," he said. "You understand?"

She nods, childlike, and hops on her bike and rides down Mim's bumpy, rutted drive, out to the street.

He broods all afternoon about the conversation. He feels himself strangely implicated, and wonders if he should now tell Grace that Stella has gone into the jungle and shot off a machine gun. He tries to imagine Grace as an eleven-year-old girl, her blonde hair radiant, her skin pale, counting in German, the blue sailboats on her pajamas. The idea crushes him somehow.

Chapter 7

When he plays cards with Mim that night, the jars of marmalade and the small fastidious crackers on the flowery tray make him feel the encroachment of age, as if he is already old and grayed.

Mim disappears into her room when they finish, saying she feels tired. He comes later, knocks softly on her door, pokes his head inside. She lays on her bed in a gray housecoat, propped on her pillows. Small knitted white slippers cover her tiny feet. He's seen her room only once before—a large bedroom with a great teak bed, surrounded by a whisper of mosquito netting. Ivory tusks adorn the walls, along with black-and-white photographs of Mim and Harold on safari, the two of them standing in their tea gardens alongside dark-skinned pluckers, them hosting elegant dinners for other British tea-garden owners on their lawns.

"May I borrow the car?" he asks.

"You don't need to ask, Will," she says. "You take the car when you want it."

But she raises her eyebrow, as if she knows where he is going, and he thinks he detects in her a trace of disgust over his inability to reign in his passions. Perhaps it is his own disgust.

Mim's Ambassador is again let into the Tagore Estate without question. When he climbs out, he notices Vikram in the window. It is one of the first things he does. He waves, and Vikram waves back. So this is how it is done? Right under his nose. He feels sheepish walking up the sidewalk to the verandah. Dozens of blue-black crows hop on the lawn, pecking at the bread crumbs someone has tossed on the ground. Beneath a thicket of trees, the groom circles the black Arabian horse in exercise.

Through the window on the verandah, he glimpses Grace and Stella inside. They are seated on the sofa, Stella sitting behind Grace; she rubs her shoulders, while Grace types on a small electric type-writer. It would not seem so strange except that Stella's legs, instead of being tucked beneath her, are loosely wrapped around Grace's waist. Grace sits, as it were, between Stella's legs. It is the first time he imagines them as lovers. When he senses in their coupling a warmth, a love between them that they do not easily display in public, or not at least in his company, a pang of jealousy strikes him.

An air of the British Raj hovers above the dining room table, where the three of them sit beneath the oppressive portrait of Vikram's father, Jugdish Tagore, a man with large almond eyes and mustaches. The only sound is Vedeshpra's quiet progression around the table, the light touch of teacup to plate, a high bonish sound, and the deep, rising percolation of hot water flooding into china cups. Stella is his rival again, and shoots him narrowed glances. When Grace laughs at something he says, Stella sulks. She thumps her knuckles against the table, and Grace must tell her to stop.

Vedeshpra disappears on muted feet, and when they hear the tray settle inside the kitchen, Grace says, "Stella, you better make sure he brings mango and not papaya." It happened often enough that Stella gets up and goes into the kitchen.

Will turns his spoon in the tea. "I shouldn't have come," he says.

"No, no," Grace said. "I'm glad you did."

Still, it is awkward. He reaches out and touches her bare knee beneath the table. She freezes for a moment, then she slides her knee closer.

When Stella returns, he takes his hand back. She looks from Will to Grace and then pushes her chair back from the table. He is not certain what it is in their eyes that tells her that something more has passed between them, but she has seen it.

"Where are you going?" Grace says.

"I've lost something and must find it," she answers.

"What?"

"A letter," Stella says. She looks over her shoulder and shoots Grace a dark look of victory.

"Don't start with me, Stella."

Stella laughs wildly and runs up the back stairs. Her laugh is heard vanishing down the marble hallway above them. It is wild and loonish.

"She's a child, you know," Grace says. Will watches as her fingers fold and refold the edge of the napkin.

He cannot imagine their bond, what holds them together, so much so that they lived in Paris together for a year.

"Now, wait and listen," Grace says. "She'll go into my room and search through my things."

They are both quiet for a minute, and then they hear Stella above them going down the hall to Grace's bedroom.

"What is the letter?" he asks.

"It's nothing," she says.

She takes him out to the verandah, where he is aware that Vikram watches from the window. His head appears for a few minutes, then disappears. He hears Stella upstairs in Grace's room: the sound of pulled drawers, of doors opening and closing. Stella makes no point of being quiet. He senses their claims upon her time, the burden they are to her. A dying man and an adult child. She is held fixed on the verandah.

Next, they hear Stella down in the living room, tearing through a closet. Vedeshpra steps out to the verandah, nervously. "Memsahib," he says quietly. "Miss Stella is going through everything." He makes a wild gesture with his arms to indicate that she is throwing things over her shoulder.

"Just ignore her," Grace says. "And please bring us some tea."

"Yes, memsahib," he says, and he retreats.

She sighs and puts her legs up on the round table. She wears a pair of short black pants, a white blouse. He notices that the skin at her ankles is so white, luminous even. She says, "Oh, God." The sounds in the house do not diminish.

He is afraid it was only a fluke, that what he had felt last night, that precision of understanding, may never come again.

"Are we just supposed to drink our tea and pretend Stella's not down there going through the rooms?" He throws his arms up comically and moves them the way Vedeshpra did. It strikes her perfectly, and relief floods his heart at the sound of her laugh. Then, perhaps he is not wrong.

He doesn't mention that Stella was out to see him in the afternoon, that as well she had confessed to shooting the machine gun. He knows by not saying it, he is colluding with Stella, but he cannot bring himself to tell her, not when Stella is running amuck downstairs.

"Did Mim tell you the rumor about me?"

"Yes," he admits.

When she does a small but deft imitation of Mim's bored nonchalance—a slight drop of the mouth, an exaggerated inhalation, followed by a quick, heavenward gaze, she captures the essence of Mim.

"Yes," he says. "Exactly."

There is nothing else to say. But he feels it again, the sensation of minds meeting, without the attending words.

They laugh, and he realizes quite suddenly that he adores the way she falls forward when she laughs. He imagines he could watch it over and over and over without tiring of it. He would be happy to glance across any table and find her there. This has become a benchmark of sorts to him now.

They hear Stella in the living room, pulling off the sofa's cushions. She has stepped up the sound of it, adding grunts and the exaggerated breath of struggle, as if to remind them of her.

"What is she doing?" he asks.

"Pay no attention," she says.

He does not ask again what the letter is.

He sees the anxiety in her hands, the way she taps them on the arm. She is embarrassed, he thinks. She feels powerless to stop the sounds emanating from the house. Yanked-open doors, drawers, ferreting. That is all he can think of. A ferreting.

"Oh," she says. "I can't stand it. You'll have to excuse me for a moment."

She gets up and then pauses at the door, looks over her shoulder at him. "I'm sorry," she adds. There is something about the crushed look in her eyes, the nervousness she suddenly betrays, and he imagines himself holding her on a bed, touching his lips to her forehead.

He does not strain to hear their voices coming from the dining room, but there is something about the acoustics of the house, which carries their voices to him, and he hears every word.

"I didn't come all the way over to India to wait around while you fuck Will."

"I'm hardly fucking Will."

"You can't be with him."

"Can't I have tea with someone? Am I not allowed? Am I not a human being first?"

There is a moment's silence. The words, *Am I not a human being first,* hang strangely in the air. They are unexpected, words that do not logically follow.

"If you mention that letter again, Stella, I swear, I will not write another word for you."

The wordless understanding, the adoration of her laugh notwithstanding, he suddenly wants out. He remembers his place; he is only here for a few days. He does not live in India. He has a small two-day job in the Kazaringa.

He is standing up when she returns to the verandah.

"Oh, don't go, Will," she says.

"I shouldn't have come."

"Oh, that's not true. I'm sorry about Stella. I can't control her. I can't control anyone, but it doesn't mean you have to go."

"No, I should go."

She walks him to Mim's car, and after apologizing again, he puts her at ease. "Please, don't worry."

When they reach the car, he glances up at the window of the Small House and sees Vikram in the window. He withdraws himself immediately, and Will realizes he feels self-conscious about his need to watch. He and Grace shake hands good night, and she applies a pressure, her touch lingering. A secret message without the words, as if she is a prisoner, he thinks. But what is it? Left to interpret it, he is at a loss. *I am sorry that it is so awkward. I like you. I love you. Wait for me.* It is impossible to know.

On his way back to Mim's, he isn't sure if she has really tried to communicate anything. It was so brief, he can't be sure if he has made it up or not, and then decides it is true. He wants to interpret it wildly, but he quickly holds his thoughts in check. There is a dying husband up in the window, an insanely jealous lesbian lover. There is nothing but ruin that awaits him. He should leave for the Kazaringa in the morning. But in the next instant he is privy to his own secret thought: that she belongs to neither of them, but rather to him.

The passenger pigeon of America had evolved to the point where it had to live in vast numbers or not at all. To find food and to protect itself against natural enemies, it required millions of pairs of eyes.

In the 1700s, it was so numerous that when flocks were seen flying overhead, they darkened the entire sky. In 1810, an ornithologist estimated a count of over two million birds in a single flock, and James John Audubon described another flock that took three days to pass overhead. And then no more than eighty years passed, and a sighting of 180 birds was considered noteworthy. Finally, in 1914, the last known passenger pigeon, named Martha, died in the Cincinnati Zoo. Her body was frozen in a block of ice and shipped to the Smithsonian.

There were mass exterminations. It was an easy massacre, because pigeons were virtually challengeless to hunt. Their instinct for coexisting in large flocks was so strong that thousands of birds needed to be killed before the others would spook. Professional hunters transmitted nesting sights to the railroad, and then they massacred thousands—they trapped them and fumigated them; they shot them with guns and clubbed them to death with wooden bats.

Men wearing old clothes and rubber boots knocked the birds' nests down with wooden bats. This went on day and night. The terrified pigeons made a cackling scream, husky and breathless, that was unlike any other known sound. Trains took them out in an unbroken procession, but they could not keep up with the slaughter. The ground was covered with the living, the dying, and the dead.

From Notes on Extinction, *by Will Mendelsohn*

Chapter 8

*I*n the morning Mim's servant, Latisha, knocks cautiously on his door. "Memsahib feel no good," she says, and she drops her head to the side, her eyes fluttering shut to indicate Mim's condition.

He finds Mim in bed, the shades pulled against the strong morning sun, her breakfast tray untouched on the side table. She is listless, and when he touches her forehead, he knows she has a high fever.

"It's malaria," she insists. "Call Dr. Chaund, and tell him it's malaria."

He stands near Mim's bed while Dr. Chaund checks her heart, takes her pulse, inserts and then reinserts the thermometer. Her fever is so high, he cannot believe it and must check it twice. Dr. Chaund is an amiable man, in his early fifties, with thinning black hair and a small paunch which rises beneath his white safari shirt.

On Will's way into Dibrugarh, to buy quinine, the traffic is so slow it unhinges him. They get stalled alongside of diesel buses. The windows of the buses, open, yet barred, frame dark faces packed so tightly they are disembodied heads, animated solely with eyes riveted to him in the backseat. On the other side of them is a slower tide of bicycle rickshaws propelled by men with dark skin papered thinly over taut muscle. Men drive oxen yoked to bullock carts loaded with green shoots of sugarcane. He feels like a grain of sand, amid pepper, a starfish in a sea of dark mollies.

He spends the next few days between his rooms and Mim's. She has malaria, and alternates between terrible fevers and violent shivering. He works in his room, and returns to her, living out, he cannot help but think, Grace's own life. He must try in the mornings to get her to eat. He sits with her again at noon, and at tea, but it is the nights that she takes from him.

On the fourth night, her fever rises so high, he sends Latisha to Dr. Chaund's house. The electricity has failed, as it does so often in India, and the phone lines are temporarily down. He hurriedly lights the hurricane lamps and sets one on her bedside table, another on her desk. He holds her hands and watches helplessly as she rolls her head back and forth on the pillow, moaning. Her lips are parched, her eyes half closed and without focus. She's lapsed into delirium, he thinks, and though Latisha should be the one to bathe Mim, she is gone so long, he must finally take Mim from the bed, in his arms, and immerse her in a tub of cold water.

He tries to set her small body in the bathtub, but her weight is dead, and he is afraid that she will slip under the water or crack her head against the porcelain. He panics when she slides from his arms.

"Latisha," he calls, but she isn't back yet. The servants who live with Mim are asleep in the hallway and do not hear him.

Quickly he climbs into the tub, a great sprawling movement, and holds onto her. His own heart beats fast. He gently bathes her shoulders and head with handfuls of cold water. Without her spirit animating her, he is suddenly aware of how tiny she is. Her head lolls against his chest, a small head of dark hair. She barely comes awake. Enough to mutter his name.

He holds her, dousing her shoulders, her neck, while he waits for the cool water to bring her fever down. Her blue gown swirls in the water just above her thigh, ballooning. He can see through it, the ghostlike shape of limbs less withered than he might have imagined.

Her arms lie heavy beneath the water. His eyes chance to fall on the numbers tattooed on the back of her wrist, the spidery numbers in blue ink, which usually lay hidden beneath the Indian bangles. In her sickness they have been taken off. The water distorts the numbers, causes them to waver. He feels her shame suddenly and wraps his arms around her more deeply. She is the closest thing he has ever had to a relative, a woman made his own by the fact of the Holocaust.

When Mim begins to shiver violently, he takes her from the bath, carries her into her room, and lays her on the bed. She has come awake now, and asks weakly for a nightdress. "There's one in the top drawer of the bureau," she says. Latisha should redress her, he thinks, but she hasn't returned, and Mim is shivering violently. He quickly rummages through her drawers, coming up with a white gown, which he brings to the bed. She is barely able to help him. The intimacy of such an act, had she been well, would have been intolerable, but the sickness lays between them.

He peels the cold, wet nightgown from her body, and hurriedly prepares to pull the dry gown over her head. He means not to, but he sees the scars on either side of her abdomen. The fact of them, their red jaggedness, startles him.

He has not remembered this particular detail until now—what his mother told him about Mim when he was a boy. "They'd strapped her down on a table, and took her ovaries without any anesthetic. And she was lucky. The boy next to her—they cracked open his skull and scooped out a ball of his gray matter."

He piles blankets on top of her to ease her shivering. Even after she sleeps, he sits next to her all night. He has lived a charmed life.

In the morning, Mim is feeling better, and asks to have the papers read to her. Another Moslem has been thrown dead into the Brahmaputra River. It is a single, isolated incidence, but it makes her hands shake. The People's Liberation Army of Assam, a more militant organization, has assumed responsibility.

The malaria has weakened her resolve, and now it is enough that she is a foreigner, that foreigners are being yanked from their beds at night. It does not matter that she is not Bangladeshi, that they are not going after tea-garden owners. Nothing he says can soothe her.

"I know the vagrancy of thought," she says. "It is only a matter of time before it occurs to them that the tea-garden owners are not Assamese either. Perhaps you do not know it, but evil has great wit."

Later, when she is asleep, he is drawn to the few things in her house that remind him that she is Jewish: a mezuzah nailed inside of the front door, a small Star of David above her clock in the kitchen, a prayer shawl in the bottom drawer of the bureau in his room.

He searches for their effect, listening for the quiet murmur of his own thought, but it is not overwhelming, their effect upon him. They perhaps mean more than they did—objects once familiar and long lost take on a new meaning when rediscovered. But he cannot push the feeling to any height. It is a strange, muted longing, but there is no conversion.

He thinks vacantly of the poem he wrote in the third grade. *If my mother weren't a Jew, she would have nothing left to do.* When she found it, she had slapped his face.

He has always felt separate, the Holocaust not his own, a Jew somewhere in between, not quite American, not quite European, a Jew for whom there is a small world.

He finds a few books Mim has in her library—*The Rise & Fall of the Third Reich* by William Shirer and *Invasion, 1944,* by Speidel. He leafs through them. He wants an accounting of what it has done to a person's soul, but there is nothing. It is only in the silence between he and Mim that he is able to understand anything.

Chapter 9

When Stella comes early in the morning, he is reminded of how exclusively he has drifted into the world of Mim's illness. He has given himself to the preservation of her life, as Rita had once given herself to the salvation of the rufous fantails on the island of Guam.

When he comes out of his bedroom, Stella is sitting at the table, helping herself to the breakfast Aruun has brought him. She acts as if nothing happened when he was last with them, as if she hadn't been pawing through the contents of the bungalow when he and Grace were outside on the verandah. Oddly, he is already accustomed to the split in their relationship. He is at once her fellow Jewish friend and her rival.

He sits down and pours some milk into his tea.

"I hate this fucking place," Stella says. "I want to get the hell out of here." She has helped herself to his toast. As she eats it, he envisions her as an old woman, crumbs jamming in the corners of her mouth. Everywhere he looks now, he anticipates age.

"What's happened now?" he asks.

"When I came out of the bungalow to ride my bike into town, Bhupen was standing outside the gates, waiting for me," she tells him.

"Good morning, Stella," he said. His voice lifted over the wall of traffic sound. She got off her bike and walked over to him.

"Hey, Bhupen, my man," she said, and made as if she were boxing him.

He laughed and mimed a few punches, keeping his lightly sealed fists close to his own chest.

They spoke of a few mundane things, the weather, Anup, and then Bhupen leaned closer and said, "Do you have the money, yet?"

"It's a lot of money. I don't know if I can get it."

"We can't keep him forever," Bhupen said quietly. He smiled, as if he was speaking about something inanimate, something for sale, something perishable that he could not keep.

Stella felt his voice creep up the back of her neck, as if it were a dark hand that held on too tight. She took a step back.

"Couldn't you ask your friend Grace?" he said.

"Don't bring her into it," Stella said, "and don't wait on me either. I didn't tell you guys to wait for me."

"Okay," Bhupen said. "It's okay. There's no problem." And he laughed and Stella eased a little. But when she climbed back on her bike, he reached out and grabbed the handlebar.

"When do you think you can get the money?" Bhupen said.

"I told you," Stella said, "it's not that easy."

"I'm sure it's not," Bhupen said quietly, "but Chetia is waiting."

"Tell him not to wait, then," Stella yelled.

"You don't understand Chetia," Bhupen said. He smiled again.

"Well, fuck him. I don't have to understand him."

Bhupen looked out at the traffic, his eyes focused beyond, as if in dark clairvoyance. When he looked back, he smiled again and said quietly, "You must understand him. It is important for you to under-stand." His voice was casual, his smile fixed.

Sweat trained down her spine, and the road, filled with rickshaws and oxen-drawn bullock carts, distorted.

"We'll give you two days, okay?" he said gently.

"Two days!" she said. "I can't get it that fast."

"How many days, then?"

"At least a week," she said. "It's not that easy, you know."

"I'm sure," Bhupen agreed, "but we have an understanding now." He smiled and nodded and then added, "We'll keep him for you. Okay?"

He stepped out to the road and raised his arm. Within moments an auto rickshaw stopped, and he climbed in. Stella stood still, and watched the auto rickshaw being swallowed by the vast throat of traffic.

"They are trying to blackmail you," Will says. He must play the role into which he has been cast. "Maybe you should leave India."

"I can't leave India," Stella yells. "We're just starting to write that screenplay. If I go, Grace will never write it, and she can't write it without me."

He knows already the starring role this screenplay plays in Stella's hopes.

"You have to tell Grace, then," he says. "Tell her what happened. She will know what to do."

"I will," Stella says, but it weighs on his mind all afternoon.

When he goes to the Tagore bungalow later that afternoon, he is prepared to tell Grace that Stella has gotten involved with the students.

He finds her in the kitchen making a chocolate pudding cake. She has sent the cook away, who now sulks on the back porch unable to find something else to do. The room is filled with sun that lights her blonde hair, her pale skin. She is in the midst of breaking eggs in a bowl, so he sits down at the table near an enormous English hutch filled with white-and-blue china and watches her. He detects in her brisk whisking movement that she is upset. It is Stella she tells him.

"She wants a thousand dollars, but she won't tell me what it is for. It seems a reasonable thing to ask, doesn't it? If I am going to give her a thousand dollars, I want to know what it is for. I'm afraid she's done something. She has all these associations in town. She knows all the whores and the racketeers at the back of the market. God knows who else she knows. She's probably friends with the students now too."

"Where is she now?" he asks.

"She's out in the garden. She has a passion for pansies and violas, and spends half the day watering and shading them."

This surprises him.

"Will you give her the money?" he asks.

"Yes, but I want her to tell me what it is for."

"Will she tell you?"

"Eventually," she says.

"When is eventually? A week, a month?"

"By tomorrow she will tell me. But I will have to press."

He considers that he has done enough. He doesn't need to say anything, then. It is not in his interest to be a tattletale.

His sexual attraction to her comes up on him quite suddenly. The open-backed soft shoes she wears, the apron tied around her waist, the way she moves so gently from her mixing bowls to the sink are alluring. It has bloomed as if overnight; as if in the gloom of Mim's illness, it has progressed without his knowing it.

He is drawn to the most minute details of her movement: the hem of her dress rising above the backs of her knees when she leans over the counter, the overflow of her breasts above the round neckline of her blouse when she bends to open the oven, her finger pressing into her mouth to lick the chocolate batter away.

When she walks past him on her way to the refrigerator, he catches her by the wrist. "Are you and Stella lovers?" he asks.

She makes no effort to retrieve her hand from his loose grasp around her wrist. "No," she says. "Stella wishes, but never."

He cannot mistake the hot interest that radiates from her pale blue eyes, and he pulls her gently into his lap. He hears her voice in his ear; such a mixture of relief and sadness that it is nearly confessional. "I thought you were never coming back." She puts her arms around his neck and holds him tightly.

He leans his forehead against hers and finds her eyes. Their mouths meet and the kiss is incendiary, perhaps even more than the first time.

They hear Stella come in through the front verandah. The door bangs behind her, and then her voice. "Where's Grace?" she says loudly. He imagines that the two of them must know where the other is at all times.

Grace rises quickly from his lap and flits back to her bubbling pot on the stove. Stella appears in the doorway and stops when she sees him. She looks to Grace, whose back is turned, then eyes Will. In the span of three hours, he has become again her rival. She strides across the kitchen and hands Grace the flowers she has picked for her from the garden, an act of courtship, he cannot help but think. She then bends over the stove, looking into the bubbling pot. "What are you making?" she says.

"Chocolate pudding cake."

"That's how I like my ladies," Stella says in a mock man's voice. "Cooking in the kitchen." Then she whacks Grace on the butt. Will is surprised by her coarseness, however put on it is, but Grace just shrugs it off.

"So you're speaking to me now," Grace says.

Stella glances quickly at Will to see if he's said anything to Grace about the students. He does not give her a look either way.

She asks for a bowl of cut mango, and he watches as Grace goes into action cutting one up, carefully shearing the yellow flesh from the flat white pit, bringing the bowl to the table. Stella takes a bite and looks at him over the rim of the spoon, as if she has scored a victory. Her eyes seem to say, "She may be attracted to you, but don't underestimate my privilege here."

They all sit in the kitchen, and Grace serves them her chocolate pudding cake. There is something about the way her hands move so surely through this small, devotional act that rivets both him and Stella.

They have not even picked up their spoons before Stella says, "I got three letters today." Then she mentions that she will go upstairs later and write some letters.

"Stop it," Grace says. He is again surprised to hear the brusqueness of Grace's voice when Stella has offended her.

"What, I can't talk about letters?" Stella says.

"It's not funny, Stella."

"What's wrong with my mentioning letters? People do write letters, Grace. I write letters. I get letters. I send letters. Letters come to me. The world is made up of letters. Your name is spelled with letters. G-R-A-C-E," she said.

Will feels embarrassed for Stella—the winner's pity for the loser, he thinks. Even so, Stella's mention again of the letter has unnerved Grace. He wonders what this letter could possibly be, but he knows without asking that the whole reason Stella mentions it is because he is not to know about it.

Vedeshpra suddenly appears in the kitchen and says quickly, "Memsahib, sahib is coming now for dessert." Grace rises immediately, excusing herself, and calls out the back door, *"Usko suno sahib mut,"* and there is suddenly a flap of servants, hurrying in through the back door for sahib's arrival.

Stella smiles knowingly and says, "This I've got to see," and gets up from the table and wanders into the living room. Will hears Grace's voice, so filled with concern, so tender it is aching. "Are you sure you feel well enough, Babu?"

"I've come for your dessert," Vikram says. "I heard you've been cooking."

"Yes, of course. You have dessert with us. Will is here," she says right away. "Should we have dessert in the living room?"

"Yes, yes," Vikram says. It is a forced gaiety.

Will lingers at the table a moment, then walks slowly through the dining room into the doorway of the living room, where he stops. They are at that moment transferring Vikram's thin, wasted body from a palanquin onto the sofa. He has had himself dressed in a pair of blue jeans and a black T-shirt that are now two, if not three sizes too large. Will does not know what to do with his eyes, and busies himself straightening his shirt. It is bad enough he has kissed the man's wife in his own house, without gazing insouciantly upon the man's infirmities. When he looks up, Grace is putting pillows at his hips to prop him up. His neck is so thin, it seems it could wear a bracelet. An ampoule of pity breaks open inside him.

"Well, I see you've come to get a taste of my wife's cooking," Vikram says. He is aware that Will has seen his wasted body in transport and tries now to gain whatever advantage he can.

And Will must do his part: he must carry on the pretense that Vikram has risen from his sickbed to get a taste of Grace's chocolate pudding cake. He must walk into the room now and remark that he had not known that Grace was cooking, but now that he knows, he eagerly awaits the tasting—the sort of talk that he loathes, but which is nonetheless unavoidable.

As he settles himself on the sofa next to Stella, he is stricken by a thought: has he become a man who goes through a dying man's house, stripping its riches, before the man's dead body has even cooled? It is a strange, cold feeling—how little regard the living sometimes have for the dying.

The only one who is remotely at ease is Stella. She sits back, bemused, and observes. Will must watch as Grace hands Vikram a bowl of chocolate pudding cake, flaps out a napkin for him, and makes his tea. She all but puts the teacup to his lips. All her attentions buoy Vikram's presence in the room.

It is nearly unbearable, the three of them struggling to make conversation, Stella doing absolutely nothing to contribute. They finally end up discussing tea, Vikram explaining the difference between CTC tea and orthodox tea. Will must feign an interest in knowing the difference, and a cup of each is brought to him by the servants. As he sips first one, then the other, he glances at Grace. Her eyes, filled with mirth, hover above the rim of the teacup, catching his. He now must comment on the difference he notices, which is so minimal to his inexperienced taste buds that he is hard-pressed to come up with the defining words. He says, "Well, I think the CTC tea is more, well, liberal, and this one is, well, frankly, much . . . stronger." He catches her eye, and she suppresses a laugh; he feels that they alone are aligned in this room.

He tries, for the sake of his conscience, to imagine that Vikram is stupid or insensitive or cruel, but he must confess that he is none of these things. At the very worst, he is a distant man, cut off from himself.

It is obvious that he takes pleasure at his wife's presence by his side, pleasure over the dessert she has made, pleasure at the sound of her laugh, pleasure in her obvious concern for him. But not pleasure in her, Will thinks, in the woman beneath the guise of wife. Vikram does not know her. It is his eye she catches when something is funny; it is to him she makes a face of exhaustion. She gives Vikram her public side. He wants nothing more. Yet, Will concedes, it is only a first impression.

As soon as the desserts are finished and the cups of tea set aside, he gets up to leave. He shakes Vikram's hand and thanks him for his hospitality. The words echo in his mind as he walks out of the living room. It is a ridiculous thing for him to say, but what is there to say when something has to be said and there is nothing to say? Grace walks him to the door, and they speak the requisite words: It was nice to see you. Thank you for dessert. Come again, won't you?

He is not back at Mim's for more than ten minutes when the phone rings. It is Grace. She apologizes for the terrible awkwardness and wants to know if he can meet her at the country club at one o'clock the next afternoon. When he agrees to it, she tells him to come to Room 3B, the room she keeps as a studio.

He sleeps fitfully that night. He drowses off, only to jerk awake minutes later, confused as to where he is and what he is doing here. He considers that his restlessness might be premonitory, and entertains the idea of not going, but in the late morning, after he has sat for hours with dry tables of genetic drifts, he finds himself preparing for their meeting, taking a careful bath, even going so far as to trim his nasal hairs—a middle-aged manifestation that particularly unnerves him. He is driven into town in Mim's Ambassador, then sends the driver back, taking an auto rickshaw to the country club, which Grace has recommended he do, for discretion, he imagines.

The country club is out in the middle of the jungle. Once elegant, it is a large white Victorian building with wide verandahs and balconies, all of which have fallen into serious disrepair. The golf course has been long lost to vines and dense undergrowth.

The jungle has not been beaten back in years and crawls onto the porches, writhing up between the floorboards; it abuts the house on all sides. It would not have seemed strange had a monkey suddenly swung down from a vine and plopped onto one of the sodden armchairs.

The long red draperies inside the main hall are tattered and dusty. Sun shines through the holes in bright pinpoints. The bar is attended by a small Indian man dressed in white, who goes into action mopping the bar when Will walks in, as if on cue. There are a couple of Indian tea-garden owners sitting at a table, speaking in English, drinking tea from English bone china.

Through the open back doors he glimpses the pool in the center of the courtyard. It was once grand and is now stagnant and smells of backwater. The sides are a velvety green. She has told him to go up unannounced to Room 3B, so he climbs the decrepit stairs under the unhooded gaze of an older Indian man wearing a bellhop's uniform who sits behind a small desk, the now defunct concierge.

Through this man's eyes, he feels himself to be what he is—a middle-aged man on his way to an illicit affair. Yet the hammering in his heart is no different from what he felt as a younger man on the verge of a coveted interlude. He detects a trace even of the same evangelistic hope.

When she opens the door, she's wearing a pair of dark capri pants and a tight white silk sweater, which shows off her figure—a figure more womanly than he has imagined. She has dressed to be alluring, adding a faint trace of red lipstick to her mouth.

Her room is large, and was once opulent. In one corner stands a mahogany desk with a computer, on which a small gooseneck lamp lights a stack of pages, as if she has been working before he has come. There are small touches of her—white roses in a vase, twenty towers of books that stand on the floor; the navy blue silk robe he has touched between his fingers now lays over the back of the chair.

The bed, a four-postered mahogany affair, is dressed in a plush white coverlet. He wonders if they will end up there, imagines their naked bodies entwined on top of it.

She sits down in one of the twin red armchairs and offers him the other. She's ordered up a tray of small crustless sandwiches and a large bottle of sparkling water. It is awkward, as if they are suddenly two actors onstage, after having had only the barest of rehearsals. It is quiet except for the crows that caw, hoarse-throated, from the plantain trees that ring the pool downstairs.

Her nerves are easy to see. She pushes her blonde hair behind her ears and crosses her legs. She looks across at him and smiles a knowing smile that works in unison with her eyes to convey a consciousness of the awkwardness, of hers, of his.

"That was awful when Vikram came in," she says.

"Awful," he says, but yet beneath it there is a suppressed smile.

She pours them each a glass of water, holds one glass aloft, then the other. "Well, I think this one is more, well, liberal, and this one is, well, frankly, much . . . stronger."

She folds over laughing, as he does, at this reference to his undistinguished defining of Vikram's teas. It has the effect of vanquishing the awkwardness, and she rises from the chair and turns on the ceiling fans, moving freely through the room.

"I don't get here often enough," she tells him, "but it is my own room. It costs only twenty dollars a month. I would like sometimes to sleep here, but I can't because Vikram needs me at night."

Surprisingly, she tells him a great deal in the next hour, more than he has expected. She tells him easily, breezily almost. Yet all the talk has a haste to it, as if they are so many words that she needs to go through.

She was married for seven years to Vikram, she says. Not happily, but not unhappily either. They were a couple, like others, dulled in the routine of marriage, but when she made her second film, *And Some Chose to Forget*, she fell in love with one of her actors, a man named Louis. She thought he was the man of her life, she says, rolling her eyes, as if such a foolish thought has now been stricken from her mind.

She left Vikram a month later, she tells him, and for nearly two years Vikram pined for her, a fact, he notes, which she now seems to relish. He called every morning to wake her, every evening to say good night to her. He slept by her bedside on several occasions when she was sick. She lived for two years with Louis, seeing Vikram often for dinner. They were two of the happiest years of her life (it is terrible to admit, she says, that she has liked having two men) but then she got pregnant, and Louis left.

"He walked out of my apartment and never came back," she says. "Then four months later, I lost the child, a son, and by then Vikram had found someone else. It was Stella who took care of me. A year later I moved to Paris alone and wrote a screenplay that didn't sell. I had no money and had to work as a translator. Then Vikram called and told me he was sick, and I came to India."

She sighs, as if to say, "There, now you know," and then an unexpected and profound sadness falls over her. Her face slackens, the age showing through briefly, and she flushes, looks down at her hands.

"Love is nothing much," she says. "One must never count on it."

He doesn't believe her, and thinks perhaps she wants to be convinced otherwise, but he is not so sure she is wrong.

Despite what she has said or because of it, he makes love to her on the opulent mahogany bed. She does not give him her body so much as she shares it. It is hers, he senses, and he is not certain why, but he likes this. He does not want to be given too much, to be given things that are not his. But he is not prepared to have their lovemaking surpass his expectation and nearly cries afterward.

There is one moment that he can't erase from his mind—when he is pitched above her, and their eyes catch. A contact of spirits, he thinks, disembodied, and he can think of no way to conceive of it, except to say that in those moments their solitary confinement is broken. And again, he feels what he can only call the exquisite absence of loneliness.

When he gets home, he finds Mim collapsed in bed. He knows it has nothing to do with his having made love to Grace, but it recalls his past, an echo of the time his mother saw him in the park with Heather Holden and was in bed when he got home.

The servants lose their heads at the sight of Mim, her head thrown back on the pillow, her mouth opened, lips parched, as she pants for breath. He sends Latisha to get Dr. Chaund and sits down next to her. Though he knows little about medicine, he at least knows to touch his index finger to the back of her wrist, to check her pulse.

"Your heart is racing," he says.

Her hand moves slowly to her forehead, to wipe the thin layer of moistness away. "So what is new?" she says. She is a small mound beneath the covers.

"It always races?"

"For years," she says.

He touches his finger again to her pulse and counts the beats. Using the second hand on his watch, he calculates that it is beating 118 beats per minute.

"Since when?" he says.

"Since when they parted me from my parents at Auschwitz."

It is the first time she has ever mentioned the Holocaust. Its mention while her heart beats against his fingertip crumples him.

Mim rests herself, rolling her head on the pillow, a slow back and forth he has seen old people in hospitals do in their restlessness.

"The driver says you sent him back," Mim says.

"I don't like to make him wait for me," Will says.

"He can wait. He has nothing else to do. This is India. If he doesn't wait in town, he comes and waits here instead. What difference does it make? You shouldn't take the rickshaws. It isn't safe. You are a foreigner, just like I am."

He doesn't argue with her.

Mim studies him for a moment, and all at once, it appears in her eyes—the realization of where he's been. She shakes her head. He is not certain what has given him away. Perhaps the lightness of his mood. Perhaps a trace look in his eyes when she mentioned the rickshaw, the memory of his lovemaking appearing there momentarily.

He and Latisha stand at the foot of her bed when Dr. Chaund comes. They watch as he listens to her heart, checks her blood pressure.

"The malaria has weakened her," he says, "and her blood pressure is very high."

The doctor teaches him how to take her blood pressure, to check her heart rate. He must do this three times a day. He is not eager to be pressed into this job—it is too reminiscent of playing nurse to his mother after his father died. It sends up a claustrophobic feeling, one of panic almost. But he wants to make himself useful to Mim. Let him not deny it; he is extending his stay for the purpose of having his affair.

Will walks Dr. Chaund out, and as soon as they step onto the verandah, the heat assails them.

"Thank you," Will says.

He shakes Will's hand. "It is nothing." He takes hold of his bicycle and climbs on. Already his forehead is beaded with sweat.

"I'm told you are an expert on extinction," Dr. Chaund says.

"Well, I write about it," Will says.

"The boy who lives at hospital is very interested to learn about extinction. His name is Ramu."

"He speaks English?"

"No, but I do, and I make a very good interpreter." Dr. Chaund smiles. "Will you come?"

"Of course," Will says. "I will come." How could he refuse? His throat constricts at the thought of how much it might mean to such a boy.

He watches Dr. Chaund ride away, and then returns to Mim's room and sits by her bedside, while she drinks an herb tea the doctor has prescribed.

"You are seeing Grace at her room in the country club," she says. It has only just occurred to her that this is the scheme.

She has always been frank with him about others, but never directly to him. There has been a line between them that neither has crossed, but he supposes that taking care of her has entitled her in some way to this breach. He wonders if he's going to have to hear these things now.

"Yes," he admits.

"I know she rents a room there. They say she writes there, but rarely. I suppose now she is going to be telling them at her place that she's gone off on a writing jag."

"I suppose," he says.

So it is out in the open. So much the better. He does not want to be sneaking around, like a teenage boy.

She doesn't say anything when Grace calls the next afternoon, and he quietly leaves the house an hour later. Sitting in the back of the rickshaw, he savors his life, if only for these moments. He walks by the bellhop's knowing gaze, and glides up the decrepit stairs of the defunct country club.

When he opens the door, she runs toward him and throws herself in his arms. It has been a long time since anyone has run into his arms, and he accepts the novelty, the thrill of it without question.

He falls back on the bed with her, as eager as she is to resume.

There has been nothing in his recent history to compare to the joy he feels, the desire that is suddenly awakened in him. The way her aliveness unites with his, produces something in the nature of tenfold. It is even better than the day before. She is not an inhibited lover, and responds quickly to his touch.

Afterward she explores his body, prowls across it in a way he is not accustomed to, but he allows it. She loves the muscles beneath the skin and follows them with her fingers, feeling like a blind woman where one group leaves off and another begins. She bites him too, the fleshy part of his shoulder, his cheeks, the thin skin of his forearms. But it is the hard, round stone of his Adam's apple that makes her love him, she tells him, the crookedness of his legs.

He is fond of the ridge of her clavicles and presses his fingers under them, then into the hollows of her pelvis. He touches the palms of his hands against her sharp scapular bones, against the two dramatic outcroppings of her pelvis. He draws his thumbs down her ribs and presses his fingers beneath them until she says it hurts.

She tells him shyly that she has not had a lover since Louis. She is like him, that way—she will go for long periods of time without anything if it isn't right. She has slept for years with books on Louis' side of the bed.

It is unexpected when she cries. She has slipped into the blue silk robe and sits near him, crying into her hands. It is not a few tears, moved by a fleeting emotion. It is a deep cry and grows in force, and for a few moments he feels entirely at a loss. He finally takes her into his arms where she sobs against his chest.

"What's the matter?" he whispers. "That you slept with books on the side of your bed?"

"Yes," she manages to say. "And more."

Whatever the more is incites a new flood of tears. He holds her tighter, feeling her body convulse against his, when only a half hour ago it had shuddered in pleasure.

"What more?" he says.

"I am so happy to have met you, and then I have such guilt. I mean, Vikram . . ."

He holds her tighter, feels her mouth against his chest, the wet warmth of her breath when she sobs. He makes no attempt to stop it, to shush her. He moves his hand instead lightly across the expanse of her back.

Only when she settles does he say, "What should we do?"

She pulls herself up and looks into his eyes. She is beautiful to him—her eyes wet, her mouth swollen. "I don't know," she says. "I'm in love with you."

He moves his thumbs across her wet cheeks.

"I'm in love with you too."

"It's not our fault, right?"

"No, it's not."

"It's our fault that we slept together, though," she says. "We are guilty of this."

"It's true," he says. "We are."

She kisses his mouth deeply, her tears wetting his face. Then she presses her forehead against his. Mirth fills her eyes now, when only moments ago it had been sorrow. "It's your fault," she says. "You shouldn't have come down to the banyan grove that night."

"You told me to come back," he says. "You walked me to the car the day we met and told me to come back."

"I know," she says. "I have such a weak character."

He doesn't know what to say. He wants to tell her that it is understandable that a woman in her position would yearn for love and affection, that it is a very difficult thing to do, to take care of a dying husband, but he can't find the words.

"My character is no better," he says.

He doesn't know what more to say, and they lie in the quiet. The silence gathers, their weight together in that bed, growing, until she takes his hand and squeezes it. When he squeezes back, he has agreed with her—they will live with their weak characters.

"I actually walked around my room yesterday thinking to myself, I have a lover, I have a lover," she says. She turns to him and smiles. "You will probably break my heart."

A flicker of pain passes through her eyes, as if she is convinced of the truth of this, and he reaches out and traces the outline of her jaw with his finger.

"I make a laughable playboy," he says.

"When are you leaving for the Kazaringa?" she says quietly.

"I've made no plans," he says.

"Why not?"

"Because of you."

It is the right answer, and they make love again more passionately, proclaiming things he could not have imagined proclaiming earlier, say in the morning, declarations of love, the absurd, foolish, endearing things one utters when seized by love. It is unavoidable, he supposes, and forgives them for it.

When he climbs into the auto rickshaw thirty minutes later, he marvels at how the lovemaking lingers on his body, like climbing off a train and still feeling its motion.

He eats dinner with Mim in near silence. She does not approve of his affair, but manages to say only, "At least don't take the rickshaws." When he tells her that Grace has asked him to, for discretion, Mim sighs, rolls her eyes heavenward. It saddens him to know that she holds her tongue because she is lonely and does not want him to leave, that there are times when one must compromise their principles so as not to be left.

When Stella comes in the morning, the three of them eat breakfast together in Mim's garden. It is not easy to get Mim to laugh, yet Stella does. His form of self-deprecating humor has no effect on her, but Stella does not mind making a fool of herself and hobbles through the gardens like a hunchback and speaks in lisps so that Mim will laugh.

If Stella knows anything about him and Grace, she doesn't say, nor does he. Grace has asked him not to. When they talk in his rooms later, they talk about motorcycles. She wants Grace to buy her one.

"She won't even buy me a moped," she says. "She thinks I'll kill myself on it. She worries about me too much." But it pleases her that Grace worries about her.

"Why do you like motorcycles, Stella?" he asks.

All animosity toward her melts away in her single utterance: "They are the hottest thing on earth."

Before she heads out on her bike, he asks, "Did you take care of the Bhupen problem?"

"Yes," she says. "It's okay."

Her eyes slide away, so he asks her again.

"You're sure?"

"Yes."

It leaves his mind then.

Late in the afternoon, he walks through three tea gardens to Dr. Chaund's hospital. Mim has told him the shortcut, and he learns the small signs that distinguish one garden from another. The pluckers have discarded their open umbrellas in the gardens after the morning rain. They are like the cheap black umbrellas he has often bought on a street corner in New York when caught in the rain. A familiar object found in such an exotic setting is strange, yet lovely. The sun glares now off the still water in the moats that surround the gardens, and crows fly like black boomerangs against the blue sky.

He carries a notebook where he has jotted some notes on extinction. He will teach the boy about Krakatau today, he decides.

Dr. Chaund receives him warmly and shows him around the hospital. He is surprised by the small room where uncomplicated surgeries are performed. The equipment Will has only seen in photographs, museums perhaps—a wooden gurney table, an ether mask, surgical instruments with wooden handles. It soothes him somehow. A place that hasn't devoted all of its energy to progress. A place that makes due with what it has.

There are a few women resting inside the rooms on small beds. They shift uncomfortably when they see Will walk past. "There is nothing really wrong with them," Dr. Chaund explains. "They are feeling weary and need to rest a day."

Ramu is wheeled out to the porch in a wooden wheelchair. Will is struck again by the boy's unabashed enthusiasm. His head wags, his grin taut, his spirit, a deep rope of flame within him. Without the sheet covering him, Will sees now his emaciated, inert limbs; arms and legs the size of a five-year-old boy.

Dr. Chaund pulls up two chairs on either side of the boy's wheelchair, and after an awkward start, they find a rhythm: Will speaks a few sentences about Krakatau, then Dr. Chaund interprets, the boy asks questions, Will answers, Dr. Chaund interprets.

They are interrupted often by a steady stream of patients, who wander in from the fields complaining of headaches and stomachaches. "It is Monday," Dr. Chaund explains. "Many have been drinking all weekend and are feeling hangovers. There have been brawls between the men. It is always this way," he says and cheerfully excuses himself.

While Dr. Chaund attends to them, Will draws small sketches for the boy—of Krakatau, of Rakata, of the airborne fern spores, of the frigate birds and toddies, of the flotsam that floats to the new, sterile island carrying plant life and insects.

Despite the heat, Will finds the experience energizing. The boy's desire to learn, to hear of such a place as Krakatau is refreshing. The flood of his questions is surprising. How exactly did the birds repopulate the island? How did the fern spores get there? He requires Will to conjure the journey of a spore from Java to the newly made Rakata, to its taking root in the soil, to its prospering and multiplying. The shininess in his eyes, a boy who will never take root and multiply anywhere on the earth.

He spends the afternoon at work, until Latisha interrupts him. She wraps her arms around her stomach and bends forward to suggest

that Mim is sick to her stomach. He goes to her room and stands outside her bathroom door listening to sounds of her retching. The
sounds are so deep, so guttural, he must knock on the door.

"Are you all right, Mim?" he asks.

"Yes," she says.

"Should I call the doctor?"

Between heaves, she manages to say, "No."

When she comes out of the bathroom, she is drained and feels her
way to the bed. She asks him to open the blinds and let the sun in.
She can't bear the dimness.

"Are you sure you're all right?" he says.

She tells him that it is nothing, not to make such a thing over it.
She has thrown up many times; it is nothing. Yet to him it is a strong
occurrence. He wants to send for the doctor, but she says no. He has
thought it was attached to the malaria, but she says no, that it happens sometimes.

"What did Harold do when you threw up?" he asks.

"He did nothing," she says. "What can he do? He got used to it,
just as I have."

He can't imagine this. A wife whose heart races, who throws up violently, at times. To act as if it is nothing. He imagines Harold reading the papers, shrugging at the sound of his wife retching in the
bathroom, thinking, "Ah, well, there she goes again." But it is true.
There is nothing to do. Still, he hovers for a while. The sound of her
retching is strong and pervasive. It is unforgettable, really, and seems
attached to things one cannot hope to shrug off. But she tires of his
concern and reminds him that it is nothing more than a spasm, a moment's discomfort, for which she has a certain patience.

"Go, Will," she says. "I am all right." She leans over and kisses his
forehead.

By the late afternoon, she is recovered and is out in the garden,
bent over her flowers. She grows roses and won't let the gardener
touch them. A large sun hat obscures her face; her hands are small and

delicate—the hands of a violinist, he thinks—and work steadily. As he watches her through the window, it occurs to him that it is as she says—this has all gone on before him; it is only now that he knows, now since the malaria, now that he has become attuned to her body. Had it not been for the malaria, he would never have had the occasion to draw so close to her.

When Grace calls, he goes. Mim says nothing, as if she has gotten used to it already. He supposes they now have an agreement—as he will get used to her retching, she will get used to his leaving for an affair. She doesn't say anything about his taking the rickshaw, and of course she will know before the hour is out that he has taken it—the driver will return with the car.

Grace wears chic little sailor pants and a white top, delicate sandals from Italy. She feels so young in his arms, so vital and vibrant. Mim's age, her infirmities have gotten under his skin.

Their lovemaking is not wild as it was the day before, but quiet, even solemn, as if now they recognize its significance, its greater nature, beyond the pleasure of the bodies. Afterward, she orders up room service, and within fifteen minutes, the bellhop arrives with a tray of fruits, cookies, and teas. She says nothing about her guilt, about Vikram, except to tell him that she has more time today. "I've got the priest from our temple to teach Vikram the Upanishads."

They spend the afternoon in the room, talking. The sun moves from the right side of the room, to the left. At first, a burning triangle of light, later a soft, edgeless puddle. She stretches out by his side, leans on one elbow, then the other and asks him many questions. What was it like growing up in Manhattan? What was your mother like? Your room like? Where was your bed? What kinds of things did you keep? Such questions as this. If he does not tell enough, she stops him. "No, go back. Now, tell me everything."

It is an odd love of details; he has rarely come across this before, but there is nothing more seductive than rapt attention, and he finds himself searching his memory for the small details she desires.

He finds nearly everything about her a wonder—the way her fingers curl her blonde hair behind her ears, the way she moves through the room, languidly, as if there is no hurry ever, the way she sits in a chair, with one of her legs draped over the arm, or her legs pulled to her chest, or folded coltishly beneath her. She has an unstudied grace, and his attraction to her is so clean and strong, it surprises him. Rarely has anyone or anything struck him so purely.

Niche-partitioning is an adaptive phenomenon. It is particularly noteworthy when it occurs between species that share the same ancestry (having been isolated at various times geographically, they have evolved into different species). When they live sympatrically—that is to say, co-existing without competing for the same food source—it signifies that they have evolved a system of niche-partitioning.

The three species of bamboo lemur on the island of Madagascar are an example of this sort of niche-partitioning. David Quammen, in his book The Song of the Dodo, *speculates on how this might have occurred: the gentle bamboo lemur was the most likely to first occupy Madagascar. It flourished on a diet of the bamboo plant named C. perrieri. The giant bamboo lemur, perhaps having evolved on a different part of the island, arrived later, and though it was bigger, it suffered the disadvantage of being a newcomer. It was unable to displace the gentle bamboo lemur from its niche. But because the giant bamboo had bigger jaws and teeth it adapted by eating the tougher giant bamboo plant, C. viguierie. This plant itself adapted: to withstand the attacks of the giant bamboo lemur it concentrated cyanide in its most vulnerable parts.*

When the golden bamboo lemur arrived, it faced competition from the gentle bamboo lemur and the giant bamboo lemur. Unable to displace either of them from their niches, it adapted itself to eating the tender leaves of the C. viguierie *bamboo plant that was laced with cyanide, this being all that was left.*

What is remarkable in this example, however speculative it is, is the deeper pattern that it illuminates: the various, improbable ways in which nature turns to preserve itself; the unpredictable departures within a solid pattern, such as niche-partitioning, which defy all reason, as if there is a will, a dumb, blind determination, at the ineffable heart, to survive, if need be, on the scraps.

From Notes on Extinction, *by Will Mendelsohn*

Chapter 10

*H*e meets Grace in Room 3B, maybe four times a week. Sometimes, but not usually, he cannot get away when she phones, and occasionally he feels he must say no so as not to seem at her beck and call. Whenever there is time, he hurries through the streets of Dibrugarh to find something to bring her—flowers at the market, fruits. This desire to bring her something surprises him. He has never been a man to lavish gifts on a woman.

He takes Mim's car to town, then an auto rickshaw to the country club and walks up the stairs under the steady gaze of the bellhop, who sits behind the desk. He wonders how the information does not travel back to Vikram; it seems it might easily, given that Vikram is a member of the club, that everyone knows him, but he supposes that no one would want to tell a dying man that his wife is having an affair.

He allows himself the luxury of savoring every moment of his present life. He does not remember a time when he has felt so happy. He does not consider if it will last or not. He has no thoughts about the future.

He discovers in Grace many of his own sensibilities; their internal world replicated so similarly that at times the understanding is so immediate as to transcend words. Their traumas and consequent troubles have manifested themselves in so similar a way that he sometimes feels as if they are brother and sister. All other relationships he has had begin to pale in comparison.

He confesses that he had to take care of his mother after his father died; she tells him that her father confided his sorrows.

"This pain I have in my shoulder," he tells her his mother said, "it starts in the second digit of my finger, and is like a red-hot pain, a lightning bolt that travels through my wrist and elbow to my shoulder, where it embeds itself in the bone and goes deep into the marrow. Mice chew at the small of my back with sharp, greedy teeth."

"My father took me with him to the metal shop," she says, "and while I sat on a bench inside, he told me how he felt like a failure. He had wanted to build naval ships, and now he had a metal shop and two children. He would cry into his big hands. His cry was so high and crushed, it pierced me. I would say, 'You're not a failure, Dad. You have this shop, and you're going to build ships one day.' My voice was high, like a choir girl's."

But it is when, one afternoon, she tells him the story of her mother that he understands the root of their affinity. "My mother went to Paris to study opera and married a man named Claude Chabon," she says. "When Germany occupied France, she was Madame Chabon living on rue Saint-Denis. Claude was in the Resistance, and on May 14, 1943, was taken prisoner from the rue Saint-Denis. She found out in July 1944 that he was killed. That August, she met Ed Tubor, pronounced Tu-ber by his Midwestern relatives, pronounced Tu-bor by Vera. She met him the day Paris was liberated, when de Gaulle led a parade down the Champs Elysées. Ed was a sailor and impressed her with his ambitions of building great ships. They knew each other only one month and married in this hillside town in the south of France, Cornillion Confoux, and allegedly, I was conceived on their wedding night in an iron bed. He brought her back to the United States, and opened a metal shop that made parts for ships he wished to build."

It is a strange moment when she says, "Living in my mother's house was like living in German-occupied France. She spoke to me and my little sister in German and French. She hoarded everything, and she told us the story of Claude Chabon over and over and over again. How every day she went to the prison to find out about him. How she went down to the train tracks where the prisoners dropped scraps of paper, telling where they were being taken, to see if Claude had dropped one for her. How she spoke every day to his mother, Renée, who lived in the small town of Soissons. How she had to go in July of 1944 after the Invasion of Normandy, because Renée was sick. How she went into town to find some insulin and was picked up by a German convoy, and how when she got back to Renée's house, she found the woman dead. Then she found out Claude had been shot."

Will is of course astonished. It is his own story, more or less—of a mother caught in time, a mother whose mind has frozen on the details of a certain time, one now long past. And not just any time, but the time of the war, a time when their mothers were coincidental in time and separated by distance—her mother in German-occupied France, his mother in a German-run concentration camp.

He does not want to make too much of this affinity; he does not want to give it meaning where there is perhaps none. Yet, he finds it extraordinary.

There are, of course, facts about her life, things that have happened to her, for which he has no parallel experience. He has nothing in his experience remotely like the one where her father, finding some opportunity in the misery of her loss (first Louis, then Vikram, then the child) takes her to a restaurant and tells her that his affair with Mrs. Henry has never ended. He wants for Grace to meet her.

When Grace tells him in horror that what he has proposed is unnatural, and that furthermore she never wants to hear of it again, he says, "You are not my daughter anyway. Your mother was pregnant when I married her."

"Ice is too light, too clear, to describe the look in his eyes," Grace says. "His face reminded me of a bat I'd seen caught in a glass jar."

She rises from the bed, as if she has said nothing important, and pulls a blue silk robe over her naked body. She walks to the table and opens the bottle of water.

"Are you his daughter?"

"No," she says. He hears the glug, glug of the water as she pours it into two glasses, her back yet turned to him.

"Whose daughter are you?"

"I don't know."

"You asked your mother?"

"I told my mother what my father told me, and then a letter was sent to me. That's when I left for Paris."

He has forgotten about the letter. He doesn't go to the bungalow anymore, where Stella would mention it.

She returns to the bed and hands him a glass of water, takes a sip from her own.

"What is this letter?" he asks.

"It is nothing, really." When she looks up, sorrow floods from her eyes. He touches the side of her face, asks what is wrong, but she closes down, and slips away to the chair.

"What happened?"

"My parents divorced. My father moved somewhere, I don't know where, and my mother traveled awhile, and ended up in a sanitarium for a bit."

"Do you speak to her?"

"Yes, now and then," she says. It is eerie the quiet that suddenly falls over the room. He is aware of a great omission.

"It is ridiculous," he says, "but I feel a bit slighted that you have shown this letter to Stella and you won't tell me what it is."

"Believe me, it was under strange circumstances that I gave Stella that letter."

She tells him the story, not of the letter, but of the circumstances under which she gave Stella the letter, as if to distract him from it.

It was when they were in Paris, in the small apartment that she rented on Montparnasse on Edgar Quinet Boulevard, she says. She took it for the windows, which overlooked an open-air market. She put a table before one of them and finished a screenplay about a black man and a white woman on the road together, running from the law. The light came in late in the afternoons and lay in the corners a grayish blue, like sleeping dogs.

Nights, she walked along the Seine, as if drawn by an invisible string that pulled all creatures living along. It was a line you weren't aware of until you skirted the edges of life.

Paris was to supplant the past, but sitting on a bench in the Jardin de Luxembourg, memory was never far away. There was always a clear path that could be traced from your birth to the bench where you sat in a garden in Paris. She had thought then, I could die now.

When she couldn't stand the solitude anymore, she called Stella and invited her for Christmas. She had not told Stella why she'd gone to Paris. After Stella agreed to come, Grace bought her ticket and cleared space in her dresser.

She took her to Notre Dame on Christmas Eve. They walked in the chill, along the Seine. It rained lightly, a cool mist that behaved like steam. Once they were inside, they walked up the side aisle along with the crowd, and stood in the transept, tipping their heads back to glimpse the apse. They drifted with the crowd and came to sit in the back in the rows of folding chairs.

Perhaps it was the belling of sound inside the cathedral, the way in which every voice, every footfall echoed, darkened by stone, sound falling into sound, which transported her thought, for suddenly the image of Jesus on the cross ravished her. The unexpectedness of it shocked her. The serpentine curve of his body, skewed from his hanging weight, was an agony that was suddenly erotic. His nakedness awoke in her a longing.

Grace leaned near to Stella. "I am sexually attracted to Jesus," she whispered.

A moment passed and Stella whispered back, "I'm attracted to Mary."

Then they bent forward in their laps and could not hold their
laughter, and had to leave the cathedral, tunneling through the mass
of people in the narthex. When they got outside, they fell against the
railing along the Seine, Stella bending over it, Grace arching backward. Their laughter was too loud for Paris; it was sprawling and
undignified. It rolled across the Seine and was heard on the other side.
It was the wrong laugh for the dourness of the hour, and broke the
solemnity, through the imposing, sneer-nosed silence of Notre Dame.
It mocked the great cathedral.

But it lashed Grace and Stella together. It was all right between
them then. And they walked home through the slick, wetted streets,
together now, good friends again.

It was early evening, when Stella took Grace's body into her hands.
She began at Grace's feet and worked her way slowly up the length of
her. She dug into the muscle, pressing out the pain that had pooled
in the pale hollow of the bone. She coaxed it up with the points of
her elbows. She rolled over Grace's body, like a pin, resting in the valley of Grace's back, in the slight cradle at the underside of her knees.
She knelt next to her then and touched Grace's skin so lightly with
her fingertips that gooseflesh rose, and when she turned her head over
and ran her hair over the fields of Grace's bare legs and arms, the plain
of her naked back, Grace cried. No one had touched her in months.

"Why did you leave?" Stella asked.

And Grace put the letter into her hands.

"So what did she read?" Will asks.

The phone on the desk buzzes, and Grace answers.

He puzzles over the details of this story, while she goes down to the
courtyard to settle a bill. He watches her from the window as she talks
to the bellhop. He feels that she has concealed something of grave importance to him, by refusing to tell of the letter. Perhaps it is the
furtive look of her in the courtyard, his inability to make out what
they are saying that gives him this thought. He thinks of her line, "I
could die now."

He has rarely had the chance to observe her from a distance, to perceive her without her knowing it. They always meet in this room, never downstairs or in Dibrugarh. She has come to mean too much to him, he thinks. They tell each other minute details, riffs of thought that he could not imagine telling anyone. He has never had such a thing, and now it seems he cannot do without it. He has told her his deepest regrets—his burned book, his wife's leaving—and she has listened. Her attention has the quality of a summer sun—intense, immediate. She has a way of artfully putting herself at his disposal so that he comes back for more. It is what Stella came to India for, what Vikram has asked her back for. Attention is a priceless thing.

He has come to need her—a thought he can barely tolerate.

When she comes back into the room, she puts a slip of paper inside of her notebook. He is oddly suspicious, as if she and the bellhop are in cahoots about something. He wonders if she is paying him off so that Vikram might never find out.

"What was that about?" he asks.

She tells him that the bellhop has given her the bill for room service separate from the rent, as she has asked. When she is in the bathroom, he cannot keep himself from looking inside the notebook at the slip of paper. It is as she says—it is a separate bill for their room service.

What he knows of her is confined to this room. It cannot be quite real. What would it be like, he wonders, to do something ordinary? To go shopping in the market? To sit at a breakfast table and read the newspaper? He would like to see her rise in the mornings, recline on her bed at night, watch her bent over in the garden, but he is prevented from doing this.

He leads two lives, as she does, or rather a life divided. One in this room, another with Mim. To Grace he gives his thoughts, his body, his emotion. To Mim, his ordinary life.

When she comes out of the bathroom, he asks one more time. "So what is the letter?"

"It is unimportant," she says.

Chapter 11

*H*e finds himself journeying to the country club, spending time with Stella, taking care of Mim, teaching Ramu about extinction. The instruments he uses with Mim take on an aura they have surely never held. He comes to love the feeling of the stethoscope in his ears, the black plastic pump in his hand, the dark cuff, the cold metal listening device, which he touches to the hollow of her elbow. He comes to expect the sounds, the pump-pump, the inflating cuff, then the greatest pleasure, the sound of Mim's heartbeat, the throb in his ear, the accompanying twitch on the sphygmomanometer.

He enjoys making the elixirs the doctor has recommended, and watches with satisfaction as she drinks them down and hands him the empty glass. He charts her heart rate and blood pressure, and feels a sense of accomplishment to note that under his care, her heart rate has slowed, her blood pressure lowered.

Once a week, late in the morning, he gives Ramu his lesson on extinction. Occasionally, Dr. Chaund enlists him to help, once by distributing polio boosters to the workers, another time by shaving the heads of children with lice, dusting their bare scalps afterward with powder.

Late in the afternoon, after he's spent a few hours with Grace, he often meets Stella in town. She becomes the companion Grace cannot be; they walk down the narrow alleys, past the shops filled with plastic buckets and saris, electrical appliances. Stella knows many of the stallkeepers—people, realities he would never have come to know on his own. They pick the best fruit at the market and sit in a small restaurant and marvel over the waiters who tend them barefooted. They talk sometimes about the things boys discuss—motorcycles and cars and guns, and gradually he grows accustomed to finding these interests in her.

In a moment of weakness, he buys her a small blue moped she's been eyeing for weeks, one Grace has refused to buy. It is easy to play Stella's father, her big brother, her more fortunate boyhood friend. She offers no resistance. He cannot keep himself, at times, from straightening her papers, from holding her wallet for her so that she doesn't lose it, from buying her small trinkets that light up her eyes, things he knows lose their value just hours after they have fallen into her hands.

Grace has repeatedly asked him not to tell Stella that they are having an affair, and so he holds this back. He gathers that Stella thinks she is working on their screenplay when she goes to the country club. He wonders what she imagines he is doing staying on in Dibrugarh with Mim, but doesn't ask. Stella rarely mentions Grace, except within the context of the screenplay they work on together. It is a source simultaneously of pleasure and frustration. Pleasure when Grace finds the time, frustration when she does not. He discovers that Stella's character is a woman named Miranda, who not only leaps from moving trains and fords swamps teeming with alligators, but one who, pitted against men, wins. Grace never mentions it.

His work goes well now. When he confesses to Grace that he feels hopeless about the situation in the world, and hence about his work, disclosing the revelation he has had outside the caves of the Vanikoro swiftlets on the island of Guam, she says, "Oh, nonsense. You do not know what is going to happen. No one knows."

Such small words, but somehow they work, and he is writing again. He writes with a lighter touch now, with humor even. She takes his pages from him, and returns them the next day with edit marks and suggestions. He follows her scribbles along the margins of the page, the drift of her intelligent thoughts in her scrawling along the margins of the page. He is surprised to discover that her suggestions are better than his own, and he takes them willingly.

He can no longer write it for himself, so he writes it for her. It is simple, sentimental even, he considers, but nothing has worked quite so well. And when a postcard from Rita arrives, announcing that it was a brown tree snake, *B. irregularis,* which has driven the birds of Guam into extinction, he is forced to reconceive his moment of revelation outside the caves of the Vanikoro swiftlets. Instead of seeing the world unraveling by a dark, mysterious hand, he imagines the skinny snakes slithering through the tangle of forest, devouring the birds' eggs from simple hunger. He teaches Ramu about extinction now with a measure of hope.

He begins to work in their room, sometimes sleeping there. Slowly he begins to keep some of his clothes there. The bellhop discusses things with him, as if he is the lawful tenant. The maid becomes so familiar with him that she brings him lassies when he is there working. She washes his clothes, as if this were his home.

When he is with Grace, he is filled often with a strange gratitude, as he imagines a man condemned to death might be.

He does not pretend that Grace is a woman any man would want. He has not idealized her. He is not ignorant of her shortcomings. She is nearing middle age, her body no longer entirely youthful; she cries too easily, she is too generous with the servants, on occasion giving things away that are his, she pries too deeply into his emotion, but she is who he wants. When she is playful, there is a flash of light in her eyes, mischievous, dark, which he adores. There has never been anyone who has been quite so near to him, who has filled his life in quite the same way. He finds himself carrying small things she has given to him in his pocket—a round stone from her garden, an amulet the priest once gave her.

At night sometimes, he wakes up with a racing heart. The darkest fear fills him then, unnamed and before this, unimagined, and he must turn on the light and wait for it to pass. It is fear that he has become sentimental, the sort of person he has always loathed. Fear that he has fallen so far that he is willing to take what he can get—the free times Vikram allows him, the beat of Mim's heart, Stella's need of a father. In these awful moments, what he has gathered for himself appears to him as table scraps, which he takes so eagerly. Is he so desperate not to be pressed out of life?

He is like an insect blown randomly to an island not its own, he thinks, where it takes up the only niche available to it. The life he is leading is not quite real, as if he's living on borrowed time, like the time one receives on a train, as it moves from one point to its destination. It is India too, India, deceptive in her rags, concealing an ancient heart that is like no other.

Chapter 12

*A*fter the rain stops, Will walks to the tea gardens, to Dr. Chaund's hospital. He passes by the factory where the tea leaves are dried and processed and packed in wooden chests, to give the manager, Mr. Patel, a note from Mim. He walks inside, past great drying bins and large machines that churn and tear the leaves. They are attended by the tribal men, who wear lungis, a knee-length wrap of plaid cloth tied around their waists like a skirt. They pay scant attention to him, as if he has business there that needs no explaining, his white skin, the passkey.

He walks through a sun-filled room, where a dark-skinned man spreads the loose brown processed tea evenly across a white-tiled floor with a rake for its final drying. The smell is strong and earthy, pleasant. He stops just outside the door to the office. Inside are two young men, obviously not tribal men. They are no more than twenty years old, students most likely, dressed in Western clothes. He knocks lightly and they look up, startled.

"Is the manager in?" he asks. He thought perhaps he should introduce himself.

"He will be back in an hour or so."

They make no attempt to hide what they are doing—one

stands at a small Xeroxing machine, making copies of an Indira Gandhi photograph. The other paints large black X's across them. The X'd out photographs are spread across the floor to dry. He knows then that they are with the All Assam Students Movement and wonders if Mim has any idea that her factory office is being used by them.

He leaves the note on Mr. Patel's desk and walks to the hospital.

He teaches the boy about the passenger pigeons of America, his first example of extinction. He's taught him so far about niches, about samples and isolates, about islands. The boy listens as if to a spellbinding story and asks many questions. When they are finished, a few women come with sick children, and Dr. Chaund asks Will to take Ramu back to his room and put him in bed.

"Scoop him up, like so," Dr. Chaund says. "He is light, like a feather. Be sure to keep his hands outside the covers."

Will wants to object. He has never lifted a paralyzed boy from a wheelchair and does not want the responsibility, nor the intimacy. He is not Dr. Chaund's assistant either. He's already walked through the blistering heat, given a lesson when he didn't have to, but he feels himself unable to object.

Though the boy understands nothing of what he says, Will speaks to him while he maneuvers the wheelchair back into the room, next to the bed. He confronts the boy's inert body, recalling the scooping motion Dr. Chaund made. He puts an arm beneath his knees, the other across the boy's back and lifts him. It is true, he is very light. His arms and legs are like rubbery noodles, yet he can hold his head on his own. Will has never carried anyone anywhere in his arms, and now in the last month he has carried Mim, and now this poor fragile boy.

Will lays him down on the bed, the boy's legs landing crookedly, one falling open, the other stubbing on the mattress and folding under. He must straighten them, picking them up one by one, laying them flat. When he draws the sheet over him, he must pull the boy's arms outside the covers, positioning them at his sides.

The boy gestures with his head, the seesawing motion that Will is beginning to understand can mean just about anything. At this moment it means, Thank you so much. At other times, it can mean, yes or no or please, or I'm happy, I'm mad, I'm certain, I'm uncertain . . .

Before he leaves, he stops into the room where Dr. Chaund is measuring out small cupfuls of cough syrup.

"Why are there young men from the All Assam Students Movement using the office in the factory?"

"Oh, they come and go from all the gardens," Dr. Chaund says. "The managers have great sympathy for their cause, and they let them use the phones and such things."

"Does Mim know about it?"

"It is harmless," Dr. Chaund says. "They are not terrorists. They are very democratic young men. It is the People's Liberation Army that you should worry about, but you won't find them here on the gardens."

It grows cooler. The sun is a great monocle held in place by the blank cheek of blue sky. The women pluckers are replaced by the men in the gardens, who do the heavy work of pruning and replanting the shade trees. The Brahmaputra River, swollen fourteen miles wide after the monsoons, thins and then slows.

What Mim has predicted since he's come, happens. On January 6, Indira Gandhi's government decides to put an end to central government in Assam. Twenty-one rounds of talks between the government and the students have produced nothing. Now there will be three separate elections in Assam in February.

Within a week of the decision there is a sudden blackout of publications, news reports, editorials, advertisements, and photographs about the campaign against the Bangladeshi. Students are arrested, the president of the All Assam Students Movement, Profulla Mahanta, among them. Will is surprised, while Mim takes it in stride. It is when there are bomb blasts and attacks on bridges that her heart rate rises again. Although no group takes responsibility for it, she is certain it is the People's Liberation Army.

A week later, there is a two-day strike. There are no phones, the electricity goes on and off. All businesses and schools are closed. A small railroad station in Upper Assam is set on fire, a train engine is derailed, wooden bridges are attacked. When he goes into town, there is a heavy presence of paramilitary troops, of policemen. He is surprised when he sees the Xeroxed likenesses of Indira Gandhi with the brutish black X's painted across them posted up here and there. When he and Mim play canasta in the light of the hurricane lamp, he finally tells her he's seen the students in the factory office. "I saw them painting X's over Xeroxed pictures of Indira Gandhi."

"I know this," she says. He is surprised she has never mentioned it before. "We tea-garden owners can't afford to alienate them. There is nothing to be done. It is not the students who worry me. It is the People's Liberation Army. They are a radical faction, and they will grow. If I know anything, I know this: One day they will turn on the tea-garden owners, because they have prospered as well, and not one of us is from Assam, especially me."

Chapter 13

On the way back from the country club a few days later, traffic is stopped while police look into every vehicle. A bridge has been blown up by the People's Liberation Army of Assam. He sees plumes of smoke coming from the horizon, and his heart quickens. He notices then that the men trudging along the sides of the road keep glancing over their shoulders.

He is easily spotted sitting in the back of the open rickshaw, and they stare at him with a frankness that is chilling. He has very little idea what possesses these men who tread the sides of the road—where they are going, where they have come from. He does not know who among them are students, who are not.

Mim is upset when he reads her the news of the bombing. He tries to soothe her again, pointing out that it is still quite removed from them, but she cuts him short. By the evening, she develops a pain beneath her right shoulder blade, so deep she is prevented from moving her head, her neck, her right arm. For thirty years she has managed to live without painkillers, but now that her husband has died, she has given up.

It is fear. It leaves her heart and travels to her stomach and sometimes lodges itself beneath her scapula bone.

When he tries to soothe her again, she snaps, "Ask Grace's husband if he is nervous, and then you will understand what I mean."

She has meant to wound him with her choice of words—Grace's husband, rather than using his name—and later she comes to his rooms and apologizes.

"I am sorry, Will," she says. "I am not myself since Harold died."

They play a game of cards in her dining room, but her words have their effects. When he lies in bed that night, he considers that he is Grace's mistress. While the idea is slightly amusing, he chafes under the yoke of it.

When he sees her next, he says to her, "I am your mistress," and she laughs.

"You can never be a mistress," she says. "I am the mistress. However you look at it, I am always the mistress, whether you are married and have a wife, or whether I am married and have a husband, I am the mistress. Men are never mistresses. They are spared this disgrace."

"A mistress is a woman who consorts with a married man. So by some stretch of the imagination, I am a man who consorts with a married woman, and would therefore be a mistress."

"You misunderstand the ways of the world, Will." She smiles. "On this point you are sadly mistaken. In any situation, I am the adulteress. I am the mistress, as well. I am your mistress. My husband is being cuckolded by you, and you are the cuckolder, if there is such a word."

He looks at her. What does it matter who is the cuckolder and who is the mistress. "I want you," he says. The want is bare, and for a moment he is ashamed.

She understands what he means by this and skirts away from him, crossing the room.

"We would be disastrous together," she says. "We are too much alike." There is something final in her tone, as if she has considered and has arrived at her decision long ago, independent of him.

The wounding is immediate. He has, of course, thought the opposite. He senses that an exit is required and slips on his sandals and stands up.

"Where are you going?"

"I am not sure," he says.

"Are you coming back?"

"I don't know." It is true. He doesn't know. He only knows that what she has said requires that he leave.

All the way back in the auto rickshaw he feels dulled. He can barely move. India passes before his eyes, as if a movie, and he is nothing now but a cardboard figure cut from America and superimposed. The rules of humiliation do not only apply to women, he thinks.

When he gets home, he goes numbly through the motions, taking Mim's blood pressure, checking her heart rate, mixing her an elixir the doctor has advised, of papaya and crushed vitamins.

"You are home so early," she says.

"Yes," he says, though he says nothing of why.

She sits at the dining room table. She is still thin, but she has regained something of herself. She is dressed again anyway, wears even a trace of lipstick on her mouth. The servants have stopped walking so quietly around her, as if she will break.

He is quiet as he pumps the black rubber ball of the cuff. He is now her sole attendant. A mistress to one, a nurse to another. Is this what is left to a man his age? Is this his penance, to bow before the altar of women, from whom he has either fled or too often ignored?

He listens through the stethoscope for the sound of her heart, watching for the pulse on the sphygmomanometer. It has been a mistake, this entire affair, he thinks.

"What happened that you are home so early?" she asks. She knows his rhythms, as he knows hers.

"I have been playing the fool," he says.

From the look in her eyes, she's been quietly waiting for him to have this realization. She touches his hand gently.

"Don't worry. Love turns all of us into fools. But you are a reasonable man." She brushes back a lock of dark hair that has been displaced by the revolving fans overhead. "We've all fallen at least once."

It is precisely this that he senses over the next few hours as he works at his desk, writing about the last dodo bird. A falling.

Late, when there is a knock on his door, he thinks it is Mim come to soothe him. But it is Aruun, woken from his sleep in the hallway just outside the door. He opens the door a crack, squinting in the light, and says, "Miss Tagore here to see you."

Immediately his heart starts, and he steels himself for a final good-bye scene, for which he does not feel prepared. "Let her in," he says.

When she steps into the doorway, he can see his leaving has had an effect. She has been crying. Her eyelids are puffy, the whites are red, the pale blue, stark. Perhaps he has intended this.

She walks into his rooms with a certain determination, yet he knows she feels herself to be at a disadvantage. She is dressed in black: black pants, a black shirt, a simple pair of Indian sandals.

"So this is where Mr. Mendelsohn works," she says. Her eyes pass over the room, and catch on a photograph that stands on a small table. She walks over and picks it up. "This must be your mother," she says. "Who is the dog?"

"It is her dog, Sally. Mim put it there," he says, and then goes silent. There is no need to defend himself.

He watches as she looks at the world maps Mim has hung on the wall behind his desk. She feigns a great interest in them.

"So are you leaving for unknown places?" she asks. Her nerves are easy to see in the quick way she pushes her hair behind her ears, her fingers lingering on her neck.

"I don't know," he says, though he has made no plans, not even tentative ones.

He reaches out for her and pulls her into his lap. She folds into him and presses her face into the hollow of his neck. "I am attached to you," she says. "I don't want you to leave."

How perfectly, how precisely the words rush to the wound she has made and soothe it. He is not yet sure what game it is that they are playing, though he is sure they are playing some game. He feels himself weaken, his resolve to hold her off, to deny her access, drain away, and he stands and walks to the window, where outside the old gardener does a late evening puja. The man sits with his back perfectly erect, in front of a statue of Durga, which stands in the midst of Mim's garden.

"What do you want me to do?" she says softly. She has stood up from the chair, and her arms hang at her sides, girlishly, helplessly.

He hasn't expected this question, and for a moment he wonders if he can ask her to leave her husband. Is this what he wants her to do? Leave her dying husband? No, he cannot ask this. And yet the situation is impossible. It has been from the start. It was just supposed to be an affair—a quick entrance, a quick exit. He was to be gone by now, and yet weeks have passed, and so too has the opportunity for an easy out. They have become attached to one another. This is the problem. To become unattached is to invite suffering.

"I don't know," he finally answers.

They both experience relief. They can exist in this no-man's-land of not knowing. She finds her way back into his arms. He has lost his advantage, he thinks. And yet who is it that is leading? Is it him, or is it her? He has never known.

She takes them to his bed, and they make love quickly, but passionately. Afterward they subside in one another's arms, and he rests his head on her breasts. Her legs wrapped tightly around his waist, her arm draped over his shoulder, her hand on his back, fills him with a deep sense of well-being. It is elemental, primary, a need that should not go unmet. It is all impossible, but yet here is this moment, perfect in its own right, deeply satisfying.

When she leaves, it is nearly three in the morning. He walks her out to the car, where inside the front seat her driver sleeps curled up, his feet tucked beneath the steering wheel. A few crows fly up from the eaves at the start of the car.

When he returns to the house, he hears Mim stirring in her

room. He worries that his lovemaking has been heard. He wonders how much of it has traveled through the thin walls of the bungalow. He tries not to recall his throaty moans, her higher feminine echoes.

At breakfast in the morning, Mim spreads marmalade on her toast brusquely. Her lips are pinched, and the papers lay unopened.

"What is the matter?" he asks.

"It is one thing to go off and have your affair in private. It is another to bring it into my house."

So she has heard. Aside from the humiliation he feels, he is not so certain that he is wrong. Does he not have any rights in her house? No right to bring a woman to his rooms? So he has made love in the room he lives in, with a woman he loves. He is not going to apologize.

"So what did you two decide to do?" she says. She tamps the fallen crumbs with her fingertips and presses them to her lips.

"Decide?" he repeats.

"I take it that there was a parting yesterday," she said. "Then, tearful, she turns up late at night, and so what?"

He is surprised by her sudden nosiness. It had begun to seem as if in taking care of her that they had entered a tacit agreement—for his care, she would say nothing more about his affair. But now she is breaching their unspoken contract. Is he going to have to listen to this now?

She returns the glass top to the jar of marmalade, the small spoon dropping into the thick orange jelly. "Do you intend to break up their marriage?"

He stares, saying nothing.

"She is in love with you, and her husband is dying. You have no place in this."

"Should I leave?" he asks.

She resumes putting marmalade on her toast, recapitulates. "I'm just asking, Will. I want you to be aware of what you are doing. This is an awful business you've gotten yourself into."

"You speak as if from experience," he says.

"I'm telling you, she is not going to leave that husband. And if you hope you can get her to, you had better think again. Hope is a horror, Will. You must cast it out at all costs."

All morning he can't get her words out of his mind. *Hope is a horror. Cast it out at all costs.* He has never considered it before, but it is true. Hope is a horror. It should be cast out. Yet can one ever really go forward in hopelessness? Is this what one must ultimately learn? That there is nothing but to go forward in hopelessness?

He imagines her concern for his love affair to be personal. Whether there was a man she tried to take from a marriage, or whether she was the married woman who could not be taken, he will never know.

Mim in the throes of passion with another tea-garden owner? A younger Mim, stealing out in the middle of the night, or slipping off in the afternoon, a woman of forty, say, greedy for life. Try as he might, he cannot imagine Mim with the bloom of youth still upon her. He sees only her withered flanks, with which he has become too familiar. Old age repulses. One had better get their loving out of the way before it descends.

He hears her in her room, and knows that she is washing her underclothes in the bathtub—something he has seen her do. He wishes not to know these things about her. He suspects there is something unnatural about the knowledge—the knowledge that a mother has of a child, a nurse of her patient, a lover for his beloved, a tormentor for his victim, none of which he is. He is a friend, no more.

Perhaps it is time to leave. Certainly he has received his signals. But he doesn't go. A man whose needs are fulfilled is disinclined to move on. It does not seem to matter either that they are cobbled together, needs met by an old woman, a married one, and a lesbian. Somewhere inside of him, his mind does not make this distinction— that he receives what is his due, not from one woman, but from three.

He thinks what another man might do in his situation. Another man would pack his bags and go off to the Kazaringa, do his two-day stint with the rhinos, and go off to Africa, as planned. But he is not this other man, he is himself, with all his broken and misplaced parts. He is not whole, nor are any of them: Stella, Mim, or Grace. When the end comes, he tells himself to remember this.

The Tasmanian Aborigines are emblematic of the dangers of insularization. They were not a separate species, but rather an isolated population who had diverged culturally and genetically from the Aborigines on the mainland of Australia.

At the time of European invasion, there were no more than three or four thousand of them. They were hunter-gatherers who lived in bands of forty, with band names like Luggermairrernerpairrerbad and Loontitermairrelehoinner. Their main sustenance was kangaroo.

They were without metal working skills; their spears were made of stone points, their canoes of bundled bark. They were known for their passionate singing and dancing.

Without question, they were unprepared for an invasion of Europeans.

Truganini's life embodies the story of the Tasmanian Aborigines. She was born in 1812 into the Trawlwooway band. The Europeans began arriving in her childhood. British seal hunters came first, a rough, brutish type who immediately began taking the Aborigine women for concubines. Then a British penal colony was founded.

The European population grew very fast, surpassing the Aboriginal population during Truganini's childhood. They put land under cultivation, brought in populations of sheep and cattle, all of which interrupted and impinged on the Aboriginal way of life.

When the Aborigines began to kill the white intruders, measures were taken. First, a mission was established, providing food rations, European clothes, and Christian education. The Aborigines weren't particularly interested, and when the killings didn't cease, a more extreme measure was instituted: bounty payments for captured Aborigines—five pounds for an adult, two for a child. Later, The Black Line—a human chain of soldiers—swept across the land to capture and kill every Aborigine that was found. Only two were captured, just two shot.

George Augustus Robinson arrived on the scene, employed to settle the Aborigine problem. He first established a model village at the Burning Island outpost. Here the Aborigines would be civilized. To speed up the *process, the children were taken from their parents so as to be more effi-ciently indoctrinated.*

The Aborigines didn't fare well. Besides the food being of poor quality, they were also exposed to European diseases for which they had no natu-ral immunity. Some died, while others wandered away. The model vil-lage failed.

But Robinson had another idea. He took a half-converted band of Aborigines, the ones he'd succeeded with marginally, and they went through the country to convert the rest. Truganini was among them.

To be fair, Robinson was not a heartless man. He understood that a people whose children had witnessed their parents' massacre, who had seen their relatives carted away, their country taken from them, their chief sus-tenance—the kangaroo—slaughtered and sold for a meager sum, would have reason to hate.

In way of atonement, Robinson came up with yet another disastrous idea: the Aborigines should be given their own island. Thus, the first Abo-riginal Establishment was founded on Gun Carriage Island. He assigned them huts and garden plots. It was not long before they began dying.

The Establishment was then transferred to a slightly better place, to Flinders Island. For almost three years, Robinson persisted with his plan. At gun point, the Aborigines were shipped to the Establishment on Flinders Island. Most of them died in transit camps. Others made it to Flinders Island and then died. Influenza, pneumonia, and tuberculosis killed them. So too did despair. Truganini was confined, on and off, to Flinders Island.

For cost reasons, the Establishment was moved back to the mainland, to Oyster Cove, Truganini among its inhabitants. It was nothing more than run-down, cold, vermin-infested wooden buildings on a mudflat.

They kept dying.

In 1876, Truganini, supposedly the only full-blooded Aborigine from all those Robinson tried to convert, died. She asked one thing, "To be buried behind the mountains."

She was buried, not behind the mountains, but on the near side of the mountains, at the site of an old prison for female convicts. Her body did not rest long in its grave. It was exhumed by the Royal Society of Tasmania. They studied its parts, then prepared her skeleton and hung it in a museum. It went on a traveling exhibit, and until 1947 was on view at the Tasmania Museum.

In truth, she wasn't the last full-blooded Aborigine. Another woman named Suki survived. She managed to elude Robinson. She lived until 1888.

From Notes on Extinction, *by Will Mendelsohn*

Chapter 14

*T*he tea-garden owners gather in Mim's living room in the evenings. Indians, he discovers, are fond of such discussions and there are endless rounds of them, from which he holds himself apart. He finds the occasions interminable, the long period before the discussion where social pleasantries are exchanged, trying. There is some light division among them: there are those who feel the Bangladeshi should be deported, those who merely want them denied the vote.

"I say they should not be allowed to vote," one Indian tea-garden owner shouts. "If they are allowed to vote, they will vote for their own, and we will be out, I tell you, out. Our concerns will be forgotten. I say they should be denied citizenship. Let them stay, but don't give them the vote."

"They are illegal immigrants, by God," another man shouts. "They should be deported. They are not citizens of India. I say they return to their country. They have their country. We have ours."

There are a few who, less vocal, don't like either idea, but worry that if the Moslems assume power their own interests will be forgotten.

Mim says nothing. Will wonders if her only part is to supply her living room, to grant them hospitality. She concerns herself instead with the flow of drinks and trays of food. She is the last vestige of the British Raj, one of the few Europeans still living on a tea garden. He is not fully awakened to this until the tea-garden owners have gathered in her living room. They are all Indian, and though not Assamese, they are nonetheless from India. Even in a country where people from another state are looked upon as outsiders, still it is better to be Indian than European. Mim is the last of her kind.

She is careful not to commit herself to any ideology. If she takes anyone's side, she will draw attention to herself, lay bare the fact that she has even less to do with Assam than do the Bangladeshi. When she is asked how she feels, it is with great reluctance that she says, "I am more for disenfranchisement than I am for deportation." The word *deportation* hangs ghostly in the air. Perhaps only he has an ear for it.

They rest on Mim's chairs, on her elegant sofas, mostly men, a few wives having come to sit silent by their husbands' sides. He and Mim sit in two upholstered English chairs, apart. If Mim feels like an outsider, he feels like an impostor.

After they leave, Mim comes to his rooms and sits down in the chair near him. She tucks her feet beneath her, slips her hand around a warm cup of tea. It is cool now and she pulls her sweater over her shoulders. "I'm going to tell you something, Will," she says. "I have never spoken these words out loud so long as I've lived in Assam, but I am going to say them now. I don't want to see the Moslems either deported or disenfranchised. It comes off my tongue bitterly when I am forced to say they should be denied their citizenship. Less than forty years ago, they were all the same people. All this nonsense about who is who, Jews, Moslems, Hindus," she says acidly. "It all sticks in my throat. They have been here a long time, yes, but that is not the reason they are hated. They are hated because they are an industrious people. They are hated because they have prospered."

She gives him a long look.

"Would you leave?" he asks. He wants at this moment to shepherd her safely out, to spare her. He has been awakened to her rarity in Assam, to her vulnerability.

"No. I won't leave here. This is my home. Where would I go?"

He suggests America, but she shrugs the idea off.

"An old Polish Jew who has lived in India most of her life, in America? What would I do? When you are old, you will understand." She touches the back of her hand delicately to her forehead, a gesture she makes at moments of grief.

The following week, there is a boycott on the elections. The students are asking the Assamese to stay away from the polls, to protest inclusion of the Bangladeshi on electoral rolls. At first the violence is contained, Hindu attacks on political candidates and their security guards, but its not long before bridges are being burned, communication lines cut, roads blocked. The Moslems take advantage of the general disruption, and attack Assamese settlements. Three Assamese Hindu girls are hacked to death in the village of Samaria. Hundreds of people armed with axes mount an attack on Samaria after rumors that Moslems in other parts of the Boko area have been attacked.

Mim's nerves are wrung out, and Will has to watch her pulse and blood pressure more carefully. Half the time they are without the phones, without electricity.

Every morning Mim reads to him another atrocity: Armed gangs kill a hundred people in a cluster of villages in northwest Assam, in the Gohpar area of the Darrang district. In the Mangaldai area, mobs of immigrant Moslems surround and attack a group of Assamese settlements. On the second day of elections, one of Indira Gandhi's candidates is assassinated. Smoldering shells remain of mud-and-thatch huts in the devastated village of Chamaria, sixty miles from Guwahati. Seventy thousand paramilitary troops and twenty thousand extra local police are called in. But despite their overwhelming presence, they aren't able to contain the violence. By the second February election, Indian Army troops are called in.

What sends Mim to bed one morning late in February is a report of a Moslem village being attacked without warning, the victims killed by machete slashes to the neck and head.

"Police say the count is higher than reported because they still haven't turned up all the bodies of those who were pursued and hacked to death as they fled into the forest. Mostly women and children, and the old," she says. "It was every man for himself and they couldn't run as fast." She lays the paper down on the table and pushes her chair back.

He finds her in her room, propped up in bed against the pillows.

"It sickens me, Will," she says.

The tea-garden owners gather in her living room in the evening to discuss what is happening. More have begun to come, sometimes as many as thirty men crowd inside. The servants have to bring in the chairs from the dining room to accommodate them all. Despite all the violence, the elections are being held. They argue deep into the night about it, Mim saying little.

Even after the elections have taken place, the violence doesn't stop. When they are counting the ballots, there is more killing and troops are called out to restore order in the Nowgong district, then in the Goalpara district. Every morning there is more news of death.

When one night Aruun wakes him, Will's first thought is that the terrorists have come, as Mim has predicted. The boy lightly touches his shoulder, and he comes awake. He carries a hurricane lamp.

"Mr. Mendelsohn," the boy says. "Miss Fars is here."

Aruun, always slightly nervous, appears unhinged. Coming upon one another in the dead of night, master and servant, unsettles them both.

"The electricity has gone out again?" Will asks, and Aruun nods.

It is so cool now, he pulls on a sweater.

Will finds Stella sitting in the chair at his table. Even in the soft webbing of light from the hurricane lamp, she looks harrowed.

"What happened?" he asks. He sits down across from her and folds his hands on the table. He feels his patience coming to an end.

"That son-of-a-bitch Bhupen," she says. "That asshole. That little motherfucker."

He has grown accustomed to her flow of curse words, to the mask of rage that overtakes her face when she is angry; it is heightened by the light, ratcheted up a notch, the lines at her mouth, between her eyes deepened by shadow.

He calls for Aruun to bring them some Limcas, two teas.

It spills out of her in no particular order, and he gathers she's been hiding on the banks of the Brahmaputra for the last six hours. Even in the sparse light, he can see the dirt stains on her green shorts and white T-shirt. Through a trail of questions he inserts, he discovers she has never given Bhupen the money, that she'd asked Grace for the money, but had not told her the truth. She'd said it was for a Buddha head she wanted to buy from the hucksters at the back of the market, that she would later resell in New York. But Grace had said no.

"And then nothing happened," Stella says. "I never heard from Bhupen. I forgot all about it even. But then this afternoon I was coming out of Sari's Newspapers, and he was standing there waiting for me, the little motherfucker."

He said, "Good afternoon, Stella."

"You were following me," Stella accused him. She felt the impulse to shove him up against the storefront, but people were already staring.

"It's been much longer than a week, and we had agreed to meet up in a week." Bhupen smiled, civility over cunning.

"I changed my mind about the prisoner," Stella said. "I don't want to see it anymore."

"I'm sorry to say it's too late for that," Bhupen said. Still with that smile seeping out from the iron brackets of his lips.

"What do you mean it's too late? What are you talking about? I don't want to see it anymore, and I can't get the money." Her voice was loud, but the traffic was a great open mouth of sound.

"It is too late," Bhupen said. He shook his head and looked up the street, as if he were reviewing the bleakness of the future that stretched ahead of them. The traffic, thick with tinkling bicycles and auto rickshaws coursed by.

"You asked Grace?" Bhupen said. His voice was casual, as if he asked something ordinary.

"She wants to know why I want it, and she won't give it to me unless I tell her, and I can't tell her because then she wouldn't give it to me."

"Tell her you need an operation," Bhupen said.

Her hand formed a cliff over her eyes to block the sun.

"No, I'm not going to tell her I need an operation," she said.

"I know you would be very sad if she were not around anymore."

"Why all of a sudden do I have to give you the money?" Stella yelled. "I said I don't want to see it. Okay. Forget it. It's not possible."

"Things have changed," Bhupen said.

Stella stared at him. How was this possible? she thought. How had this happened?

"I'll tell you what," Bhupen said. "You can have another day, but . . ."

"But what?"

"But if you don't get the money, I can't guarantee the safety of your friend, Grace."

Stella begins to cry now. She has taken this threat very seriously, and Will must now calm her, tell her that it is doubtful that Bhupen will really do anything.

"He is preying on your fears. It is highly unlikely that he would kill an American for one thousand dollars."

"You don't know him," she says. "He is evil. He has no feelings. I swear it." She holds her forearm out in front of her and picks the tall hairs from it. He has seen her do this before, when she has been upset, but it looks particularly deranged, isolated as it is in this light.

He thinks it is all the violence that has unnerved her. Americans know nothing like this—America is bland in its politics, stable to the point of boredom. "There is still a lot of chaos," he says.

"No, it's not that. I know an evil man when I see one. And, believe me, I've known all kinds of men."

He must take her at her word on this point, that she has known all kinds of men. But, still, he can't take the threat seriously.

"He has found a victim in you, Stella. Your fear is his opportunity."

"I think he is part of the People's Liberation Army," she says. "Those guys are terrorists."

"I doubt it," he says. "Still, even so, he is not Aban Bezbaruah. Even if he is a member of the People's Liberation Army, he is a pudgy college boy working the Dibrugarh outpost, living in the back room of some clay shop. Let's not turn him into Che Guevara. He is just taking advantage of all the disruption."

Stella pulls a wad of bills from her shorts and lays it on the table. It is crumpled and damp. "I called my father and told him I needed an operation and that he had to wire me a thousand dollars," Stella tells him. "I waited around all fucking day to get it, and he only sent me five hundred. I hate his guts."

She stares at it, as he does, a mound that is only half.

"You can't tell Grace," he says.

"No," she says and starts to cry. "I would never hear the end of it. She would send me back and never write that screenplay. I can't ask her."

The screenplay has become a savior to her, the chariot that will rescue her career and drive her to the gates of Hollywood. She stares at him, blinking, and implicit in the silence is her request for the five hundred dollars. He feels the press of their friendship. All the hours they have spent together have gathered a weight of their own. His fathering has its consequences.

He goes to his room and takes five hundred dollars in traveler's checks from his drawer, and though he considers that it is not the best thing to do, he gives them to her.

"What is Bhupen's name," he says.

"Bhupen Ram."

He writes Bhupen Ram on the line of the checks and hands them to her. He knows that it only prolongs her dependence, but it has gone beyond her, and he knows that she cannot summon a solution herself. She can no longer look him in the eye. She is aware that a woman her age should not find herself in such circumstances, and in her humiliation, she can barely thank him.

She slips out of Mim's house with her head bent. He hears the high whine of the moped and the crunch of the gravel as she drives off. It has been a mistake, taking her under his wing.

In the morning, Mim tells him that there has been a death in the Tagore gardens. News has traveled through the servants. His heart begins beating violently. It is Grace, he fears. Stella has bungled the affair, and Bhupen has gone after Grace.

"Who?" he asks.

"It was a Moslem."

"Who did it?"

"Most likely the People's Liberation Army. The Moslem was killed with a machine gun," she says.

Perhaps Stella is right, he thinks, and he gets up from the breakfast table. The phone lines are down, so he climbs into the back of Mim's Ambassador and requests that he be taken to the Tagores'.

As the car drives bumpily over the rutted roads, he cannot forgive himself for having gone back to sleep after Stella left. He should have gone with her. He should have insisted. He has a way of letting things drift, of not acting, of believing that things have nothing to do with him. He has always been this way, a fact that he has never admired in himself.

He has not been to the bungalow in almost six months, but his car is let in without any questions. He scrutinizes the gatekeeper for any sign that awful things have happened in the night, but the man reveals nothing but tedium, a weariness at the boredom of sitting all day, waiting to open and close the gate.

When Will climbs out of he car, his eyes shift instantly to Vikram's window, but he is not there. He walks down the arbored sidewalk, which is nothing more than a pale wooden rib cage now that the yellow hibiscus has withered.

He asks for Grace and Stella when Vedeshpra answers the door, and is relieved to find that Grace is in the garden, that Stella has gone to town.

"There was a death in the gardens?" he asks.

"Yes, in the eleventh garden. Mr. Patel found him in the morning. A Moslem."

So it was a Moslem, not Grace, not Stella. Grace is in her garden. It gives him some relief, but still there has been a death.

As he walks around to the back of the bungalow, to the garden, he is going to tell Grace about Stella. He is certain that the Moslem dead in their garden has something to do with Stella. He realizes he should have told her from the start, when Stella first went into the jungle. Why he did not, he cannot now say.

He crosses the small bridge that arcs over a pond and leads to the garden. It is overcast now and cool, and he shivers, something he has done little of while in India. There is a vine-covered trellis that surrounds the garden, and as he approaches the gate, he hears Grace's voice, a plaintive strain, followed by a man's soft reply. He cannot imagine who she is talking to and pushes away the vines and peers through the trellis. She sits on the stone bench outside. He is not certain, at first, who sits next to her. The man is Indian, youthful, dark-haired, and Western dressed. It takes him a moment to recognize that it is Vikram. It is a profound shock, akin to discovering that someone you've thought was a woman turns out really to be a man. No longer is he the emaciated man Will last saw in the living room of the bungalow, propped up on pillows, his neck so thin it could have worn a bracelet. No, this Vikram, though not a picture of health, is certainly on his way to it. He sits on his own now, his back erect. His hair has even grown back, a thick shock of shiny black, and though he is still thin, he no longer has the look of a dying man. He has risen, as if from the dead.

And she has said nothing of this extraordinary transformation! In all the weeks that they have been meeting at the country club, not a word about Vikram's journey from his bed on the second floor of the Small House to his place next to her on this stone bench in the garden. There must have been triumphant days, days when Vikram took his first steps, when he walked down the steps of the Small House unattended and walked out into life again. They must have been momentous. And yet not a word about it from her.

She is crying, obviously upset by the death in the gardens, and Vikram is comforting her. He is surprised by the tenderness Vikram shows her. He takes her arm into his lap and begins to stroke the soft, white underside methodically, his fingertips making a practiced, delicate, lengthwise sweep. It is not something, he, Will, knows about her. It pierces him, this intimacy between them: he has come upon a married couple in their garden. Grace and Vikram Tagore, consoling one another over the death in their tea gardens.

He leaves immediately, walking uneasily around to the front of the bungalow and down the barren arbored sidewalk. He sinks into the backseat of Mim's car, sick to his stomach. He marvels over Vikram's return to health, Grace's shrewdness at concealing it. It is a stark betrayal, one he cannot yet calculate. He has not realized how much he has counted on Vikram's dying—a secret he has concealed even from himself. Without quite realizing it, he has figured on an easy ascension.

He broods all afternoon in his rooms, uncertain of what he should do. He retraces his life with Grace, thinking of what she has said, what she has done. Their life has been a fiction, he thinks. Confined as it has been to one room, it has very little reality. That is why he often touched the round stone Grace gave him—he carried it as proof, evidence of their experience together. Grace's real life unfolds on her tea gardens with Vikram. His unfolds at Mim's with Mim and Stella, with Dr. Chaund and Ramu at the small hospital.

Aruun comes in later with a note one of the Tagore servants has brought. The phone lines are still down, and Grace has sent it. "Vedeshpra told me you came this morning, and then left without seeing me. What has happened? Meet me at our room at three o'clock. Love, Grace."

It isn't easy to get an auto rickshaw in town. In all the trouble, they have disappeared. The streets are oddly deserted, filled now only with young men with shifting eyes, rush lights of hate, with the presence of the Indian Army. He is forced to take Mim's car to the country club and now must ask the driver to wait. The man will of course talk to the bellhop and to all the others who make up the idle work staff of a place long ago gone to seed, but what is he to do?

When he walks inside, the bellhop nods to him, and he nods back. It is as it always is. But once inside the room, he sits down in the chair and feels immediately a chasm between them. He watches her and listens as if from a distance. For her it is the same, she is distracted by the death in the gardens and tells him that instead of Vikram she had been the one to go in the morning. Between a narrow row of tea bushes, the Moslem lay faceup, she tells him, his arms and legs flung in a way that bespoke death—one arm against a tea bush, the other half wedged beneath him, his legs thrown open and bent inhumanly, one backward, the other skewed at the knee, in ways a living person would never position themselves, not even in sleep. A machine gun had been emptied into his chest, and where there had once lay a distinction of flesh and bone and organ was now a bloodied pottage. A flap of heart poked out from a sinkhole filled with blood and shattered bone. Someone had touched his eyes closed. Grace, along with thirty women pluckers and a half dozen managers, stood ringed around him.

"A few days ago Vikram forbid the tea-garden managers to let the students hold meetings in their bungalows," she says. "Mr. Patel said this was why they threw the dead Moslem into the gardens."

Tears have begun to brim in her eyes, and he says nothing. Strangely, he feels no sympathy for her, for her ordeal. Ordinarily they would have talked about it. It is only when he says nothing that she notices his remove.

"What is the matter?" she asks him. When he angles his eyes away, she drops to her knees in front of him and gingerly laces her fingers through his. He allows this, but her hand feels alien, and when his remains rigid, returns no warmth, she soon retracts hers. He looks at her and wonders who she is. Perhaps he has attributed qualities to her that do not belong to her.

"You came and then you left without saying anything," she says. She has now retreated from him a bit, moved back on her knees.

"I saw you in the garden with your husband," he says.

She hadn't guessed that this is what made him leave, and she looks, sadly, down at her hands.

"You never so much as mentioned it to me."

"I didn't think you would want to know."

"Want to know," he yells. "All this time I think I am making love to the near widow Tagore, only to find out now that I am merely her lover, the man she has on the side, that after she is with me, she returns to her husband at night, a man supposedly in the throes of dying, who is secretly recovering, and they eat a quiet meal and retire."

"He has gotten better," she says.

"I have made him better," he says. "I have made him better." He is immediately sorry that he has said this, but then she concurs saying, "I've thought the same."

He stands up from the chair and walks to the windows, where down below the rain patters into the slimy pool. The usual unbroken blue skies of India are entirely overcast. He cannot feel happy that he has saved Vikram's life. He is not proud either that he has harbored the dark desire that Vikram simply perish.

"I can't believe that you didn't tell me," he says. "You could have at least done that." He clutches the long red drapery in his hand. It seems to have wiped out the fact of their life in this room, to have betrayed that which he has believed was lovely, beautiful. His late-night fears have not been unfounded—he is a sop, standing at these windows. When he considers that all the times she has run into his arms, has kissed his face, his body, she has concealed from him the fact that her husband has risen from his sickbed, it arouses a violence in him. It is a grievous breach, he thinks.

He hears her voice now, small, contrite. "I didn't tell you because I thought it would upset you."

He turns to her. She is still crouched on the floor on her knees in the bent, limp pose of one caught, of one found out. "You didn't tell me because you didn't want to lose your good thing. A husband at home who provides you security, and a lover you meet in a room who compensates for a husband whose lovemaking and conversation bore you to tears."

She says nothing, just bows her head.

"I saw your marriage," he says. "When I was in the room with the two of you, you were in the room with me."

"It's changed now that he's well. It is better now."

He stares into her eyes. They seem so freakishly pale that he is unnerved by them, these eyes he's spent hours gazing into. He can no longer discount the idea that she is capable of great cruelty, of being so self-serving as to actually be a person he must now defend himself against.

"So I've made your marriage better," he says. "I have come along and helped raise your husband from the dead, and in addition, I have made your marriage better."

She says nothing.

"He's not dying anymore, so leave him."

"I can't leave him again," she says.

"Why not?"

"I have done this before and have ended up with nothing," she says. "He took me back—"

"And you are cheating on him again. Let the man go. You are not his and you never will be. Don't you see that? It is unfair, and it is cruel, Grace. And it is beneath you."

Grace has hung her head. Her white neck is bent, like a flower stalk. He has kissed that whiteness so many times.

"Whatever he gives you, I will give you and more." Words from a dime-store romance, but yet he feels them to be true.

While he waits for her to say something, he is struck by how beautiful she is to him; she is a woman for whom he realizes he would do just about anything. When finally she looks up, she says, "I can't." And he knows instinctively that it is not a tentative, I can't, not an unsure posture, unstable and easily overthrown, but rather one which is adamant, stony, final. I can't.

She looks limp now, broken. A death in her gardens and now this.

He stands again, this time to go, but she won't allow him. She grabs hold of his wrist.

"You wouldn't be happy with me," she says. "I am not unscathed from my life. You'd grow tired of me and then you'd leave me, and then I'd have to do something drastic, like throw myself off a bridge."

"But I love you, and it is impossible for me to believe that I will tire of you. I have never loved anyone so much in my life."

"I know," she says, "but you don't understand. I left my marriage once, and you don't know what that was like. I didn't fare so well after Louis left. I didn't fare so well at all. I was so far gone that I fell into Stella's hands. I can't do it, Will. I can't leave my marriage."

"Have you ever once considered a life with me?"

And then she says it, without pause, without consideration. "No."

To see into her eyes is for him to have a revelation that he doesn't want to have: she wants him to stay on in Dibrugarh indefinitely, come to her room to meet her, for as long as their intense physical relationship exists, and nothing more.

As he moves down the hallway, he hears her cry. It is a cry not often heard; it is deep, unbearable. When he passes the bellhop, he can still hear it, and he knows the man believes he has ended his affair with Mrs. Tagore and has left her heartbroken. He nods to the bellhop, and it is with a cold sureness that he knows he will never see this man again, that he will never tread across the carpet before his hooded eyes again.

In the backseat of Mim's Ambassador, he sinks down, his hands trembling. He is oblivious of the ride and is surprised when the driver turns off and they are back at Mim's. He walks into his rooms, moving past Aruun, brushing off his polite, "Mr. Mendelsohn, would you like your afternoon tea?"

He closes the door to his bedroom and sits on the edge of the bed, his heart pounding, his eyes blinking rapidly. He is not a man made for sudden, abrupt changes. He finds himself weeping into his hands, the grief churning out of him without grace. He is not accustomed to such strong, full emotion, and it does not flow naturally. It is like a river forced out through a garden hose.

By dinnertime the phones are working again, and while Mim is out in her garden, pruning back her rosebushes, he calls the airlines. Flights have resumed and he makes a reservation to fly to Guwahati in the morning. Impulsively, he makes another for three days later to Kenya.

He dreads telling Mim, but goes to the garden and sits down on the marble bench inside. Today, as if to claim her right to be in Assam, as if to erase her foreignness, she wears a sari. It's so cool out, he shivers. It is still overcast and drawn, dark clouds scuttling across a sky that has most often been an unbroken cheery blue. The crows are small in number now and caw thinly as they hop among the rosebushes. Quietly, he explains to her that it is time for him to go. "I've imposed upon your hospitality long enough," he says, as if that is the reason he must be leaving.

She puts down her clippers, and her hand goes to her heart. Her eyes are suddenly rush lights of sorrow. Her face slackens, shadows suddenly deepening the hollow of her cheeks, her lips puckering open dryly. "Oh, Will," she says, expiring a breath of air.

She pushes back a few stray wisps of hair. "You can't go now. There are riots. The elections may be over, but the trouble is not. This is the worst time to leave. What is the rush?"

Should he say? he wonders. He looks down, then finds her eyes. They are like two fierce points which burn from deep inside her eye sockets. "You were right about Mrs. Tagore," he says. "It is over now." He smiles wryly, and her eyes melt in a pity he can barely tolerate. When she touches his hand and tells him she is sorry, he does not doubt her.

"But, Will, you can't go."

He looks away for a moment, struggling against a tide of guilt; he considers staying to care for her until after the situation has settled, but the urge to leave is so strong, panic rises inside at the prospect of remaining. He quickly reasons that he has been good to her, generous beyond measure, that there is no debt on his side.

"I have to go," he says. It is only after he touches his throat and his hand trembles that she understands his deep upset. He feels ashamed and excuses himself from the garden.

When she comes to his rooms later, she is careful with him. While he packs his suitcases, she sits in the chair near his bed, a small, delicate figure dwarfed by the large teak chair with its gargantuan arms.

She twists the bangles on her arm, a stack three inches wide, which cover the tattooed numbers on the back of her wrist. "I know all about these disappointments, Will, but this is not a time to go running off in India. Don't forget that you are a foreigner here, as I am. This is a very unstable time; who knows what will happen to you. So you stay here for a few more weeks and avoid her. There's no saying that you would have to see her. Their tea gardens are miles from here. Why don't you stay for another few weeks, until this has blown over."

For her sake, he should, but he has made up his mind. It is not just a flight from Grace, but a flight from the foolishness of passion, from the indignities that affairs bring—the lying, the betrayal, the secrecy, the gilded hope.

Mim leaves the room in defeat, and later they eat a silent dinner together. Afterward he teaches Latisha how to take Mim's blood pressure, her heart rate, how to record the numbers on the chart he's kept. Mim sits patiently on her bed, resigned to another loss, her arm proffered as they take the cuff off and on, place the hearing device in the hollow of her elbow, over and over again until the girl gets it. It is only because Mim speaks haltingly the language of the tribal people that he is able to make himself understood at all. It is with honest sorrow that he hands over these instruments—the stethoscope, the blood pressure cuff, his watch with a second hand, the ingredients for the elixir, the charts he has carefully kept.

Mim feels deserted, he knows, jilted as if he were a lover, and is silent now. She doesn't come to his rooms all night, as if to punish him. He takes the maps from the wall and rolls them alone, and when he goes later to take her blood pressure, to make her drink, Latisha has already done it. The glass sits on her side table as evidence.

"Mim," he says. "I am sorry."

"I know you are," she says. "I am sorry too. I will miss you. You're very dear to me." He is surprised when the tears come. Never through her malaria, through all the retching, through her violent heart rates and high blood pressures has Mim cried, but now she cries, and he holds her hand, a hand he has come to know perhaps better than was necessary. He sees the hurt it has caused. She will suffer when he's gone.

Chapter 15

Late, Will hears the sound of the front door opening. When he detects a woman's voice, he regrets that he does not have time to compose himself. He never imagined that she would come; it is unhoped for, unexpected, and he is astonished at how quickly his heart races. He stands up, quickly tucking his shirt into his pants and smoothing back his hair. He doesn't know what to do with himself and moves over to his table, makes as if he is straightening his papers.

To have a hope raised when moments earlier it has not existed, then to have it dashed, is the bitterest form of disappointment: It is Stella. The flight his mind has taken in just those moments. Stella stands there as if to mock his illusions, to throw up to him the vanity of his hope.

He is certain the look on his face has betrayed his expectation, and he acts quickly, inviting Stella in, offering her a chair at his table.

"So it's true," she says. "You are leaving."

His suitcases stand testimony, the maps he's taken from the walls that lay half rolled on the floor.

He knows then that Grace has told Stella, at least, this. And now he has to bear witness to the look in Stella's eyes—an odd coupling of pity and sorrow. He is now a defunct rival as well as a friend lost to her.

"Where are you going?" she says.

"To the Kazaringa for a few days," he says. "Then to Africa."

Aruun brings in a tray of tea, and they watch quietly as he sets the teacups in front of them, places a blue sugar bowl and a matching creamer of milk on the table.

"I trust that everything worked out with Bhupen," he says.

She bends down to tie her shoe. "Well, not exactly." When she sits up, her eyes angle away.

"What happened?"

She touches the edge of the napkin indelicately with her fingertips, then looks up. "I need more money," she says.

His disappointment is merely deepened.

"I need four thousand dollars," Stella says. Will watches as she quickly stirs her tea and takes a sip that she neither wants nor tastes. He can sense the narrowness of her thought, now a single, tunneling thread, a hope so determined there is nothing else that she considers.

He must again listen to her story: She did not take the money to Bhupen early in the morning, as he had required, but rather later, after the Moslem was found dead in the gardens. She waited around for him all day, going back and forth between town and the clay shop, where Bhupen worked for an old man named Mr. Hazaracki. She finally found him just an hour ago, and they spoke outside the shop, while the old man went upstairs to bed.

"That was the prisoner thrown into the garden, wasn't it?" Stella said. She could not conceal her anger.

"You must keep your voice down, Stella," Bhupen said. "The old man living upstairs hears very well."

"That was the prisoner, wasn't it?" she whispered loudly.

Bhupen said, "I don't know what you are talking about."

"The Moslem you showed me in the jungle was in the garden this morning, dead."

"How can you be sure?"

"I recognized his face," she said. "I remember what he was wearing."

"Many people in India look the same, especially to the Western eye, and many people in India wear the same clothing. The important question is, Stella, did you bring the money?"

Stella dug down into her shorts and pulled the rupees and the traveler's checks from her pocket. She dropped them to the ground, where they fanned out and scattered near Bhupen's feet. Without the slightest annoyance, Bhupen bent over and picked them up.

"It is not enough," he said. "You make a mistake about the money. It is no longer a thousand dollars. It is five thousand now. You did not bring it to me on time, and I am forced to raise it."

"You can't do that," Stella yelled.

"Shh, Stella," he said, putting his finger to his lips. "Interest rates are high in India," he whispered.

"Why are you doing this to me? You know I don't have any money, and you're still doing this. I haven't done anything to deserve this." Her breath seethed out of her.

"The river floods, people die," Bhupen said. "Tell the police your story." And then he laughed, a profoundly hollow sound.

"I can't get four thousand dollars," she whispered. "I barely got this."

"I will take this for now," he said, putting the rupees into his pocket. "But if I don't see you tomorrow morning before eleven o'clock with the money, you will not find your girlfriend Grace waiting for you at home."

Stella waits for Will to say something, but he is silent, struck again by the shoddiness of human affairs, the shabbiness beneath it all, time spent in such inglorious pursuit: hacking people to death with machetes, now a death in the gardens, a threat of death to Grace, an adulterous affair come now to a bad end.

He is amazed at how easily indelicate matters slip from her lips, as if they are so much a part of her everyday life that to report them is commonplace. But to look at her now, her shoulders rounded, her brown eyes wide with fear, and yet narrowed upon a thought so singular he can almost hear it, like a train chugging doggedly down the tracks.

"I'll pay you back," Stella says. "I promise."

"No, you won't, Stella," he says. It is absurd to pretend that she will.

"No, I will."

He rubs his eyes with his index fingers.

"I have that letter," Stella says suddenly. "The one Grace won't tell you about." Her short fingers close over the handle of the delicate teacup, and she lifts it to her lips. He shudders now to see the look in Stella's eye, lurking behind the raised teacup, the look of a feral creature caught.

She pulls the letter from her shorts and lays it on the table next to his teacup. He gathers she means to give the letter for the money. It is visibly dampened, the edge where it has been opened softly jagged. The return address is MSMH, Vera Tuber, Marcy, New York. So the letter has been written by her mother, he thinks.

"Put it away," he says quietly, and Stella retrieves it and stuffs it down into her shorts pocket. It seems another grievous breach of propriety, of honor, in a line of many.

"Why would you betray Grace?" he asks her.

"She uses people," Stella says. There is bitterness in her voice.

"She's been good to you."

Stella tosses a fragment of cookie into her mouth. "I thought this whole time that she was writing that screenplay when she went to the country club."

She narrows her eyes on him. He is again her rival, at least for the moment, and he knows then that she has found out that Grace has been meeting him in the country club, rather than writing the screen-play. He wonders how it came out. Did Grace finally tell her, or did Stella guess?

"I could have told you she would never leave Vikram," Stella says. "You should have seen her without him, in Paris, after Louis left her. It wasn't a pretty sight."

So Grace has confided in Stella, he thinks. His hands tremble again, and he feels the need to compose them in his lap. He thought perhaps he would get better at loss, the more he lost, the easier it would be to lose, but in fact, he feels the other way.

When they are in the backseat of Mim's Ambassador, on their way to see Bhupen, it is quiet between them. Stella is silent to preserve his will—she doesn't want to say anything or do anything that will loosen him from assuming her responsibility. He cannot imagine what he will say to this young man.

The rain beats down on the windshield, the wipers loud and me-chanically inept, and he cannot help but to think, How has he ended up riding in a car with Stella, heartbroken, on his way to meeting a thug. Shouldn't he be doing something else? Running around a yard with his own children? Sitting at the kitchen table with a wife? Writ-ing his book in the comfort of his own office?

Yet, he must admit it has an odd symmetry to it. It was Stella who had given him Grace's whereabouts in the banyan grove in exchange for money, which had paid for her visit to the jungle. Now it is he and Stella again, returned to their original transgression, Grace faded into the tea gardens with her husband as she seemed to him the moment Stella first mentioned her.

"Are you afraid?" Stella asks him.

"No. You said he was pudgy and docile. Right?"

"Yes, both."

"So I'm not afraid."

"What are you going to do?" Stella asks. "Are you going to beat him up?"

"Jews don't beat people up," he says. She laughs nervously.

Bhupen is surprised Stella has brought him. He has come, as if Stella's father, and for the moment much of the bravado he has had when he thinks Stella is alone folds. His eyes are darting and unsure beneath Will's gaze.

Bhupen takes them quietly through the shop crowded with the dull clay bodies of countless Durga statues of all sizes, and leads them back to the storeroom, where Will discovers that amid boxes of clays and plastic jars of paints, Bhupen lives alone.

Stella sits down on one of the boxes, her sneakers touching the floor, while Will stands next to her. Bhupen leans against the wall, his arms folded. He has retreated behind a seriousness that is studied, never true in a man as young as he is.

A barren bulb hangs from the ceiling, carving a six-foot circle of light out of the darkness. Along its perimeter lies a thin mat where Bhupen sleeps.

When Will gets a look at Bhupen in the light, he cannot believe that this is the guy who has terrorized Stella. He's fleshy, barely out of his teenage years, with a slight case of acne lingering yet on his chin, a patch on his forehead. He has great big doe eyes, the eyelashes of a girl. He is not certain how Stella has read evil in these eyes.

It takes Will little to inhabit Bhupen's mind. He has taken advantage of Stella's fear, her inexperience in dealing with men who don't have much to lose. It is conceivable that he has nothing to do with the People's Liberation Army. Perhaps he has simply seized on the opportunity to extort money from this odd woman who will pay one hundred dollars to shoot off a machine gun in the jungle. He may be no more than a poor boy trying to better his prospects in a country where a poor boy doesn't stand a chance.

He says, "Bhupen, Stella's given you the money, now, leave it alone."

Bhupen says nothing. He's suddenly filled with that Eastern inscrutability, but it is only faintly real.

"She hasn't got any money," Will says. "She's given you money she's had to borrow. You've had your time, you've squeezed her enough, and it's over now."

Bhupen looks off, as if through a window, his eyes blinking furiously against thought.

"I'll put it to you another way," Will says. "I know the general of the Indian Army. It would only take a phone call, and I could gravely damage all prospects you might ever entertain for a future."

He is surprised to find himself enjoying this rouse and would go on except that Bhupen relents. His shoulders give way first, then the cocksure look in his eyes vanishes, replaced with a dewy, boyish fear.

"All right," he says.

"Thank you," Will says, and he reaches out and shakes Bhupen's hand. Bhupen opens the door, and Will shelters Stella under his arm, shepherds her out of the shop.

In the backseat of Mim's car, Stella thanks him profusely. She even takes his hand and kisses it. She calls him the only Jew Bad Boy she's ever known. Somehow he takes this as a compliment. He isn't sure why. Perhaps he needs all the compliments he can get.

They ride for a few moments in a victor's silence. He savors his success. He must admit that he has enjoyed asserting his power over this pudgy little man. He might even have, if the situation had required it, shoved the fleshy Bhupen up against the wall, pushed his forearm against the boy's throat.

"She's in love with you, if that makes you feel any better," Stella says.

"It doesn't."

"I told you right from the start that she was *very* married."

He never thought he would be riding in the back of Mim's car, in cahoots with Stella, sharing the same heartbreak, the same failure with the same woman. Who knew what indignities awaited one?

Stella is so grateful that he has settled her troubles that she helps him pack. She is as inept at it as she is at handling her affairs, and puts things in that are not his—Mim's books on World War II, a small ivory tusk, a silver flask Mim has used as decoration. He tells himself to remember to take them out, but he knows already he can't be counted on to remember. He feels his thoughts at a great remove, his body going through the motions.

Stella has the buoyancy of a person who has been redeemed, rescued from something harrowing. She talks without thought, saying whatever comes to her mind. She tells him how Grace has been crying up in her room, pretending that the death in the gardens has set it off. Vikram, not knowing how to console her, finally went off for a walk with his cane, taking Gandhi-like strides through the gardens.

"She's up in her room with a splitting headache," Stella says. "Believe me, I'm going to have to hear about you for a long time. The reason she can't leave Vikram is because she is a coward. You should have seen her in Paris, after that letter."

Now Stella has the look—a winner's pity for the loser; her words are like consolation prizes.

"Where did you find the letter?" Will asks.

"All the time it was underneath Vikram's mattress in the Small House."

"You went up there looking for it?"

"No, after he moved back into Grace's room, his servant found it under his mattress and brought it over to the bungalow, not knowing what it was, and I happened to be there when he came."

He knows he shouldn't ask, but he asks nonetheless. "How long has Vikram been staying in Grace's room?"

"For two months now."

It makes him sick to his stomach, but he goes on folding his pants, laying them in the suitcase one after the other, careful to hide his feeling.

"While we were in Paris, she cried all the time, and went to the Louvre every day and sat in this one window, where all she could see was the square below, where you could see nothing of modern life. She went to Parisian astrologers, this guy named Jean-Paul Louis, and spent all of her money, and I mean all."

A Parisian astrologer? he thinks. His Grace?

"I slept with her every night in the bed and held onto her and listened to her cry."

He could imagine Stella, feral, lying awake, with the prize in her hands, trembling with joy over having made it into Grace's bed, slipping her hand under Grace's nightdress when Grace was most vulnerable, Grace pushing it away idly. Then, Stella, undeterred, laying back for a few days, then trying again. It took a special diligence to turn a straight girl from men. Stella had had dreams for the two of them. They would live in L.A., Grace would write the scripts, Stella would star in them.

Stella is eager to tell him all manner of things about Grace that he could, of course, not know about her. It is ill-gotten knowledge that darkens his impression of her, but he nonetheless listens.

"She has insomnia and takes sleeping pills. You should see her when she's really stoned on them," Stella says. "Her voice gets slurred and she staggers around. She doesn't always remember either what she's done when she's taken them. Like, she'll get something to eat, and when she wakes up in the morning, she doesn't remember it. Sometimes she'll talk to me, and then she won't remember what she's said. It's freaky.

"She always has pains too, headaches, jaw aches, backaches, and she takes little nips off painkillers all day long. I wouldn't be surprised if she is addicted to them too. And I know while we were in Paris, she was taking antidepressants. I don't think she takes them anymore, but she did while we were in Paris.

"She goes into these stupors sometimes too. Her father locked her in this trunk when she was little, so he could fuck the hairdresser,

Mrs. Henry, and sometimes, I'll find her just staring, like she's in a coma, and I know she's back in that trunk. It's eerie."

There is the sense while they are talking that the reason Grace must resort to these things is a problem that stems more from her being a repressed Gentile than it does from anything else. They've forged their solidarity again—the Jews against the goy. Finding fault in the Gentile, a sport he has occasionally participated in.

After Stella leaves, he feels sickened. The words always have a way of falling off the person defamed, of creeping back to the mouth from which they've dropped. It has done nothing to diminish his feelings either, a futile hope that had led him to do it in the first place.

He's lost again, borne along as if by a rope he is unable or unwilling to let go of.

In the morning he and Mim have their last breakfast together. Indira Gandhi is coming to tour Assam, Mim tells him. "She's blaming the massacres on the students. They are blaming it on her." She puts the paper aside. "You must promise me that you will be very careful, Will. Don't be out on the streets. Stay in your motel room."

He promises her.

Mim walks him out to the car and before he climbs in, she puts her arms around him and he draws her, small and frail, into his arms. "I thank you for everything, Mim," he whispers.

"And I you," she whispers back.

As he is driven through Mim's third tea garden to the hospital, a lane down which he has so often walked, he feels his throat constrict. The vibrancy has been lost, the women in their colorful saris gone now from the gardens, the green vanished from the bushes as they've been pruned back, rows now of grayish brown.

He finds Dr. Chaund in his office, bandaging a young tribal man who has been wounded in a love battle the night before. "It seems his girlfriend was with another man, and he lost his reason," Dr. Chaund says.

Will doesn't know how to say good-bye to Ramu. He cannot shake his hand, nor hug him; the boy lays inert in the bed. He finally kisses his forehead. The boy draws his lips into his mouth, his head seesawing forlornly, as if to say, I'm sad, but it's all right.

Under the Free Zone incentives, big swaths of the Brazilian rain forest were cleared to plant pasture for cattle. A land rights provision that applied to a number of ranches stipulated that fifty percent of the forest on any given fazenda had to be saved.

A scientist named Lovejoy had a brilliant idea: with cooperation from the ranchers, the mandatory insularization could be shaped into an experiment; the destruction of the forest, which was now fated to happen, could be carved up systematically, according to certain patterns: a large remnant here, a smaller remnant there, the rest clear-cut. The lessons would apply not only to the Amazon, but to the world, which was experiencing a similar fragmentation on a far larger scale.

Reserve #1202 was a small patch, ten hectares in all. Immediately following insularization, the reserve lost its large predators—the margay cat, the jaguar, and the puma. Then the deer, the white-lipped peccary, and other small prey vanished. The reserve was too small to provide the necessary food and shelter for these large mammals.

The avifauna population declined, the ant-following birds in particular. They needed a lot of ant colonies to sustain them, and in the small isolated ten-hectare area there simply weren't enough ants. After six months of isolation, the birds had eaten all the ants, and it wasn't long before the birds followed the ants into extinction.

The trees along the perimeters of the reserves, unused to such exposure to sunlight and wind, declined. Their leaves were scorched, and with weak root structures unaccustomed to the elements, they began dying and falling. When one tree went down, it sometimes took another with it. With trees falling, there were now large gaps in the forest. Hot breezes reduced humidity and raised temperatures within the reserve. The leaf litter on the floor of the forest dried, those creatures and plants unaccustomed to heat and light began to decline. After a while, the number of standing dead trees in the center of the ten-hectare reserve increased dramatically.

Little by little, the ecosystem within the ten-hectare broke down, the intricate system of interdependencies destroyed: a domino effect, forcing one species after another into oblivion. A cascade of extinctions.

From Notes on Extinction, *by Will Mendelsohn*

Chapter 16

On the flight to Guwahati, he feels dull, leaden, his intellect and emotion split from one another, a psychic act his mind chooses in moments of bewilderment. He knows it's been accomplished when he tries to retrieve his feeling for Grace and cannot. He isn't even able to conjure her face. What Stella has said about her takes a strange precedence, and all he can see now is the woman who stumbles through the night, drugged on sleeping pills, this woman who lies. He thinks, for some reason, of the times when she has asked him to repeat the names of things he knows, how he has lain on that bed saying, "There are ailanthus and bald cypress, cassia and catalpa, trembling polars and upas, wayfarings and wicopies. Cyclamen, delphiniums, harebells, and kingcups," while she listened with what he could only call rapt attention. Had he been like a boy before his mother?

Once in Guwahati, he cannot get a private car or a taxi because of the trouble and must ride in a crammed bus to the outskirts of Guwahati, to a motel near the Kazaringa. He is the only Westerner, and unshielded by Mim's car, without the remove of an auto rickshaw, it is suddenly disconcerting to feel so many eyes upon him at once, every movement he makes watched. Their eyes are not discreet. They are open looks, probing every inch of him, without the slightest self-consciousness.

To escape their scrutiny, he watches out the window, but the sight of torched villages, their thatch huts collapsed, still smoldering from a night raid is no more quieting. A few bloated corpses float darkly in voluptuous green rice paddies, vultures circling them. When he sees a band of refugees, some of whom are maimed and bandaged, trudging down the road with their bony cows, he feels the fragile thinness that separates people harmed from those in tact.

Perhaps Mim was right. Perhaps he has been too rash. It is not the first time, and his mind offers up to him his most impetuous acts, none of which have ever brought him any fortune. This in itself is unsettling—to imagine that he brought yet another burden down on himself.

He checks into a dingy motel on the outskirts of Guwahati that causes him to fall more deeply away from his feeling. The room is spiritless, without hope. It has a rickety single bed, that seesaws when he sits down on it, a wicker desk and chair that one might find in a K-Mart sale. The walls are painted the color of mustard, spidery lines of musty black mildew creeping up from the baseboards. There are huge dirty smudges on either side of the doorway, as if some hulking and filthy figure has brushed past, time after time. He opens the windows to clear out the musty smell, and a cloud of dust wafts in from the busy road outside.

He misses Mim's orderly rooms, his servant, Aruun. They stand now in his mind as monuments to his loss, that to which he will again have to aspire. He misses Stella too, her easy camaraderie. But for Grace, he still feels nothing.

All day he feels divorced from himself. He hires a car and is driven to the Kazaringa, and then must go on elephant back through the elephant grasses with Colonel Bandopatai, to the site where a rhino lays slain. Its nose is hacked to pieces, where the horn has been cut off, its body already strummed by vultures, riddled with flies. They don't get down from the elephants, but rather sit atop them and gaze upon the death from this distance.

He asks Colonel Bandopatai the requisite questions, and discovers that the rhino has been gunned down with an AK-47, by a poacher, one of the many Bodo tribesmen who are part of the People's Liberation Army of Assam.

"They use the proceeds, my dear man, to fund their revolution," Colonel Bandopatai says. He is a middle-aged man, with a rounded paunch and the wispy forelocks of a man balding.

"How do they get into the preserve?"

"There aren't guards enough, ol' chap. This is India, after all."

"Why aren't the rhinos systematically dehorned? If they have no horns, it only stands to reason that the Bodo tribesmen would lose interest in killing them."

"Yes, Mr. Mendelsohn, it does stand to reason, but such reason is immaterial in India, and what could you possibly know of India?" He says this with an almost tactile disdain. It is through his eyes that Will understands him; they are dark and small and inaccessible. There are no dreams in these eyes. If he at least enjoyed his role—sitting atop an elephant, using his dear mans and ol' chaps, but Will senses instead a man packed deep inside of himself, who has come to find every human encounter an unfortunate necessity.

They return through the elephant grass, in silence, Will rocking back and forth as the elephant lumbers forward. With all that is happening, his visit to the preserve and his concern over the rhinos seems whimsical, indulgent.

When Will gets back to the motel, his mood has darkened. The room in its ugliness, only enhances his gloom. He washes his hands and face in the small bathroom and stretches out on the rickety bed, which feels made of stiffened cardboard, the mattress a bag of sawdust. He feels the encroachment of depression, a tunnel down which he will, if he does nothing to avert it, begin to spiral, where his thought will become more and more narrowed, more and more convinced of doom.

He stirs himself into action, opening his suitcase, taking his papers out, hauling the typewriter out from beneath the desk. He arranges his papers and opens the black case to his typewriter, only to find Grace's letter wedged down into the roller. Stella has put it inside. He pulls it from its pinch between the rollers. *Grace Tagore. 302 West 12th Street, Apt. 18D, New York, New York 10014.* The return address again: *MSMH, Vera Tuber, Marcy, New York.* He thinks of the possibilities: he could read it, he could lay it aside, he could rip it to shreds and flush it down the toilet.

He knows already that he will read it, and reasons now that he is under no moral obligation not to. He has not asked for it, he has not paid for it. In fact, he has done everything in his power to avoid having to read it, but now it is here with him.

He puts off a reading and goes downstairs to the road, a rutted road that leads into Guwahati, where on either side are clustered stalls selling such things as sugarcane juice, coconut milk, fruits, and paan. He buys a cold Limca from one of the vendors and leans an elbow against the blue counter while he drinks it. He watches the endless chug of people pass, on foot, on bicycle, in rickshaws, crowded on the diesel buses. It is as if they are being drawn along, pulled by some invisible hand, to a distant heart.

When he returns to his room, he turns on the lamp at the desk and makes himself comfortable in the wicker chair before he slips the letter from its envelope. His heart beats fast, because he knows already that whatever it is, it cannot be good. He is reading it now, he tells himself, so that he may lay bare this woman he has become so foolishly attached to. But he knows it is not true—that he reads the letter because it is hers, because there is nothing else he has of her. He reads the letter because he is bereft without her.

Dear Grace,
There is something I have never told anyone about what happened to me on June 17, 1944, when I went to Soissons to take

care of Renée. It was just eleven days after the Allies had landed in Normandy.

On June 16, I arranged a car ride to Claude's mother. She was quite sick when I got there. She had ulcers on her feet and legs, and she had no insulin at all. There was no car, so in the morning I had to walk the five miles to town.

I walked a mile, maybe two, and a truck of German soldiers stopped and asked me where I was going. I told them I was going into Soissons to get medicine for my mother-in-law, and they said they'd give me a ride. I didn't want to get in the truck with them, but they insisted. They didn't want to hurt me. They just wanted to be around a pretty girl who spoke German.

They were young, no more than nineteen or twenty, and their morale was very low. I think they knew they were losing the war.

When they found out that I was an opera singer, they asked me to sing something for them. I had not sung in a while, not since they arrested Claude, and I had not sung Wagner since Germany occupied France, because I knew, as everyone did, that Wagner was Hitler's favorite. But they wanted to hear Wagner, so I sang Wagner to them. I sang a bit of "*Dich Theure Halle*," from Wagner's *Tannhauser*.

The truck was stopped by a car of SS officers. We were told to pull off to the side of the road, to wait there until the motorcade passed. A few minutes later, we saw the motorcade come down the road. There was suddenly a lot of excitement. The soldiers thought it was the Führer's motorcade, but no one knew for certain. They quickly lined up on the shoulder of the road, in full salute, and at the very last moment, I was pulled from the truck and placed in their midst. "Sing Wagner," one of them said. Someone else said it too. They were caught up in the moment. So I sang the opening aria to Wagner's *Parsifol.*

When the motorcade passed, it slowed, but it was impossible to see who was inside. Some said they saw the Führer, but I didn't.

A few minutes later, maybe as many as ten, one of the cars from the motorcade returned and pulled up alongside the road next to us. The window on the passenger side rolled down, and an SS of-

ficer said, "*Das Mädchen, das so schön Wagner singt,*" and he
pointed to me.

There was no question that I had to go.

There were two SS officers in the front seat. They were part of
the SS Escort Commandos for the Führer. I never really got a good
look at the one who drove. The other one turned in the seat. He was
thin-faced and hungry-looking, no more than thirty years old. He
said, "If there is time, the Führer might want you to sing for him."

We drove to the German bunker near Margival, north of Soissons. The whole area was swarming with SS officers from the Escort Commando. Hitler was meeting there with his Field Marshals
Rommel and Rundstedt, though I didn't know this at the time. A
meeting had been called at the last minute.

The thin-faced SS officer escorted me inside the bunker, down
a hallway, and into a small room. I barely remember this. I was
afraid and can now only remember the strange look of my white
sandals so near the thick black boots of the SS officers.

The room had a small bed, a desk, a chair, and a bathroom attached. The SS officer told me to make myself comfortable. "It
might take awhile," he said. "There might not be time at all." He
said I should prepare something to sing just in case.

He seemed embarrassed and hesitated at the last moment, as if
he might say something more, but then he left.

I practiced my voice quietly. I don't know how long I paced inside the room, singing to myself. Hours, it seemed, but it was difficult for me to tell. When no one came, I thought maybe I would
be lucky, that I would get out of singing for the Führer.

But then the door opened. I saw the two SS officers, one of
them the thin-faced one, and I thought they were coming to tell
me that I could go. I was relieved, but then he came in, the Führer,
and the door closed. I recognized him instantly, of course, but still
it was strange, and I had the eerie feeling that it could not really
be happening, that it was so unlikely an outcome to my morning,
but there he was. He wore the uniform of the German soldier.

He was so nervous and distraught, that in some odd way I was
eased. I moved out of his way immediately, to the foot of the

bed, and he sat down in the chair at the desk. When he looked at me, I suddenly felt so self-conscious that I looked down at the floor.

"*Du gleichst meiner Nichte schon sehr Geli,*" he said. "*Das ist bemerkenswert, bemerkenswert.*" You look a great deal like my niece, Geli. It is remarkable, remarkable. His voice was oddly soft.

I looked up then, briefly, and I noticed how pale his blue eyes were. I thought how he did not look so powerful. He looked broken-down and old and sick. He looked small, in fact, hunched in the chair. I couldn't imagine how this man could have caused so much trouble. And then suddenly he commanded, "Sing! Bitte! Sing!" almost as if he had read my thoughts.

I sang the opening aria of Wagner's *Tristan and Isolde*, where Isolde stands on the deck of Tristan's ship with Brangäne, gazing wildly out to sea. *Entartet Geschlecht! Un wert der Ahnen* . . . He took some small black pills from a box in his pocket and quickly swallowed them while I sang.

He fixed his eyes on me then, and when I finished the aria, he began to speak. "*In ein paar Wochen ist der Alptruam vorüber,*" he yelled. "*Es wird sich herausstellen, Das Rommel falsch liegt. Es ist nicht hoffnungslos, wie man so sagt.*" Rommel will be made wrong. It is not hopeless as they say.

He stood up and began to pace. He began talking wildly of how Rommel had betrayed him, and how he was surrounded on all sides by cowards. There was something riveting about him, something terrifying and exciting—his wildly gesturing hands, the conviction in his voice. It was true what had been said about him—that he had hypnotic powers.

Then, abruptly, he told me to sing again, and I sang Isolde's last aria. It began so gently with the words, *Mild und leise,* and had a strange effect upon him. For a long time he stood and watched me, his eyes filling with rapture, a kind of ecstasy. Then he said, "*Du bist meine Geli.*" At first he spoke softly, then more insistently. "*Du bist meine Geli.*" You are my Geli. Geli was the only girl he had ever loved. She had killed herself over him many years before.

He took my hands into his. He clutched them. His voice was soft and yet strangely harsh. *"Du bist ein Zeichen göttlichier Vorsehung,"* he said. *"Lügner und Feiglinge umzingeln mich jetzt. Du bist ein weiterer Beweis, dass das Schicksal mich für diese Mission auserwählt hat."* I had been given to him in his darkest hour. I was a sign from Divine Providence; he knew it when he saw me singing alongside of the road.

He sank to the floor and pulled me down to my knees. *"Du bist ein weiterer Beweis, dass das Schicksal mich für diese Mission auserwählt,"* he said. My being there was proof that Fate had selected him for his mission. There was a wildness in his eyes. His hands were hot like irons as they moved up my arms. *"Du bist meine Geli,"* he said. I was his Geli returned. He kissed my neck, my cheeks while I sang. When he pushed me back on the floor and crawled on top of me, I was singing, *Fühlt und seht ihr's nicht? Höre ich nur diese Weise, die so wundervoll und leise.* The whole time I sang. Afterward he stood up. He said nothing, just straightened his clothes, and when I sat up, the door was closing.

Only then was I afraid. I was afraid I would be shot. He would regret his brief loss of control and order that I be shot.

By the time I was taken out by the SS officers, it was nearly dark. I was glad that the thin-faced officer was there. I asked him what they would do, but he wouldn't answer. When I asked again, the driver told me to shut up.

They stopped alongside a deserted road, and I was told to walk into the woods without looking back. I was sure that as I walked away, I would be shot. I fully expected it. I knew they were told to shoot me. I walked and I kept walking, every moment expecting to be shot, and then finally I heard the gun go off, but I was not shot, and I never knew why I was saved. Still I don't know.

Mother

Will lays the letter down on the table, where it flutters lightly in the air of the ceiling fan. He feels a throbbing at his temples. What Grace and Stella and Mim are doing in his life, why this letter has fallen into his hands, he cannot imagine. It seems to have the workings of something darker than chance, something for which he has no explanation. Yet it could not have been more perfectly orchestrated to make a mockery of his life.

He leaves his room, walking out to the road again. Here, on the outskirts of Guwahati, there is no electricity, and the stallkeepers burn hurricane lamps, which hang from hooks inside the stalls, illuminating their candies and cigarettes, their stacks of fruits and pyramids of spices in a light that obscures time.

He buys a sugary glass of tea from a barefoot boy who wanders through the crowd, carrying a metal holder for six, calling out, *"Chai, chai, chai."* The boy stands waiting for Will to drink it like a small brown crane, one dusty foot perched on top of the other, his head inclined upward.

When Will finishes it, he hands the empty glass back to the boy. He feels disquieted. Is it the idea of the letter? The remote chance of its possibility? he wonders. It is so absurd, he is tempted to laugh at Grace's earnestness before such folly.

He moves across the road, steering clear of a bullock cart, an auto rickshaw buzzing past him, the horn like a duck's quack. The words that had once made no sense come back to him: *You can't be with him. Can't I have tea with someone? Am I not a human being first?*

Has Stella held her captive with this idea? He recalls the afternoon they all met when Stella goose-stepped past the end of Grace's chaise, the bereft look that fell into Grace's eyes when Stella saluted her Nazi style and bellowed, "Heil Hitler." Is this her thinking: as the possible offspring of Adolph Hitler, she could never under any circumstances have a life with him, a Jew?

The disquiet only grows in him as he threads himself into the stream of people who walk along the edge of the road. Such a strange creature this would be, he thinks: the daughter of Adolph Hitler. He imagines her in a cage, people coming to gaze in at her. Would all of her foibles, her characteristics be seen in the light of this one fact?

Why has this fallen to him? he asks himself once back in the room. Idle, pat answers float into his thoughts: Retribution for not having embraced the culture of his fathers, a Jew for whom the Holocaust has never meant enough. After all, he was the boy who wrote the poem: *If my mother weren't a Jew/She would have nothing else to do.* But he does not believe in Divine Retribution anymore than he believes in Divine Providence. And even if he did believe in Divine Retribution, why would it be leveled on him? His sins are petty, unremarkable, dull even. Some infidelity, vanity, lust, greed, in more or less small quantities.

Perhaps it is not punishment, but rather a warning to stay away, an admonition not to return in any manner to this woman. Yet he does not believe in divine warnings either, nor in signs.

Perhaps there is simply no meaning to it. Certainly he has not always found meaning for things in his life. Often things happen, their meaning vague to him, then lost entirely in the shuffle of life, before they are even remotely apprehended. Perhaps it is instead random, some fluke of chance, some strange twist of events for which there is no logic, some improbable set of circumstances. Nature is filled with such oddities.

When he takes the books out of the suitcase that Stella has packed, it is late. His hands tremble lightly when he finds an account in Speidel's book *Invasion, 1944,* of the morning Grace's mother has written. As he reads it, his heart drums steadily against his breastbone. It is true: there had been a hastily arranged meeting at Margival in the WWII German bunker on June 17, 1944. The bunker, in fact, had a large working room on the ground level, sleeping quarters with bath, and special air-raid shelters.

Hitler had come in the morning with General Jodl and his entourage. He had flown in from Berchtesgaden to Metz, and then they had all motored from there to the headquarters. The whole area had been heavily guarded and hermetically sealed off by Hitler's SS Escort Commandos.

"He looked pale and sleepless," Speidel wrote, "playing nervously with his glasses and an array of colored pencils that he held between his fingers. He sat hunched upon a stool, while the field marshals stood. His hypnotic powers seemed to have waned."

He openly expressed his displeasure at the success of the Allied landing, for which he blamed the field commanders. Field Marshal Rommel told Hitler quite frankly that the struggle was now hopeless against the Allies—they had superior capabilities in the air, at sea, and on land. Hitler insisted the "V weapon," which the Germans had begun using in the last day, would be decisive against England.

The announced approach of Allied aircraft made it necessary to adjourn the conference to Hitler's air-raid shelter. The quarters were small and could seat only Hitler, Rommel, Rundstadt, their chiefs of staff, and Hitler's chief adjutant, General Schmundt.

It was here that Rommel urged Hitler to end the war. "Don't you worry about the future course of the war," Hitler interrupted to say, "but rather about your own invasion front."

Speidel wrote that the conference was "interrupted only for lunch, a one-dish meal at which Hitler bolted a heaped plated of rice and vegetables, which had previously been tasted for him. Pills and liqueur glasses containing various medicines were ranged around his place, and he took them in turn. Two SS men stood guard behind his chair."

There is no more about this day. It occupies less than six pages in the book. A small, nearly insignificant event in the history of Nazi Germany. There is a brief mention of it in the other book Stella had accidentally placed in his suitcase: *The Rise and Fall of the Third Reich*.

Will tries to imagine that while all this was going on, in some room in the bunker was a girl who could sing Wagner. If it was to be believed, then one would need to assume that at some point Hitler had told his SS officers to go back and retrieve the singing girl along the road. When would he have done so? At the door before walking into the bunker? In the hallway before entering the workroom? While the conference was underway? And how had his desire been conveyed? In an aside to his driver? In a whisper out in the hallway? A small note slipped to an SS officer beneath the table?

And when during the meeting did Hitler decide he wished to hear the woman sing? Before Rommel told him the struggle was hopeless against the Allies? After Hitler had told them all that the "V weapon," which had been put in use since June 16, would be decisive against England? Or still later, after they'd adjourned to the air-raid shelter and Rommel had urged him to end the war?

And what excuse had he used to absent himself from the meeting? A need to use the men's room? A desire for fresh air? Then he and the SS officers had left the meeting room, and instead of going to the bathroom or out for air, they had headed down the hallway to the room where the opera singer waited? Did they exchange a look, a wink, now in collusion, as if they were putting something over on the field marshals? Or had it been more discreet?

Could it possibly be believed that Hitler slipped out of the room to hear a woman sing when he was in the midst of a discussion of the utmost importance to him, one that had the deepest most dire ramifications? Could something so out of the ordinary happen during a time of the most unimaginable strain?

How long was he absent, then? Ten minutes? Fifteen? And wouldn't Speidel have mentioned it? After all, this was a man who wrote the details of Hitler's lunch, complete with a description of the pills and glasses ranged around Hitler's plate.

And all this before one even stopped to consider Hitler's physical condition. He was sick, and so sick he was taking a variety of medicines, one of which, or maybe more, might well have blunted any sexual drive and all ability to perform. Wasn't it unlikely that a man so physically broken down and emotionally on edge would consider a sexual liaison with a stranger in a distant room? Particularly a man who had worked quite hard at distancing himself from women, in general, a man who presented himself to his people as an unworldly man, uninterested in conquest. A man who had gone out of his way never to be found in the company of unmarried women, to whom he might be sexually attracted? Could such a man on the brink of utter and complete ruin be transported to the ecstasy Vera described, even if only for a few moments?

If not, then why would a mother tell her daughter such a lie?

Will tries to imagine Vera, a young woman no more than twenty-two or twenty-three, caught in a war. How disorienting it would be to have lost a husband, to be living in a country not of one's origins, occupied by yet another foreign power. Perhaps she was picked up by German soldiers outside of Soissons, as she claimed. Perhaps Hitler's motorcade had passed. Perhaps the night had fallen, and in the excitement and chaos of the moment, she and a German soldier had a momentary liaison, from which she took secret, guilty pleasure, and for which, consequently, she felt deep shame. Her mother-in-law was waiting. Her husband was most probably dead. Perhaps the facts had jammed in her mind. Perhaps for those hours of her life, there occurred some psychic break that had never occurred before or after, and it had amassed and overwhelmed and created from the various pieces of her experience—Hitler's passing motorcade, her own singing, the lust of the German soldiers—the story she wrote Grace. Perhaps she'd needed to create a stronger context, in which she appeared more blameless for her own indiscretion. Perhaps Grace's father was no one other than a young German soldier, no more than eighteen or nineteen years old.

He imagines Grace receiving this letter, and in a panic, disappearing to Paris. She does not know if it's true, but even if it is not, her mother has sent it to her. She is paralyzed by the thought of it, crippled by her other losses—first her lover, then her husband, then an unborn child. The man she has considered to be her father all her life has told her that he is not. Will can see her falling into Stella's hands, under the spell of a Parisian astrologer. He can imagine her sitting across from this man, asking him who she is, if she has a future or whether she should just go to the grave.

He lays awake half the night. He doesn't really believe it, but he tries the idea out on himself: I have made love to Hitler's daughter. I am in love with Hitler's daughter. He tries out all variations on this theme until it feels like nothing any longer. Perhaps the horror will come to him later. He waits, but none comes. The thought of it does not alter his feeling. It is only the idea that is repugnant, he realizes. It is not her. He is still aroused at the thought of her body, and without warning, memory of her is flung back to him; he suddenly feels a longing for her so potent and urgent, it unnerves him. It is her laugh for which he longs, the feel of her inner thigh against his hand, that mental affinity to which he has become so partial.

He seeks to understand what the letter touches inside of him, but it is vague, diffuse, and cannot be apprehended. The idea that finally brings relief is: we cannot help who we fall in love with.

Chapter 17

*I*n the morning he discovers that he cannot leave Assam even if he wants to. Flights have been suspended again. The phone lines are down as well. Mr. Patel, the owner of the motel, tells him it could be days.

"What happened now?" Will asks.

"The village of Chamaria, sixty miles from here, was destroyed by a Moslem mob. These Moslems must be deported, I tell you."

Not wanting to return to his room, to his own despair, Will sits down in the small lobby. It is a concrete block, windowless, dismal with a couple of plastic white chairs and some colored plastic beads hanging in the doorway.

Mr. Patel, somewhere in his fifties, is paunch-bellied and wears thick-lensed black glasses that are taped at the corners. He leans across the counter, glad for the company.

"But it was in retaliation for the attack by the Assamese on Saturday," Will says.

"They have taken away the rice farms of many Assamese," Mr. Patel says. "They take them over, and these men are ruined, I tell you. Ruined. They have their own country. I say let them go back there and live. They are our enemy. Why would they want to live among us when they are our enemy?"

"Maybe there is no such thing as an enemy," Will says.

"Oh, this is nonsense you talk," Mr. Patel says. Yet it rouses him. He, like many Indians, is fond of discussion, and he gets up and calls his wife to bring them some tea.

"There is such a thing as an enemy," he says. "I have lived in India all my life. I know the enemy. The Moslems are the enemy with their vengeance-seeking God."

"What if it's just an idea that people need to embrace," Will says. "What if it keeps life orderly if this one is the enemy, this one is not. It serves many purposes, the idea of an enemy."

"An enemy is not an idea, my dear man," Mr. Patel says. "An enemy is an enemy; and if you think it is an idea, then you are going to lose your life one day. The enemy will come, and you will have your idea and not your life."

"An enemy, the idea of an enemy, keeps us from having to face the fact that our way is not necessarily the only way. It keeps the path clear and clean. Otherwise, it could all fall into confusion. If this person isn't my enemy, then it means their kind is not my enemy, which means I might have to take in everyone, deny my superiority over them, accept my ordinariness, my lack of remarkability."

"Oh, my God, you're talking like that fool Gandhi," Mr. Patel says. Yet he is delighted. When his wife brings in the tea, he comes out from behind the counter and sits with Will in the plastic chairs.

"You've been in India too long, my man. The sun has touched your brain. There are clear enemies. Say what you will, there are clear enemies. Tell the Jews that Nazi Germany was not their enemy. Tell the Indians from anywhere in India that the British were not their enemies. You are an American. You are soft from America, where nothing much happens."

"I don't say that people do not have or create enemies. All that I am proposing is that they are not inherently enemies. That to make an enemy of a person is to keep them out, to keep them at bay, and when you keep them at bay, you are protecting your identity. Enemies are made so as to maintain an identity. If you're way is right, then you don't have to make way for anything or anyone else. If the Moslems are my enemy, I do not have to accept anything about them. What they say, what they do, how they are, I can reject out of hand. I don't need to let them confront my way at all. I'm only saying it is a convenience, in the service of the ego."

"What is this service to the ego? A person makes himself your enemy when he tries to take from you things that are not his. A man comes from Bangladesh, kicks you off your farm, takes over your rice paddy, and you and your children starve, then this man is your enemy."

"This man is a criminal and should be punished by the law. There are laws that prevent that sort of thing."

"Oh, what world are you living in?"

And it goes on like this for a few hours, until they both tire of it, and Will goes upstairs.

He sets his desk up and works all afternoon, without joy, with only the vaguest interest in allopatric speciation: the phenomenon of a species splitting into two different species while the two sets of individuals are living in two different places.

Mr. Patel has arranged for a woman to bring him lunch and dinner, to wash his clothes. She is a plump, middle-aged Indian woman who moves lightly, yet quickly, through his room, placing the stainless-steel plates of food on the nightstand next to his bed. Accompanying her every movement is a slight jingling sound—like many Indian women, she has tied her keys to the drape of her sari. He takes comfort from her presence.

In the early evening, he walks along the edge of the road, past the stalls, threading his way into the line of pedestrians and bullock carts, more conscious now of his difference. He attempts to decipher who is Bangladeshi, who is Assamese. Their physical characteristics are so similar that finally the only way to identify them is by what they wear. He has been told that Moslems wear beards and dark clothes, while Hindus wear mustaches and white clothes.

Detached from either side's concerns, the trouble between them does not seem so urgent, so consuming. His perspective is different, he supposes. There is no speciation here. A man who has studied specie differentiation knows that human beings, no matter what their color or religion, are not a different species.

He is stopped at a busy intersection by a traffic conductor, a small bulging man dressed entirely in white, who stands on a concrete block in the middle of the intersection, conducting traffic with wearied repetition. Through the dust, he appears a luminescent marionette.

Will looks around him and sees a group of young men standing together near a stall selling newspapers. They watch him with impassive, unbidden stares, and Will wonders whose eyes are seeing him, and what do they see? A foreigner? A Jew? They are Assamese, Hindu. They wear the white korta pajamas, the white leggings, mustaches. There is a heightened tension in the air, as if at any moment, something might snap, and he feels unsafe the way he has felt in jungles when panthers were around.

He turns away from them, and in the next moment a rock hits his right ear. Waves of shock ratchet through him, and an involuntary gasp escapes from him. His hand rises quickly to his ear, and he turns toward them, fearing they have gathered and are going to come after them. Their stillness is a mystery to him, their black eyes like a clerestory through which floods a dark light unknown to him.

Someone calls out, *"Ghar jao. Futo,"* which he does not understand, and he vanishes quickly down a thin lane so narrow no car can pass down it. He looks over his shoulder only once, and sees three of them running after him. Everyone on the street stops and stares as he races down this rutted lane that empties onto the dirt road alongside of the Brahmaputra River. It is deserted except for some goats tied to stakes in grassless yards.

He clambers up the banks of the river, and disappears down the side, which hides him, and tries to catch his breath, his heart booming in the quiet. His ear throbs, and when he touches it, a warm river of blood flows down his fingers to the palm of his hand.

He hears the young men walking toward him. He moves away and stumbles to his feet, scrambles quickly over the hard dirt bank, crouched down, on his way to the river's edge, but he trips on the rotting remains of a dead cow that is half sunken in a small hollow.

His cheek hits against its protruding shoulder, his hand dropping into a slosh of innards. Hundreds of flies swarm up and fly into his nose, his mouth, his ears. The rotting stench is putrid. He forces himself to lay still and strains to see through the thick, moving warp of flies, blinking rapidly against their frenzied assault, breathing through the small hole he makes of his lips. As the men came closer, his hand moves over the cow's body in wild search of a loose bone he can use for a weapon. But the men skirt away from the dead cow, covering their noses with their shirts, and miss seeing him. Following behind them is a young barefoot boy pulling a goat on a rope. He watches the boy walk up the bank some twenty feet away, disappearing to the other side like the mast of a ship on a horizon.

Will scrambles up. It takes only moments for the flies to reclaim their body. He stares down at it, and when the light of the moon reflects its glassy, half-eaten eye, he is certain it stares straight through him. In horror, he backs away and moves quickly to the river's edge, where he bends down and thrusts his hands into the water, swirling them frantically to rinse them of cow guts. He slaps at his pants and his shirt, brushing them with his wetted hands to make sure none of it remains on him, but it doesn't seem enough, and he finally walks into the river and crouches down and does it all over again.

From inside one of the huts he hears the high, nasal whine of India's sitar. When the music passes away, he hears the loud, collective buzz of flies on the dead cow and shudders. India is filled with portents.

He has no other choice now but to walk back to the road and get an auto rickshaw. He draws even more attention with his bloody ear and his wet clothes, but no one tries to interfere.

Once up in his room, Will washes himself and cleans his ear. It is nothing much, a small cut, a swelling no bigger than a marble. Yet, he is shaken and sits on his bed for at least an hour. He is not certain why they hit him. He thinks perhaps that in the general upset, he had been singled out to take their aggression. It is nothing more than this, but even so, it has unnerved him.

The incident only makes him recall Grace that much more. Her loss feels suddenly great, and like a child, he cries himself to sleep.

Chapter 18

*T*he stampede of feet on the concrete staircase of the Motel Guwahati wakes Will. He bolts up in the bed. It is a sound he has only heard in movies, the sound of storm troopers coming in the dead of night. The sound is unmistakable. He knows somehow they are coming for him. It is one of those instant knowledges, completely inexplicable, and immediately he retrieves his shoes from the floor and pulls them on.

He has no time to get his shirt from the bathroom, where he has hung it to dry. The door breaks open, dropping onto the floor like a felled tree, and four Indian Army officers pour inside. They wear khaki uniforms and black storm trooper boots. Immediately, they converge upon him. In the flurry he registers only the flash of their dark-skinned forearms, their sidearms, their raven-black eyes.

"What is going on?" Will asks. His heart drums hard against his breastbone.

"Your passport," the lieutenant yells. He stands in front of Will, a man in his fifties who wears a walrus mustache and a pair of big silver glasses.

The soldiers back off and loosely ring him, their guns slung at their shoulders, while Will sits on the bed, paws through his bag for his passport. Finding it, he hands it to the lieutenant, who barely glances down at it, before snapping it shut.

"Why are you in Guwahati?"

"I am doing research at the Kazaringa," Will answers.

"What research?"

"On the one-horned rhinos," he says.

As if this is evidence of something, the lieutenant nods his head, and the three officers move in and yank Will from the bed and throw his arms behind him. When he resists, they kick his feet out from under him, and while three of them pin him facedown, the other two handcuff his wrists behind his back. What is before his eyes are their black storm trooper boots. It comes to him in a little plume of thought that weaves itself in between the gusts of panic. First the letter about Adolf Hitler, and now Nazis break down his door?

"Is this some kind of a joke?" he says. But the hard blow from the butt of a gun falling against the small of his back is no joke.

They drag him out of the room and down the ill-lit hallway. When they pull him past the beaded doorway to the lobby, Will glimpses Mr. Patel, who recedes behind another beaded doorway, into the blackness of his rooms.

He is pulled through the dust of the street; his heart has begun a rapid tattooing, unlike any he's ever known. It isn't even faintly morning.

"What am I accused of? I demand to know," he says.

He is again silenced when the butt of the gun hits against his right shoulder blade, a blow so hard, he feels the contagion of nerves from his neck down to his fingers. They throw him into the back seat of an army jeep and two of the men press in on either side of him. The lieutenant sits in the front, and the driver lurches away from the curb, honking the horn four times to warn a cow that has wandered into the middle of the street. It freezes for a minute in the lights, and then with a tired imperiousness, moves to the side.

Will leans forward, addresses the lieutenant. "I am a scientist. I have come to India to research the wildlife preserves. Look in my satchel. You will find nothing but scientific papers." Sweat spills from his hairline, from underneath his arms.

No one answers him, and the jeep turns off onto another dirt road, more rutted than the last. The two blows he has sustained have injured him, and he now trusts that they are going to treat him badly from this point on. Every moment now is one passed in fear.

They stop and pull him from the jeep and drag him through the night toward a building, skirted with bamboo. He is surprised that it is a prison. Inside, a narrow swatch of concrete stretches out between two rows of cells, ten on each side. The smell of urine and feces is overpowering. The hum of many flies pervades the air. He can barely make out the men; they are thin, stick figures, as many as fifteen in a cell, asleep on the concrete floor without mats, without any kind of blanket or pillow. Only one is awake. He sits on his haunches, one of his hands grasping the bar at its lowest rung. Flies cover his face, and he sits motionless.

They pull Will into a dark room and push him into a chair. No one says anything to him, although they speak to one another in Hindi. He hears a few of them moving about in the darkness, the scrape of chair legs against concrete. Then suddenly, the scratch of a match against a flint and an eruption of light. It is startling and illuminates the profile of the lieutenant, ekes out a corner of the room where a cheap painting of Lord Vishnu hangs framed in brown plastic.

A hurricane lamp is lighted and set down on the table; he blinks in its suddenness. It is set nearest him so that he is illuminated while they are not. There is something about this yellow, meager light, that seems to give license to the night, to those who operate in its depths.

One of the men sits across from him, but Will cannot make out which one. Another sits farther back, just a dim shadow, nothing more. Two of them stand on either side of him, holding wooden sticks. From the periphery of his vision, he can see a dark arm, a bit of pant leg, a wooden stick in hand. The light is very exclusive.

Then it begins.

"Who do you work for?" a voice says. It is the lieutenant.

"I don't work for anyone. I am writing a book about extinction."

"Where is Aban Bezbaruah?"

"Aban Bezbaruah?"

"Yes, Aban Bezbaruah. Where is he?"

"I don't know him. I have never so much as seen him."

"You have heard of him?"

"I have read about him," Will admits.

"And who is he?"

"I have only read about him. I have no association to him whatsoever."

"Who is he? Answer."

"I don't know him."

The first blow descends. It comes from the right, a wooden stick against his chest. Then another blow from the left, against his left shoulder. His legs and arms turn to water, his vision blurs, and for a moment he fears he will topple from the chair.

A hush falls over the room. This is how it is done, he thinks: use a meager light, recede into the shadows, place the henchmen on either side of the interrogated, ask the same question over and over, relentlessly, ask the question as a command. When the answer is not sufficient, the henchmen move in, deliver the blows. It is methodical, precise, perhaps even boring in its execution.

"Who is Aban Bezbaruah? Answer," the lieutenant yells.

"He is the leader of the People's Liberation Army, but I have only read about him. I know nothing about him."

"I ask again, where is Aban Bezbaruah?"

"I know absolutely nothing about his whereabouts," Will says. "I know nothing about him. I have never once met him. I am in Guwahati to visit the Kazaringa. Ask Colonel Bandopatai."

The blows come again, this time harder. Three hits, one to his ribs, one against his shin, another against his right shoulder. He has no defense—they have not taken the handcuffs from his wrists. There is a sharp, flickering pain, which comes from beneath the scapula and shoots up the back of his neck now and down his right arm. The pain in his rib comes quicker, is sharper, more insistent. The one in his shin is dull, but constant.

"Who do you work for?" the lieutenant yells.

"I work for no one," Will answers. "I am a writer, writing about extinction. I have gone to the preserves around India. Look at my papers. I know nothing about the People's Liberation Army," he yells. "Who has said that I do?" His mind seeks a logic, the beating tied to a reason, but he can barely think beyond the pain. He is only able to consider that it has something to do with Stella, with Bhupen, before the next question comes.

"Where is Aban Bezbaruah?" the lieutenant yells. "Answer."

"I have never seen this man."

The blows come slowly, one after another. Two from each man at his side—one to his abdomen, another to his left lower rib, then his right temple, his left jaw. From his throat comes a dry scream, the first in a series. It is a sound he has never quite heard, a sound he does not wish to make, but he cannot help himself. It is the body itself, knowing that it is in peril that screams out its fear. For the first time he considers that his heart will give out, that it won't be the blows that will kill him. It hammers in his chest, striking against his breastbone, like an anvil. What he's felt before, what he's called terror, when he has said, "I was terrified," does not compare to this.

Pain throbs and shoots from so many sights on his body now that he can no longer keep track of all of them.

"Please," he says. "I don't know anything about the People's Liberation Army or about Aban Bezbaruah. This is the truth." His voice is soft, pleading.

As if he has not spoken, the lieutenant says, "Where is Aban Bezbaruah? Where is he?"

Will looks up and tries to find his eyes, but he cannot see him. He is a dark fog, the man behind him utterly invisible.

"Who has told you this?" Will asks the darkness. "If you tell me who has told you this, I could clear it up." The story of Bhupen and Stella tangles in his mind. He hears himself thinking, "I met this woman and she paid them ten dollars to see their machete . . ."

"Where is he?" the lieutenant yells. "You must tell us."

Will considers making up a place, any place. Nellie, the Nowgong district, he thinks to say, but he cannot bring himself to utter the name of a place. To speak the words might implicate him further.

"Answer," the lieutenant demands.

"I know nothing about Aban Bezbaruah," Will yells. "I have nothing to do with the People's Liberation Army. You know this. What is this charade? What is it?"

The two men by Will's side yank him up by his armpits and heave him against the concrete wall somewhere in the darkness behind the chair. He cannot breach the fall, his hands are handcuffed behind him. It is the left side of his face that glances off the wall, that takes the force of the impact. His left eye is now damaged and blood rushes down his face. He drops to his knees and writhes back and forth, howling.

"The place?" the lieutenant yells again.

Will opens his eyes and stares into the hurricane lamp that sits on the table, through the meshwork of white netting, into the brightness of the flame. He thinks again of naming a place, Chamaria, Nellie, Dibrugarh. This can be stopped, he thinks. If only I name a place, but some part of him lies beyond their clubs, beyond the pain they inflict, and refuses to give a name.

"You must give the place," the man in the shadows says. Will looks into the blackness, searching for the man's face. He is surprised when the man gets up from his chair deep in the shadows and comes to the table and leans in far enough that the light illuminates his face. It is a pock-marked face, one touched by suffering.

"I don't know a place," Will says.

"It doesn't matter," he says. "Just a place. Any place."

"There is no place," Will says.

The blows come again, but the men have lost their enthusiasm. Their hits are not hard. They have begun to doubt themselves. He can see it in their tentative, shifting footsteps that they realize that they are beating the wrong man. Finally, they back away, and Will rests on the floor, on his side. He can't understand what they say, they speak in Hindi, but he feels the collapse of purpose. The rousing command, the sense of duty has suddenly disintegrated. The men are no longer one unit. They have dissolved into factions. One of the henchmen, in disgust, sits down in a chair and lights a cigarette. The other one walks away. Their enthusiasm has waned like a man's toward a whore he's spent himself on.

The men come to stand around him. They speak about him, stare down at him. He sees their black boots, and he thinks of something his mother has said to him when he was a child. "Jews are not children for whom monsters are imaginary. No, they know monsters can and do come in the middle of the night and tear you from your bed, your home, your family." So, finally, they've come, he thinks.

But when they bend nearer to him, they seem less like Nazis, more like children now, who have made a mistake and are not certain what to do. He is a fallen thing, a Goliath gone down.

He wants to remember this moment, where these men have faltered, where doubt has overcome their brutishness and their humanity has seeped out like small pinpricks of light through mortared brick. They have paused over his fallen body, unsure of what to do with him. What he is now is their mistake. He is not their Jew.

One of them bends down and takes his pulse. He says something to the others, and then they try to get him to his feet. In the pain of moving his broken bones, he loses consciousness.

At the start of the sixteenth century there were three distinct groups of giant tortoises—highly improbable creatures, weighing 250 pounds and living upward to a century. One group lived on the Galápagos Islands, another on the Mascarene Islands in the Indian Ocean, which include Mauritius, Rodrigues, and Réunion. The third group lived on the remote island of Aldabra, off the coast of Africa. Piled up, they basked in the sun, their scutes polished smooth, their breathing slow and measured.

Then, the Portuguese, Dutch, and French sailors arrived. They touched down at Mauritius as early as the 1500s. The Portuguese and Dutch, though forced at times to eat the tortoises, did not much like the taste of them. However, the French did and they butchered hundreds of them.

Then came the navy and whaling ships that carted the tortoises away by the thousands. They were perfect for export: with their behemoth endurance, the tortoises could stay alive in the holds of ships for months without food or water. They simply hauled them on board, turned them upside down to prevent them from wandering away, and stacked them up.

By 1780 the tortoises were extremely rare. One generation later, the tortoise populations on Rodrigues, Réunion, and Mauritius vanished. They survived only on Aldabra and the Galápagos.

In 1778 a colony was established on Aldabra—its main export, tortoises. They shipped the tortoises out by the hundreds, mainly to Mauritius where they'd long since eaten their own supply. This is not to mention the destruction caused by cats and rats that came ashore and ate the tortoise eggs.

In 1870 Aldabra was leased for wood cutting. The severe loss of habitat combined with the systematic harvesting pressed the tortoises close to extinction. When, in 1878, a party of sailors spent three days looking for tortoises, it seemed it was the end: they found only one.

There was some alarm about it and a few protection measures were instituted. But no one had much hope, particularly after a naturalist vis-

ited the island during World War I and declared that a person could live for years on the island and never encounter a tortoise.

Against all expectation, these patient, enduring creatures made a slow, stately comeback. Today, 150,000 giant tortoises live on the island of Aldabra. What saved them was, in part, the protective measures taken, but largely what insured their survival was the remoteness of the island, its inhospitable heat, and its relative inaccessibility to human beings.

From Notes on Extinction, *by Will Mendelsohn*

Chapter 19

A loud ringing in which he has drifted for untold hours finally wakes him. It takes him a few moments to realize that the buzzing originates from inside his own ears. Then it all comes back, in one solid, harrowing piece. Instinctively, he reaches with his right hand to touch his ear, but a deep pain shoots from his shoulder and prevents him. He cannot move his other arm without the same effect. They are not aligned in their usual way, pulled now from their sockets. His wrists cannot be moved without pain either. It is with relief that he discovers his fingers are still his own.

There is a solid blanket of pain encasing his rib cage, which lays under a mound of swollen, bruised flesh. He is certain many of his ribs are broken, but it is difficult to say how many and which ones. To move his upper torso at all causes pain that is unbearable. He must not move. Even the pressure of lying on his back hurts him. His right jaw throbs, and he senses it is swollen also. His left shin is broken and has swelled beneath his pant leg like a goiter.

He screams, calls out for anyone. He waits, listening for footsteps, for voices. There are no sounds. In the silence the ringing in his ears returns to him. There are two sounds, one high-pitched and constant, the other like a muffled jackhammer. In some ways it is worse than the pain, maddening in another way. Between the two, he can no longer think. He has become these things—pain and ringing in his ears.

He is in a small, concrete room, the floor gray, the walls white-washed though rotting with mildew. It is a windowless room, no more than ten by twelve. A thatched roof pitches above him, which diffuses the light and keeps the room from being in total darkness, from being airless. Has he been put into solitary confinement?

He cries out again, a burst of words, a few screams, which deteriorate to howls. He has no idea how long this goes on before he hears someone at the door. Not the sound of a key, but rather the sound of the door being unbolted. Then the door opens, and a boy no more than nine years old slips inside. He pulls the door closed, but not entirely. He stands in the corner, warily regarding Will, one foot atop the other. The bruised swellings on Will's body frighten him. Big rounded lumps of flesh—one goitered at Will's shin, hilly blue swellings on his chest, the right side of his face, raised as if a tumor grows beneath. Why they have sent a boy to do this job, to confront a man in pain and disfigurement, he cannot understand.

"Do you have a doctor?" Will says. "I have broken bones."

But it is pointless, the boy understands nothing.

He is a thin boy with a thick head of shiny black hair that has been cut haphazardly, as if shorn quickly with a razor blade to keep it from falling into his eyes. Judging that Will is immobilized, the boy stalks closer, stopping in the middle of the room to test his theory. He is barefoot and wears a plaid *lungi*, a skirt Moslems typically wear, and a filthy T-shirt, which even in the dimness Will can see is riddled with small holes. He is perhaps one of those homeless children, who has attached himself to the prison, doing odd jobs for food. The children of India are kept from nothing.

When Will tries to shift himself to see the boy better, sharp, deep pains shoot through him issuing from as many as ten separate places. He moans, a sound that a wounded beast would make, a horrible sound from the hell of his soul that he is incapable of squelching. It frightens the boy, and he moves away to the corner, where he squats on his haunches near the door, ready at any moment to run.

Will tries again. "I need a doctor. A medic. Medic," he says. He does not know the word for doctor in any languages the boy might speak. The boy shakes his head.

"Police?" Will says.

The boy stares from wide black eyes, fringed with long dark lashes.

Will makes the gesture of cupping his hand and moving it from his mouth to his stomach, the movement all beggars make in India. He cannot make the gesture fully, because the movement of his arm is so limited, but the boy understands and slips out the door, bolting it shut behind him. He returns awhile later with a stainless-steel plate with some chapati bread and a brownish soup, dal. He sets it on the floor next to Will, then quickly moves away, across the room to his place at the door. Will tries to reach for the plate, but the pain is too great, his movement too restricted. He points to the boy, then moves his mouth as if chewing, and after a few times the boy understands that Will must be fed.

He comes slowly and sits on his haunches, looking at Will with large almond-shaped eyes, tentatively feeding him bits of chapati bread soaked in dal soup, afraid each time he puts his hand to Will's mouth that he will be bitten, but after a few tries, he loses his fear and waits patiently for Will to chew one bite while he readies another.

The boy leaves afterward, bolting the door behind him, and Will drifts in and out of consciousness. Sometimes the pain is so much that he writhes back and forth; he weeps, unable even to weep into his hands. The ringing in his ears does not subside and consumes his thoughts, until he learns to scrape his fingernail against the concrete to distract himself.

At moments he lays on the edge of madness.

When the boy comes again with food, he rests easier on his haunches, waiting patiently while Will chews his food, swatting the flies away from Will's face. When once the boy reaches out to catch a dribble that runs down the side of Will's face, it becomes obvious that the boy must take care of the man.

It goes on like this for days. Will drifting in and out of sleep, awakened by pain, then exhausted by it. He discovers if he keeps himself still, the pain will slacken. It doesn't disappear, but if he doesn't move, it is more tolerable. It is when he writhes because of it that it is made worse. So he practices lying still, scraping his fingernail against the concrete, listening to this sound, to distract his mind from the ringing.

Sometimes when he cries out, the boy comes. Sometimes he does not. There seems to be no rhythm to the boy's comings and goings. Perhaps the boy has rounds to make of prisoners.

So the boy comes and goes, feeding him with his fingers, bits of chapati and a soup of dal. Will wonders who regulates his coming and going, who gives him the chapati and the dal, who sends him in. When he hears the door being unbolted, he watches to see what lies outside, but the boy is quick and slips in through the smallest opening. There is sunlight outside the door, which leads him to believe that the structure opens directly to the outside. It is removed then from the prison, he thinks. So he is in solitary confinement.

He finds it strange that none of the prison guards have looked in on him. At least opened the door and gazed upon their handiwork, come in to kick him for all of his noise, but not one of them comes. Only the boy, according to a schedule Will cannot comprehend.

When the urge to relieve himself comes after days of eating, Will doesn't know what to do. Is he just supposed to shit his pants now? Shit them and have the boy clean him up? It is with horror that he realizes he has pissed himself time and time again. He feels a great outpost of stiffness at the crotch of his pants, which surrounds a smaller circle of wetness. He must be pissing himself in his sleep. His right leg and foot can be used without too much pain, and he is able to move himself by pushing his prone body headfirst. It is only the straw mat beneath him that makes it possible to push himself to the corner. He slides the mat from beneath him with his good foot. His hands work well enough and he is able to push his pants over his hips, then later to retrieve them. It takes great effort to return to the mat, to navigate himself back to his spot.

It exhausts him and he sleeps all morning. When the boy comes, he gestures with his head to the pile he's left in the corner. The boy stalks over to it and stares down at it, plugging his nose. Will conveys the idea that it must be taken away, and the boy leaves, bolting the door behind him, and returns with two large green leaves from a papaya tree. He uses one to push the pile from the floor, another to hold it, and in the end, he presses it between the leaves and carries it out, his arms held straight out in front of him, to keep it as far from him as possible. It is a comical sight, and Will, even in his humiliation, must smile.

The boy comes more and more often, sometimes without any reason, sometimes just to sit next to Will, to swat the flies away. They have small conversations wherein they speak their separate languages, incomprehensible to the other. When the pain is especially bad, the boy will stroke Will's forehead with the tips of his small fingers. Simple as it is, it manages to calm him.

He tries, at certain moments, to teach the boy English, making a game of it, pointing to his own nose saying, "Nose," holding up his hand, saying, "Hand," but the boy won't have it. He shrugs it off, as he would shrug off a hairshirt.

They communicate with gestures, a nodding of head, a shaking of head, a smile, a frown, gestures of the hands. Strange sounds that needed no language: Tsks and shhs, hmmms and ahhs.

The boy likes to touch Will's wounds, to prowl his body when he falls into half states of sleep. He likes to feel the humps of swelling, to run his fingers along the crusty lines of the scabbed cuts on his chest and his face, to press sometimes in the tender blueness of bruises, to watch Will wince. Sometimes Will will say, "Husk, husk," when he wants him to stop, and the harshness of the sound makes the boy understand.

Though he is only a boy, he knows this is irregular, that something has happened. He will sometimes run his small brown fingers over Will's flesh for an hour, as if trying to extract the story of how they got there. But the story is not in them. The wounds are ghosts, phantoms, nothing really. Evil is as mysterious as love, coming quickly and doing its deed, leaving behind traces that only hint.

He wonders what he is to the boy, if the boy thinks about him when he is not with him. He brings food twice a day, taking away the waste in the corner, wiping Will's body sometimes with a wet cloth he tucks into the waist of his lungi. When the swellings have begun to go down, he motions to Will the progress, pinching his fingers together, as if to suggest that the swelling is being pinched away.

It is when the boy leaves that it is most difficult. The isolation, the deprivation of sound, of sight. It is hard to maintain himself in such conditions. He tries to busy himself. Every day he attempts to sit. He tries to move his arms, but the pain is still too great. The only thing he can do is bend his toes on his left foot, lift his legs slightly. He tries to take deeper and deeper breaths, but this is least possible. Mostly, he must lie very still. He worries about how he will heal. What if his arms, having been ripped from their sockets, have incurred nerve damage? The bone broken at his shin is healing improperly—it bows out and will leave him with a limp. The thought of himself limping through the rest of his days, his arms hanging lifelessly by his sides, fills him with despair.

It is not true what they say—they may beat your body, but they can't break your soul. It is a lie. They have broken his soul. Wherever it resides, they have found it and broken it. They are not so separate. It is not true either, that love conquers all. These are things people wish to be true, but they are not true. Violence conquers. Evil has the heaviest hand. Let him never deny this again.

Sometimes the boy has to rouse him from his stupor. He will do little dances, hopping on one foot then the other. It is the animation that catches Will's eye. He will clap his hands, sing some childhood song, anything to bring Will back.

He loses track of the days. He is not sure how long he sleeps when he sleeps. Once the boy brings him a cigarette in the middle of the night and holds it to his lips while he smokes. The boy rests against him, sucking his thumb. Will begins to wonder if, like him, he is the only thing the boy has in the world.

In moments of lucidity he can make sense of what has happened to him, if only in the simple terms of cause and effect: he hadn't loved his wife properly, as a consequence her resentment caused her to burn his work, which in her guilt caused her to leave, which ultimately led him to reconceive his book, flushing him out into the world and so on. He searches for some deeper pattern, but he can find nothing.

He imagines his mother would tell him it was his ancestors, reminding him of his origins; his denial has been so drastic they've had to resort to extreme measures to bring him back. She might reason the entire thing away with this simple idea.

Will his be a story of triumph or tragedy? he wonders. He cannot believe he will ever find his way out. He must either be moving toward life or death, yet he feels no movement, as if he has been set down in the middle of the sea, without even the slightest hint of a breeze.

At moments he can hear Grace's laugh, can see her smile, her full lips parting, baring her small white teeth. But he has so lost track of any sense of his sex that, oddly, the memories of making love, which before the beating he had relished above all else, leave him. The thought of her thigh could quicken his heart. The idea of her sex would arouse him. Now it raises nothing in him. He is not even certain if his sex works, but if it is a worry, it is a distant one. There are so many broken parts, if it is broken, it will have to wait its turn.

This is his life: broken bones, a broken heart, everything broken, and this boy. It fills him with despair; it is so pitifully small. That he is alive is no testament to the triumph of the human spirit. It is instead the triumph of the human body, the body merely a dumb mechanical thing which hasn't the sense to know that it is a coffin, housing a dead spirit. It is the heart that goes on, which keeps beating.

He has other moments, strange, lucid moments which he clings to. Where truths reveal themselves in flashes, nothing more than that, like light will flash on a choppy sea. He is borne up to a state of mind for which he has no name, a state of mind where he feels joy, wonder at the light that comes through the thatched roof, wonder over this boy with the lopsided grin who brings him food. Yet, the state of mind doesn't last. It deserts him. It slips away like a breeze that has come and stirred the papers.

The boy is sometimes mischievous, hiding Will's food behind his back. He stands with one hand upturned, as if he has nothing, and then bends over to laugh, bringing the food forward. Sometimes he holds the food to Will's mouth, then at the last moment he snatches it away. It makes him laugh, a syrupy, high giggle that Will grows fond of. Sometimes Will closes his mouth against the food, and the boy hovers with it, anticipating when Will's jaw will open, trying to snatch it away before Will's lips close over it.

One day, when Will tries to raise his left arm, it lifts without pain. He first discovers a way to sit up—if he leans heavily on his arm, he can ease himself up to a seated position. The boy is shocked to find him sitting against the wall. As if this has made Will more human, the boy is delighted, and the things he carries in his pocket, he empties into Will's lap. Strange little things that excite him: a wooden top that he spins on the floor, a coil of black licorice that he licks with his tongue but will not eat, a small red dump truck, no longer than three inches. Will is as delighted to hold them as the boy is. While he turns them over in his hands, the boy squats nearby and sucks his thumb.

When he leaves, Will discovers he can scoot around the room, navigating with his good left arm and his good right leg. In the evening he maneuvers himself to the door and positions himself in such a way that when the boy opens it, he thrusts his foot against it, throwing it open. The boy freezes for a moment, frightened, and Will sees that he is in someone's backyard. When he tries to maneuver himself outside, the boy waves his arms, calling out words Will doesn't understand. He keeps looking over his shoulder, fearful, but of what Will doesn't know. He repeats the words, over and over, and looks so terrified that Will is actually cowed back inside. The idea that he is not safe, that the boy is hiding him, causes him to retreat. Once he's back inside, the boy closes the door and bolts it.

In that brief moment he has seen some goats tied to stakes, the back of a woman wearing the black veiled garb of Moslem women, who walks on a road. Between him and the shack is a long green expanse of garden. He has a revelation: The army officers took him somewhere and dropped him off, leaving him for dead. The boy must have found him.

He puzzles over this as he waits for the boy to return. When the boy doesn't come, he is unsure why. He does not come the next day either, and Will goes hungry. He thinks of nothing but his hunger and listens all day for the sound of the boy's padded footfalls, for the unbolting of the door, but there is nothing other than the sound of the goats, some music that first night.

The boy does not come for two days, and when he finally slips inside, it is in the pose of a wounded lover, his head hung, his eyes cast down. He hands Will the food and crouches down on his haunches, watches Will bolt it down. When Will looks up, there are tears in the boy's eyes.

"What's the matter?" Will says, touching the boy's tears.

The boy places his fingers on Will's mouth, to show he is sorry he's left Will to starve.

The piles of shit have grown and the place stinks, which only adds to the boy's sorrow. He goes out and comes back with the leaves and dutifully takes them out. Afterward, he sits down next to Will and rests his head on Will's good shoulder.

In the stillness of these moments, it comes to him: there are no captors, no guards. There is nothing. He is the boy's pet.

When the boy comes the next day, Will uses his small body to raise himself to his feet. His forearm must rest on the boy's shoulder. The boy must sling his arm around Will's hips, and in this way, they move through the room, Will sliding on his good leg. They learn a rhythm, a dance: the boy takes a step, Will leverages his weight and slides. A step, a slide, over and over again. Afterward Will sleeps for eight hours and wakes in the night to find the boy nestled under the crook of his good arm, the door open slightly.

For a week the boy helps Will to walk, going over and over the same sliding hop, the same choreographed steps that allow Will to move forward. Will is surprised the boy has such patience, and afterward when he lies down on the mat to recover, he lets the boy run the little red dump truck through his beard, over his lips, up the bridge of his nose and across his forehead. It amuses him, though Will is not certain why, and elicits from him the syrupy, high squeals of laughter that are reward enough.

He sleeps with Will every night, beneath the crook of his good arm, the door always left slightly ajar. A few times Will sits in the doorway while the boy sleeps and looks out across the expanse of garden, at the great Indian sky. He never sees the Moslem woman again.

He has no idea where he is nor what he will encounter once he leaves. He has no way of knowing how long he was unconscious, nor where his body was taken. Perhaps he is in Bangladesh.

Will his story be a cautionary tale? An admonition against passion? Or will it be a tale of redemption? A story of a heartless man gaining heart? Perhaps, he thinks. Will it spur him to do great things? A plan rises in his mind, then collapses. No, sadly, it will not be this.

And what of love? What would it take to be held in place by love?

he wonders. If it flowed through you and overtook your lesser feelings? He sensed it possible, but it was no more natural, he supposed, than fashioning an athlete's body. It must need constant attention, long vigilant hours. A monk's life? No, there would be nothing like this.

Simply not to flicker out seems the greatest struggle.

When he gestures for a stick the next morning, the boy brings him one, and then is patient, lending his body, until Will figures out the secret of using the stick to walk without the boy's help. It is a slow, torturous process, and sometimes the boy laughs helplessly to witness Will's contortions, his stumbling.

He makes a game of it so that the boy won't lose interest. Will is not certain how it develops, but somehow out of the play, the rules emerge. He hobbles after the boy, and when he catches him, he taps him on the shoulder with the stick, and then they reverse roles, the boy hobbles after Will on one leg, with his own stick.

When Will rises up one night and pushes the door open, the boy panics. He runs ahead of him and tries to dissuade him, waving his arms, saying something that Will doesn't understand. Will shakes his head and throws his arm out, to signal that it is over. And the boy, knowing there is nothing he can do, stands helpless. When Will puts his arm around him, the boy sobs against his hip.

The boy walks behind him, through the garden to a thin, rutted road. If he follows him, Will decides, he will not prevent him. But when they get to the road, the boy stops. Will even holds out his hand and says, "Come with me," but the boy shakes his head. He touches the boy's arm and says it again, but the boy only shakes his head more vehemently.

So Will turns and hobbles away. He can't get anyone to go anywhere with him, he thinks.

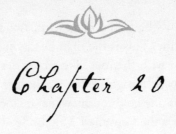

Chapter 20

The sky is flung like a magician's cape above him, studded with stars. It is dark except for the light from the heavens, which reflects in the still pools of water in the rice paddies that stretch out on either side of the road.

He is momentarily excited by the adventure of it, walking a road not knowing where he is, not knowing what country he walks in, yet the pain he feels with every step chips away at his enthusiasm, until it ceases to exist. Then worries set in: What if there is nothing and no one around for miles? What if he cannot find food, water?

But within ten minutes of walking, a few auto rickshaws buzz by, a couple of bicycles. He thinks to hail one, but he is penniless. He wonders what he must look like in the stark-white light that passes over him quickly. A beggar, in rags, his hair and beard unkempt, a man walking shoeless with a stick.

Then shacks appear along this road; the light from hurricane lamps burns inside. He sees barefoot children in doorways. His hope is raised: wherever these shack settlements are found, there is generally a town nearby. He hobbles in the direction the auto rickshaws drive.

From a mile out, he can see a road ahead, heavily trafficked. The lights are steady, a strand of moving pearls. When he arrives, the first

thing he recognizes is the traffic conductor, standing on a concrete
block, dressed in white. This is the man he saw just moments before
he was hit in the ear with the rock. He recognizes the stall where he
has bought newspapers, recognizes the stallkeeper, a man who wears
a red turban and has one gold tooth. When he looks up the road, he
sees the neon sign for the Guwahati Motel. He's been no more than
a mile or two away.

The people on the streets stare at him. Their looks are still open,
curious, but are now seeded with fear. They edge away from him,
wanting nothing to do with him. All the better, he thinks, and hobbles the three blocks to the Guwahati Motel. When he pushes back
the beads to the lobby, he finds Mr. Patel behind the counter. Immediately Mr. Patel waves his hands, saying, "No vacancy. No vacancy."

Will collapses in one of the white plastic chairs. "It's me, Mr.
Patel," he says. "Will Mendelsohn."

Mr. Patel rounds the counter, stalking nearer to him. "Oh, my
God, so it is you. We thought you were lost to us." He doesn't come
too close, stopping midway. The stench has a large radius.

Lost to us, Will thinks. He can't help but remember the look of
Mr. Patel receding into the blackness when the police took him away.

Mrs. Patel is summoned, and Will is helped into a small, dark
room where he stretches out on a thin cot, and she asks him questions, gingerly checks his body. He is sorry he stinks and mutters an
apology, but she pays no attention. Women are always left with
blood, with the wounded, with the dying, he thinks, while men pace
outside rooms, bewildered.

Mrs. Patel opens the door and tells her husband, "He must go to
hospital immediately."

Will asks for a bath first, and they take him, one at each elbow, to
the bathroom and show him how to work the shower. He is given
everything he could possibly need: soap, razor, shaving cream, even
Paco Rabanne aftershave, which is so popular with Indian men, but
which he forgoes.

He sits on the floor crookedly—with the lingering pain in his ribs, he must take the weight on his good arm—and washes his body with one hand.

Mr. Patel has not saved his suitcase, his papers, and so he must put on a pair of white leggings and a white korta top. While he awkwardly dresses in the small room with the cot, Mr. Patel hovers outside, filling him in on all that has happened in his absence. "There has been more trouble. They say the official death count has reached over three thousand. There are over a hundred thousand refugees now. Aban Bezbaruah has been arrested. Just yesterday there were more massacres. My God, it's been a bloodbath."

On the way to the hospital, Mr. Patel's eyes find his in the rearview mirror. "They came barging in late that night, and they showed me traveler's checks with your name and the name of Aban Bezbaruah. They said you were funding the revolution. They insisted that you were an American with interests in their cause."

So it was the traveler's checks, Will thinks. He does his best to explain how the traveler's checks ended up with Aban Bezbaruah's name on them, but admittedly it is a tangled story. "I had a friend who got mixed up with a young man named Bhupen, and one night I gave her five hundred dollars in traveler's checks to get her out of trouble. I had no idea his name would be crossed out and Aban Bezbaruah's name written on them."

"Oh, my God, what a terrible mix-up," Mr. Patel says. "Oh, my God. I had no idea. What was I to think? It was such a time of mayhem, I had no idea in this world, man."

Mrs. Patel starts to cry and dabs at her eyes with the end of the drape of her sari.

They don't ask him what happened.

At the hospital X rays are taken of his chest, of his legs, his arms. The gurney table is wooden, the X-ray machine large and cumbersome, twenty years outmoded. It has to be hauled over the top of him, sometimes the wooden gurney maneuvered when it gets stuck.

Will sees a wooden cart in the corner, lined with newspaper, silver medical instruments laid out on top of it.

Two nurses, wearing white saris and small-winged white hats perched in their black hair, appear phantomlike above him. Their accents so crisp, so precise, are lovely to his ears. "Mr. Mendelsohn, I must put this plate beneath your leg." He follows the gentle movement of their slender brown hands as they place cold metal plates beneath his back, his legs, his shoulders. When they discover he has been beaten and left to heal without the slightest medical attention, pity floats in their soft brown eyes.

They roll him down the hallway in a wooden wheelchair to a ward crowded with old men, and give him a painkiller, a white pill they call Dilaudin, and in twenty minutes, he is without pain. Near bliss descends. His skin is clean, there is a bed beneath him, nurses float past like sailing ships, sometimes appearing over him.

The doctor, stiff in his white coat, comes later. "We must rebreak and reset the tibia in the morning," he says. "There are two ribs, both lower, anterior that have partially healed, but have healed improperly and press too close to the lung. I'm sorry to say that they will have to be rebroken and set as well. The tibia we can cast, but there is no way to cast the rib cage."

"Will I be given anesthesia?" Will says.

The doctor laughs the short, dry laugh of the inundated, the overworked. "Yes, yes. We are not so primitive here in India. We have such things."

"Good," Will says. "That is all I care about." To feel no pain.

The Patels are there in the morning, when they wheel him in to the operating room, a room without the slightest trace of modern medicine. It could be the back room of a man who dabbles in surgery.

When he wakes, the Patels are sitting dutifully in wooden chairs at either side of his bed, Mr. Patel in his starched white shirt and black glasses, taped at the corners, Mrs. Patel in a green-and-orange sari, rolls of middle-aged flesh protruding over the waist. He notices the white cast on his left leg, feels the bandages that have been wrapped around his lower chest, then tumbles effortlessly back into oblivion.

His next few days are idyllic. A variety of foods are brought to him on trays, mangoes, Limcas, *paratha,* fried okra, *gulab jaman.* The painkillers are given to him liberally. He drifts through the hallways, pushed in a wheelchair by one nurse or another. There is not a cheerier soul in the place than he. What would have appeared appalling to him before—this hospital with its World War I–standard equipment, gross inefficiencies, overcrowding, and at times filthy conditions—is a haven. They cannot understand his enthusiasm, and are so grateful for his gratitude, they can't get enough of him. He's never alone. Even the dreary old men with their amputated limbs and their tumors maneuver themselves over to his bed, to his wheelchair to warm themselves on his cheer, as if holding their cold hands over a fire.

He wishes he could hold this state of mind forever, to be frozen in the state of gratitude that he finds himself in as he lies between clean sheets in a bed, in the absence of pain, relishing the hum and buzz of people around him, the nurses coming and going, bringing him cold Limcas.

When he is able to get around by himself, he finds a small nook in the hospital where no one goes, and secrets himself there for hours. From the window he can see the jammed traffic below, the boys with their bullock carts, the young men jockeying with wooden crosses heavy with cheap plastic trinkets, the women in their saris, moving sway-backed slowly from one stall to the other, picking out their daily food.

He is simply a man broken—broken bones, broken heart. A condition he is willing to concede may not be permanent. His being has crowded around these breaks, hovering, going over the minute details of them. He would like to believe that when he leaves India his life will get better, but he doesn't believe in progress anymore. Progress toward what? For what? He has embraced the idea of endurance. There is no promise, ever, of anything. There are only small states of grace.

A week later, he leaves India for the island of Mauritius. On his way to the airport, he stops at Mr. Patel's motel. With Will's directions, Mr. Patel has graciously gone to the hut and found the boy. Will is meeting him in the motel lobby, along with the old Moslem woman who marginally cares for him.

When he walks into the lobby on crutches, the boy doesn't recognize him. He's now so clean shaven, his hair cropped short, his clothes so new, he appears to be another person. So Will hobbles as he had once hobbled in the game, and the boy understands who he is and grins, then breaks out in his syrupy laugh. He rams softly into Will's side.

Mr. Patel has arranged the white plastic chairs around a small table where his wife has set an offering of tea and sweet cakes. The old woman sits in one of the chairs, dressed in the black *burka* that Moslem women wear. Will can only see her sunken, kindly eyes, her gnarled hands, like knobs at the ends of her sleeves. A hump rests between her shoulders, bending her forward slightly. While they talk the boy stands between her chair and Will's, shifting his weight from one chair arm to the other.

The boy's name is Abdul, the old woman says. His parents were killed in a raid made on his village two months earlier. She found him wandering down the road. He'd walked for days, perhaps as long as a week. He was faint from hunger, the soles of his feet burned. In exchange for running errands, for feeding her cows and goats, she gives him food and lets him sleep out in the hut, where in more prosperous times, she had stored rice. Her own house lies beyond the small section of forest where the hut stood. While Will inhabited the hut alone, the boy slept outside.

Will asks how he was found, and the boy's hands suddenly flap, demonstrating the presence of the vultures he'd seen circling above the rice paddy that morning. He knew this sign by now and went to see if someone was dead. He found Will faceup in the water and pushed him with his foot. When Will moaned, he stood by him all day until an older boy drove by with an ox-and-bullock cart; he convinced this boy to take Will on the cart to the hut, where they lay him down on the mat. The boy looked in on him for days, poked at him sometimes to see if he was still alive. He knew to watch the rise and fall of his chest. The boy demonstrates this by breathing in and out deeply, his own small chest filling and emptying. When he heard Will screaming from the hut a few days later, he hurried through the old woman's cabbage garden. His eyes grow big, and he bends forward to giggle when he admits he was scared.

He wants to touch Will's cast now and points to it. Will withdraws the pantleg, and the boy crouches down on his haunches and runs his fingers over the hard bumpy white plaster. He pulls the small red truck from its hiding place inside the waist of his lungi and drives it around the ankle, then up the shin. They all watch quietly.

While Will arranges with Mr. Patel and the old woman for him to be taken care of, the boy comes and sits on his lap, rests his head on Will's shoulder, sucks his thumb. It is a relief to Will that the boy will never want for food, for shelter, for clothing, for education.

He flies to Mauritius to spend a few days studying the giant tortoise in the Pamplemousses Biological Reserve. He had missed it when he was last here. He then planned to go on to Africa, but he discovers he isn't able to travel easily and stays in Mauritius for three months. He needs somewhere to heal; it is as good a place as any. It is a relief to be out of India, to be purged of its rhythms, to have them replaced by wide swaths of beach, by tropical breezes, in a place relatively unpeopled.

He hobbles along the sea, walks through the forests, struggling against a tide of inertia. The despair lingers long after his bones have healed, an air into which he sometimes feels sewn. His leg bothers him even after his ribs heal; the scar forms adhesions to the bone, and he must spend a little time each day rubbing it. His jaw never feels quite the same, but he grows accustomed to its strange new alignment. His thoughts are often confined to these things.

He corresponds with Mim; the troubles in Assam have subsided. It will grow again, erupt at another time in the future, but for the moment it has receded. He longs to hear word of Grace, but Mim never mentions her.

He works in his hotel room most afternoons. In the evenings he eats at the small restaurant downstairs. He gets to know a few people, though not well. A few of them press for his company, but he hasn't quite returned to himself and cannot find the words to tell them.

There is a young American woman staying in the hotel who tries to intervene. Wounds, he discovers, do not repel certain women. In fact, she graciously offers to rub the adhesions on his leg, but her touch only deepens his sorrow, and he shies away. He explains that it is not personal, that not enough time has passed since his last love affair, but she doesn't understand and goes out of her way after that to avoid him.

He has become an island, living upon an island.

It is never the lone or the rare that survive, he knows. Never the isolated. They are the first to go. It is the commoner, the generalist, the adapter who survives; those that are joined, that are visited by others. The lone, the rare vanish. Species go to islands to die.

Six cubic miles of lava rose from the floor of the ocean and exploded into the sky above the Malay Archipelago. It was morning on August 27, 1883. It registered on every barograph in the world. Thirty-six thousand people were killed by the tidal waves that hit the coasts of Sumatra and Java. Ships were beached on the shores of Sri Lanka.

Krakatau, an island thirty miles off the coast of Java, was reduced to a small crescent of sterile rock. Dropping the first and last letter of its original name, they renamed the island Rakata. There was not a living thing to be found on it—not one terrestrial creature, not a spore, not so much as a seed.

Three years later, the first botanical expedition was led by Professor Traub. The team discovered mosses, blue-green algae, eleven species of fern, and flowering plants. A year later there were trees and an abundance of grasses. Another year passed and there were spiders, butterflies, beetles, flies, and one species of lizard, Varanus salvator, a close relative of the Komodo dragon, known for its ability to travel. But dispersal is just the first step.

Sea birds came also—shearwaters and boobies, petrals and pelicans, frigate birds and noddies and terns. Hidden in their feathers, embedded in their skin, hiding deep in their intestinal tracts, they carried other life forms— fern and fungi spores, seeds of flowering plants, mites and lice, insects.

Having gotten there, whether spore or seed or terrestrial animal, it must establish itself. This is especially crucial for animals dependent upon sexual reproduction. To colonize a new habitat, the creature must be able to find a niche, a mate, and protection.

By 1906 Rakata was inhabited by nearly a hundred vascular plants, a grove of trees ringed the shoreline, green moss carpeted the summit. In 1936, Rakata supported 271 species of plants. About thirty percent blew in on the wind. Another thirty percent floated across the sea. Most of the others came in with the animals.

Life is insistent.

From Notes on Extinction, by Will Mendelsohn

Chapter 21

*I*t is late in October when he returns to New York. His apartment is still empty and has not been opened in well over two years. He throws the windows up to air the place out, and for lack of another thing to do, he hangs his map of the world on the wall, as Mim had done in his rooms in Assam.

Later, he inspects himself in front of the long mirror on the back of the closet door. He's older, noticeably thinner, his hair cropped more closely to his head. When he walks, it is with a slight limp. There is more gray in his hair, the lines at his mouth have deepened, the softness under his chin is more rounded. There is a look in his eyes he's never seen there, an addition, like a haunted attic.

For days he walks around the neighborhood. He finds himself standing at the railing on the Hudson River watching the ships pass. He is again confined to an island, but an island unlike the islands of the world—far from isolated, there is a constant tide of visitors, of migrations, of infusions from the outside. He trucks past vendors on Sixth Avenue and buys books from them, magazines he's missed. He visits the Strand, passing hours in its dusty aisles, looking for books on evolution and extinction. In the late afternoons he slips into the movie theater on Greenwich Avenue.

On his way home one day he walks past 302 West 12th Street, the address to which Vera sent Grace's letter, and counts up eighteen flights.

That night, he stretches out on his mattress with the phone and calls information, asks for Grace Tagore's phone number. It is with a certain relief that he discovers it is unlisted. He checks for Stella Fars, but there is no listing. He cannot remember what she told him was her given last name. It was Rosenblatt or Greenblatt, or it could have been Greenberg. He tries out the variations, but there is no listing for any of them.

On impulse, he calls information for Marcy, New York and asks the operator what the initials MSMH stand for. They were in the upper left-hand corner of Vera's envelope; he's never forgotten them. He has not told anyone about the letter; all this time it has floated about in his thoughts, untended, like a balloon left to drift, not yet punctured by any insight, seized by any realization.

The operator says, "It must be Marcy State Mental Hospital. Would you like the number?"

He writes it down, then dials. A woman's voice answers, "Marcy State Mental Hospital," and he says, "I'd like to leave a message for my aunt, Vera Tuber, if I might."

The woman pauses for a moment, as if checking a roster of names, then answers, "What is the message?"

He hangs up. So Grace's mother is in a mental hospital. He re-members Grace's word, sanitarium—*she stayed in a sanitarium for a bit*—spoken in their room at the country club. At the time it had conjured the softness of TB clinics high up in the Alps, as if Vera had gone to take a rest, to sink deep into salt baths.

He ventures up to his mother's apartment on Amsterdam Avenue. For the first time he can remember, he is glad that it hasn't changed remarkably in the last twenty years. He's only in the apartment for a minute when she notes the changes in his physical appearance. "You're thin," she says. "You're limping."

He says nothing, but he allows her full embrace and doesn't avoid her penetrating eyes, though he knows his are suddenly filled with sorrow. "Ah, Will," she says, and she strokes his cheek with her hand. "Something's happened."

They sit in her kitchen and he gives her a few trinkets he's brought her from India. She turns them over in her hands, but finally she pushes them aside, and it's her eyes he must contend with.

"What's happened to you?" she says.

He pauses for a moment to consider whether he will provide the details or give a cursory telling. It is her attention, her keen interest, he suspects, that draws him out. He is aware that he has never spoken at such length to her, provided her with such detail from his personal life. While he speaks, it is not without the memory of her own story, which he had heard so many times at this very table.

When he finishes, she cries into her hands; it is a brief squall of tears which come quickly and then are stanched. She wipes her face with a napkin, then balls it up in her hand and lays it lightly down on the table. She asks to see his wounds. But he doesn't want to show her. There is something faintly unnatural about it.

"Why not?" she asks. "A mother isn't supposed to see her full-grown son's wounds? Is that what you think? You think just because you're a grown man that I don't care anymore what happens to you?"

He argues with her, then finally relents. What does it matter? He unbuttons his shirt and shows her his rib cage. There isn't much to see but a scar, a bit of calcified bone that has left some small knobs beneath his skin. Once he's gotten used to the idea that there are moments when propriety is lost and intimacy, even if it is not wanted, is gained, he feels a certain eagerness to show her the rest of them. Like the boy, she runs her fingers over the ridge of shin that still protrudes, over his crooked rib cage, feels the place in his jaw where there is now a small hollow.

When she sits back in her chair there is a look in her eyes that he's never seen before. It is complex, a mixture of satisfaction and tenderness, kindness. But it is more—some gate, some wall has lifted. Could this be? he wonders. His suffering a passkey?

He meets Geena for lunch the next day at the Jane Street Cafe, three blocks from where she lives in the apartment she found when she left him. He has imagined that of all the people, she would be most interested in hearing about his trip, about the animals and the places they had talked of for nearly ten years. But it is not the case. He discovers he has long been replaced by a man who teaches medieval history at Hunter College. He listens patiently to her enthusiasm regarding twelfth century monasteries in Spain, while inwardly he feels a tug of jealousy. She used to speak this way about his work, but he doesn't pursue it. He feels an unexpected affection for her, and is surprised to find that he cares for her and wants to wipe the soup from the corner of her mouth, push the hair from her eyes. He settles for touching the back of her hand.

"So how was your trip?" she asks. Her fingers move delicately over the rim of her coffee cup, down the handle. They remain exquisite. He begins with, "I went first to Brazil," but by the time he gets to Guam, he sees the glaze that comes over her eyes, and he trails off, sums up his trip with the words, "It was a good trip. I got another book out of it."

"That's good," she says. "I can't wait to read it." But he knows already that it is a hollow enthusiasm, that she most likely won't.

She has come with papers for a divorce, and pulls them from her purse, slides them across the table. She and the medieval historian want to marry and have children. He glances over them and promises to read them later.

"I'm not asking for anything," she says. "You only have to sign them. I've asked for nothing."

He clutches inside. He reasons that he doesn't want to be married to her either, that certainly he has put her in this position, but this is no solace. He is not sure what he would have her do or say, but it is not this. His life operates now solely on irony, he thinks. At every juncture lurks irony.

On their way out of the restaurant she notices he has a limp. "What did you do, trip in the forest or something? You were always so clumsy."

He looks at her, and a dry despair wells inside him. After all, she has not loved him.

He watches her as she hurries down the street on her way, presumably, to meet the medieval historian. She has left him more thoroughly than he has ever left her, and his stomach churns to feel the final distance that has fallen between them.

Late in the afternoon, he retrieves his book from the safety-deposit box where he's been sending it for the past two years. He's lost only twenty pages—the pages that he wrote the last day at Mim's, those he wrote while in the Guwahati Motel.

Bundled in a coat, he reads them at a cafe on Hudson Street, sitting at a table out on the street, drinking cup after cup of espresso. They are good pages, he decides, but they are not scholarly. They are not so much filled with scientific ideas, as they are with the flesh of the earth, with its creatures. Landscapes, jagged, forested, carpeted in green, inhabit the pages; they are infused with qualities of light, crepuscular, dark, copper-colored, with airs, with the fragility of the creatures that depend upon the earth. After all, they are notes on extinction, not a masterpiece on the patterns of the natural world. It would be a fitting, nice ending to the story of a manuscript lost in a fire, that when rewritten it turns out to be greater than its first incarnation, but he must admit it is merely different.

For a long time he sits at the table, his hands resting on the manuscript. Disappointment settles slowly inside him. The sun is warm, though there is a breeze that is cool, sometimes even cold. He finds himself suddenly susceptible to an old man who is led past his table by a middle-aged black woman, either his nurse or paid companion. It is the way he holds her hand, follows her blindly, like a boy in a daze, that strikes Will.

A black man arrives from nowhere and begins to paw through the metal trash can at the edge of the sidewalk. He's dressed shabbily in dark pants, in a filthy red T-shirt, his shoes open at the toes, laceless. He goes through the trash methodically, picking through each bag gingerly, looking inside every paper wrapping. He does so without despair, with a sustained, enduring concentration. Finding a half empty Coke bottle, some bits of sandwich that he plucks from a Styrofoam container, he slips them in the plastic bag he carries on his wrist.

It is no longer with distance, with a detached, small, unrealized ache, an imagining of what it must be, that Will observes these small shufflings of life past his eyes. He's been put in touch with life's shadowy side, attuned now to its darker image. To those who have been invisible to him, his eyes have now turned; he feels a sudden, unexpected kinship. Is this what there is for him to do, to take his place among the common, the ordinary?

On his way home, he walks past Grace's apartment building on Twelfth Street and stops in front of the doors and looks inside. It is an elegant, though small lobby, filled with glass shelves on which delicate porcelain vases stand. On impulse, he walks through the revolving doors into the lobby and steps up to the doorman sitting behind the desk.

"Grace Tagore, Eighteen D," he says.

A short, round man with a mustache picks up the phone and presses the buzzer for 18D without the slightest hesitation, as if he has possibly seen Grace Tagore just this morning.

"Are you expecting anyone?" he asks whomever has answered. He slides the phone away from his mouth and asks Will, "Who should I say is calling?"

Will never imagined that she was in New York, let alone up in her apartment. It's been nearly a year, and his heart suddenly pounds. He thinks of saying, "Never mind." He considers giving a false name. Perhaps he should leave. But finally he says, "Will Mendelsohn."

"Will Mendelsohn," the doorman says into the phone.

When he hangs up, he says, "Go on up."

"Is it Grace Tagore?" Will asks.

The man regards him strangely. "Yes, Grace Tagore."

Then he is riding up in the elevator, carrying his manuscript, standing next to a woman who has come up from the laundry room and holds a basket of perfectly folded clothes on her hip. For her the ride up on the elevator is mundane. She won't recall it in another ten minutes. He, on the other hand . . .

By the time he reaches the door, his heart beats so rapidly that he considers getting back in the elevator, walking through the lobby, returning himself to the street. What if Vikram is there? What if they have a child, a child with Vikram's brown skin and Grace's blue eyes? Can he bear the disappointment? No, he can't, but now he knows Grace is here. Grace. Grace is a name. Her name. Grace is a mercy given, he thinks. Grace is a state of being. He has known grace.

It is not he who rings the bells, but rather she who opens the door. She finds him standing there quietly.

"Will," she says. She pushes her hair behind her ears, touches her fingers to her neck.

Perhaps the affair has not run its course, he thinks.

"Would you like to come in for tea?" she says.

"Is Mr. Tagore in?" he asks.

"No," she says. "Vikram died two months ago." She draws her lips into her mouth, a gesture of sorrow, and looks down at the floor.

He is surprised at how saddened he is by the news. It was news he thought would elate him, but now that it has finally come to pass, there is nothing elating about it.

"I'm sorry, Grace," he says.

"Thank you," she says. She opens the door and he follows her into the apartment. It has much the same furnishings as the bungalow in India—white, straight-backed sofas, a few framed drawings, Persian rugs. There are boxes, as many as forty, piled up inside the room, against the wall.

"Are you moving?" he asks.

"They're Vikram's effects," she says.

She offers him a seat on the sofa, and then hurries to move the assortment of Vikram's cuff links, his tie clasps, a few silver money-clips she's been sorting, to the coffee table. She is so near him, he can smell the light soap he'd once known, rose-scented. It brings with it a tide of memory. His eye moves along the curve of her hips, the soft rise of her breasts beneath her sweater.

"What happened?" Will asks. "It seemed he had gotten better."

"He got better for a while and then he slipped away. He wasted away to nothing." She finishes moving the tie clips and cuff links to the table and stands up. "He died in that bed in the Small House. Stella and I took his ashes to the city of Benares and scattered them into the Ganges River. That's what he wanted."

He bends his head, looks down at his hands.

"Would you like some Assam tea?" she asks.

"Okay."

She disappears into a small kitchen just off the living room and he hears her taking things down from the cupboard.

"Where did you go?" she asks. She speaks casually, as if it were nothing much.

"To Guwahati," he says, "then to Mauritius." He dislikes their posturing, their posing as if they are merely friends who haven't seen one another in a long time. Perhaps she has forgotten him in all this time.

"How long have you been back?" she asks.

"Only a week."

"I've been back for a month now."

Another silence settles, interrupted by the clatter of cups, the metal brush of the teakettle against the burner in the kitchen.

She appears in the living room a few minutes later with a tray, which she sets down on the glass coffee table next to the cuff links and tie clips. She kneels on the floor and stirs in milk and sugar in the amounts he likes, then hands him the cup.

She takes a sip of tea, her eyes hovering above the rim of the teacup. The images Stella had last deposited in his mind—Grace biting off bits of painkillers, stumbling in a drugged stupor through the night, have lost their edge. The idea of the letter now seems ludicrous; somehow coming upon her in her New York apartment, as she sorts through her deceased Indian husband's personal effects, the likelihood that she is Hitler's daughter takes on a dimness, an oblivion.

"So what will you do?" she asks.

"I'll finish my book," he answers. "How about you?"

"I'm going to try to direct another film, if I can find the money." She smiles, pushes her blonde hair behind her ears. "Would you like some of those biscuits. I found them here. I remember you liked them."

"All right," he says, and she gets up and goes into the kitchen.

He hears the cupboard door squeak open. "I was so surprised to find them in one of the Korean markets," she says. "I had forgotten all about them, and then I saw them on the shelf. In India they were like our daily bread."

She returns with a plate of them—round, slightly tanned flat biscuits. It is true. These small, flat cookies were always there; they accompanied every tea, joined every plate of fruit, appeared next to every dessert.

She slips one off the plate, while he takes two.

"When I found them, they reminded me so much of India I sat down on my bed and ate a whole pack of them," she says.

As he eats one, it reminds him of India. They have the simplest taste—dry, hard, a bit sweet, easily digested, common. Not rare in any way.

"I miss the sound of India's crows," she says.

"I do too. The crows here don't sound the same way."

"No, they're higher voiced."

"More like shrews," he says.

"Yes, and they don't have the shiny blue-black feathers either."

"India's poor cousins."

She laughs.

And so it begins again, he thinks, but he cautions himself against such ideas.

As they sit and talk, it grows dark, begins to rain. When she gets up to make them some more tea, he wonders if it is a sound with which he will grow familiar, or if it is confined only to this moment. Does the outcome hinge on chance? he wonders. A chance look, this said over that, this gesture rather than that, which might tip the balance one way or the other? Things that are impossible to calculate.

Yet chance is only one element. There are others. After the Brazilian rain forest was hacked into fragments, a question arose: What is the minimum critical size that a fragment of land has to be in order to sustain itself? He wonders now, is there a minimum critical feeling already present between them that is strong enough to survive the vagrancies, to withstand the onslaught of doubt, the hazard of feeling? They've suffered devastations, losses. Can they recover?

They will either rise or they will fall, he thinks. On matters such as these, he supposes, there are no in betweens, although there are crucial moments, moments when it might go this way instead of that, when there is need for care, for intervention; it requires a vigilance, to read the signs before they become consequences.

He must pay attention.